MW01622561

THE SAMPHIRE SCHOOL SERIES

Catching the Sunrise

A NOVEL BY

TAMAR SHY

Thank you, dear Esther, for editing these books and for writing — along with the rest of our dear children — the best stories of our lives. May each chapter we write and the characters we form of ourselves continuously bring more nachas to the רבש"ע. — T & M

The Samphire School Series, Book 1
Catching the Sunrise

ISBN: 978-1-60763-358-7

Originally serialized in Yated Ne'eman

Author: Tamar Shy (tamar@tamarshy.co.uk)
Editor: M. Jakubowicz
Proofreader: Elisheva Ruffer
Cover design: Rivka Lewis
Internal design: Nachum Shapiro

The Judaica Press, Inc.
Brooklyn, NY
718-972-6200
info@judaicapress.com
judaicapress.com

Manufactured in the United States of America

Contents

PART I

New Beginnings

1 Off to Boarding School

Sherry ran her thumb over the label on the top book on her pile, her stomach coiled tighter than the binding. The train that would carry her to her first year at Samphire Boarding School was scheduled to leave in less than an hour. She bit her lip and placed the stack of books on her bed with the rest of her neatly arranged supplies, surveying them one last time to make sure she hadn't missed anything.

I hope I get on well there. It's going to be hard being so far from home!

She perched on her dresser and stared at herself in the mirror on the opposite wall. Her reflection showed a worried frown. She was already dressed in the Samphire uniform—a pleated navy skirt with a yellow leather belt, a tartan shirt peeking out from beneath a double-breasted navy blazer, and a navy beret with yellow trim and the school's emblem. She wished she could tell the girl in the mirror not to worry, that everything would be fine—and maybe fill her with as much confidence as her sister, Chava, had tried to do earlier.

If the place is anywhere near as splendid as I hear it is, I'm in for a jolly good time.

She flipped back an errant lock of brown hair that obscured her vision and looked more closely at the mirror. The large brown eyes looked no less worried.

I should get back to packing.

Situated in southeast England, three miles from the Port of Dover, Samphire was a two-hour journey from the Spencers' home in the heart of Kent. Sherry had attended a local day school for first form, but would now be one of the new girls joining the second form at the boarding school. Chava was entering the sixth form, her last year there, and had talked almost non-stop for days about the ins and outs of Samphire—mostly the outs.

"And listen here, dear sister, you'd better watch out for Mrs. Davis. She expects perfect work. Hand in a scruffy report with poor handwriting and that will be the end of your break time for the week."

Sherry stared at Chava's reflection, which had appeared beside hers in the mirror. Both Chava and Sherry bore a remarkable resemblance to their mother: dark-brown hair tied back neatly in a half-pony, large, deep-set eyes that revealed intelligence, and charming smiles that were almost perpetually present. Right now, Chava's smile had a teasing quirk at the corners.

"Is there anything good about Samphire?" Sherry said. "You think just because you're in the top form, you can scare the wits out of me? Well, you needn't bother. I have my own sources, and Samphire sounds alright to me."

"Oh, it's more than alright." Chava laughed. "But what point is there in having an older sister if you can't benefit from her wisdom?" She hopped up on the dresser and sat next to Sherry, jabbing a finger at her. "Samphire is the finest school in the country. Just see to it that you're its finest student. I want to be proud of you there."

Sherry wiggled her eyebrows. "Hear, hear. The mighty head girl speaks."

Emboldened by Chava's pep talk, she shifted off the dresser and admired the figure she cut in the school uniform. In truth, she was buzzing at the prospect of being a Samphire girl. The school, which had opened half a century ago in 1934, was one of the most respected boarding schools in the country. Sherry gave the girl in the mirror a determined look. She was determined to make her *whole* family proud.

Yet she couldn't help feeling nervous that she wouldn't be able to live up to the family legacy. Ma had been so proud when Papa became the Rabbi of their small local shul, and both of their parents had invested a lot in the *chinuch* of their daughters. Chava was fulfilling those expectations, coming in top of her form practically every year—and no wonder. Chava was a serious, dignified girl, who placed great importance on matters such as schedules, order, and marks. As head girl that year, she sought to be the finest student Samphire had ever had.

Sherry, on the other hand, was impatient, struggled with timekeeping, and found herself more drawn to having fun than fulfilling duties. Still, at heart, she hoped that she and her sister had more similarities than differences. She'd had good marks in first form, which she was proud of. But as for being dignified, well ...

She frowned. *I'm also kind and thoughtful, aren't I? And I'd do anything to get someone out of trouble. Uh, is that even a good thing ...?* Her musings were interrupted.

"Chava, Sherry, hurry!" their mother called, her mellifluous voice floating up the stairs. "We have to catch the ten o'clock train."

"Come on, we'd better get these suitcases closed, Sherry." Chava huffed as she struggled to fit in her sports equipment.

Sherry slapped her forehead. "I've forgotten something. Won't be a moment." She raced down the stairs, two at a time, and galloped into the kitchen.

Her mother looked up from her coffee. "All packed?"

"Almost! Now, where is my purse?" she muttered to herself.

Her mother looked incredulous. "You don't say. Don't tell me you're still looking for that thing." She got up to help with the search. Though she was impatient, she still managed an excited smile for Sherry that made her dimples appear. "It's all the nerves getting to you, isn't it?"

Sherry laughed. "Yeah, that's it." She winked. "Otherwise, I'm as organized as they come."

"Oh, Sherry." Ma chuckled. "You'll get there. Just like I did." The twinkle in her deep brown eyes made Sherry feel understood and treasured.

A flash of bright cobalt caught her eye, and she spotted her wallet jutting out above the mantelpiece.

"Ah, there it is!"

She bounced over to retrieve it, then gazed at the photos on the shelf. They were fun snapshots of her family, many of them taken during school holidays. Her favorite was still the one of her as a seven-year-old, perched on her father's shoulder as she shoved her half-eaten ice-cream cornet into his mouth. He'd laughed helplessly, and when he tried to put her down, she'd climbed up his back and jumped onto his hat before he could say, "Enough!"

She smiled, touching the glass that covered her father's face. His blue eyes, deep as the Atlantic Ocean, betrayed the musician and storyteller in him, and they held her in check like nothing else could. She stared, her gaze unfocused, and took a deep breath.

Am I really ready to travel so far away from home?

Papers rustled and hit the floor. She jumped and turned to see her mother, usually unflappable, hurry to retrieve the pile that had just dropped from her hands. She scooted over to help, noting a letter in unfamiliar handwriting on the top of the pile. Ma was surprisingly swift, though, and scooped up the letter, along with the rest of the papers, before Sherry could even touch one. Still, she caught a few words: *Can we be certain they will get along ... new sisters ...*

Her mother scrambled to get the pages in order and then shoved them into an envelope addressed in the same friendly handwritten script. Ma's cheeks reddened and she stuffed the envelope into her handbag.

Hmm ... interesting.

Sherry wanted to ask her mother what those words meant, but Ma seemed intent on ignoring her unspoken question.

Her mother smiled, pointing to her mug. "I've got ten seconds to finish this." Her grasp was awkward as she took hold of the porcelain handle, and coffee spilled onto the coaster.

Sherry gawked. That was so unlike her.

Why is she so jittery? Have the contents of that letter upset her? Or is she worried about me starting boarding school?

She knew her mother was worried about this new chapter in her life. Samphire had done a world of good for Chava, and she suspected that her mother hoped it would polish her, too. She thought of how often she had gotten into mischief at her day school last year, and her face grew warm. She could certainly use whatever polishing she could get.

A car honked in the driveway.

"Oh no!" Her mother gasped and jumped from her seat, her eyes wide. "If Moshe is ready at the wheel, it must really be late."

Sherry's heart leaped—whether from excitement or nerves, she couldn't tell. "Let me grab my things." She bounded up the stairs two at a time and finished packing in a jiffy, throwing the last few items haphazardly in her suitcase. Behind her, Chava folded her arms and clucked her tongue.

"Come on, girls," their mother called from the landing. "Do you need help with your bags?"

"No, we're coming!" they shouted.

They loaded their knapsacks onto their backs and grabbed a small suitcase each. The bulk of their belongings had already been sent off to school the day before. Sherry scrambled down the stairs and yanked the door open. She stopped to kiss the *mezuzah*, and waved goodbye to 15 Amber Road, the house that had been her home for almost thirteen years. Then she went out to the car, Chava and Ma following at a more dignified pace behind her.

A short drive took them to the station, where their train was about to depart. Sherry found herself ushered on board so fast, she hardly had time to say a proper goodbye. She rushed to the window and spotted Ma blowing kisses at her daughters, her hand at her heart. Sherry vaguely made out the words, "Be good, dears. Take care of each other."

She bit her lip and held her breath. A strange sense of unease settled inside her, as if a can of Coke had popped in her stomach and was fizzing and bubbling over. She robotically followed Chava to the section reserved for Samphire girls and took her seat. Other similarly dressed girls surrounded them. Some of them greeted Chava cheerfully, but Sherry barely noticed them. She pressed her forehead to the window, straining to catch one last glimpse of her mother on the platform that was growing smaller and smaller.

"Chava, is this the cheeky little sister you're always on about?"

Sherry swiveled her head around to see who had asked the question. A short, freckled girl with ginger hair grinned at her from the seat across the aisle. Several other girls tittered.

Sherry turned to Chava, heat flushing her cheeks.

"Don't mind Suri," Chava said, patting her hand. "She's always ready to tease. But she's a good sort, really. Just don't take any notice of what she says. There's nary an ounce of truth in it."

"And mind you watch out for my sister," Suri warned. "Leah Felder. She's in your form, and is a lot worse than me."

She pointed at another girl several seats away with freckles and a fiery orange ponytail that matched her sister's. Leah flashed shimmering green eyes at Sherry, then resumed laughing with her seatmate.

If Sherry had known these girls, she might have made a retort to get a laugh. Instead, she forced a half-smile and looked out the window, not sure whether to believe Suri or not. She missed Esther, her best friend from her old school who had laughed at all her jokes. She wondered what Esther was doing now, and a pang of loneliness pierced her.

After a couple of hours of passing small towns, sheep-filled fields, and working farms, Chava squealed and grabbed Sherry's arm. She pointed out the window.

"Look, there's Samphire!"

All the girls in the railroad car turned to look out the windows on Sherry's side.

Perched on the edge of a white cliff, towering above the tranquil turquoise sea, was a white stone building, surrounded by lush grass, white fences, and trim hedges. Beyond the school was a sprawling village, as picturesque as a postcard. It was exactly what the most prestigious girls' boarding school in England should look like.

"Isn't it beautiful?" Chava whispered, her hand flat against the pane.

"Yes," Sherry said. "It's unbelievable."

Chava had told her so much about the place over the years, she almost hadn't believed it would live up to the hype, but Samphire was spectacular.

"Did you know Samphire was built from material excavated during that tunnel's construction?" said a tall girl, her turned-up nose pressed against the window.

Next to her, a girl with short black hair and wire-rimmed glasses rolled her eyes. "Did you know that no one likes a know-it-all, Rivi?"

Rivi closed her mouth.

Sherry felt bad for her, but was grateful for the silence that allowed her to admire the place that would be her home for the next ten months. Under the sun's rays, the ocean waves traveled in a brilliant procession of luminous arcs of light. The view was so breathtaking that even Chava, for whom this was a familiar sight, couldn't take her eyes off it. She wasn't alone—not a single girl on the train looked away.

A chill ran over Sherry's scalp—a good one. Staring at the majestic stone building, as unmoving as the cliff it stood on, the monumental weight of this moment fell on her. It infused every muscle and bone in her body, and a rush of tears threatened to spill down her cheeks. She blinked them away, but she knew this was a moment she would never forget. She tried to memorize every detail—the building, the cliffs, the sea—taking a photograph without a camera.

Perhaps she would write a story about it later. She smiled. Memories were nice, but even better when you recaptured the emotions in words.

A girl laughed nearby, pulling her out of her reverie, and she scolded herself for being so sentimental. But then she saw Chava's expression. Her sister glanced at her with a weak smile, her eyes moist. Her hand was over her heart, much like Ma's had been while saying goodbye, as she turned from Sherry back to the window.

"Chava," Sherry whispered, "are you okay?"

Chava didn't really look sad, but she didn't look enthusiastic, either. She tilted her head, her gaze fixed on the building that was growing ever larger as they came closer.

"No, Sherry, I'm not really sad." She looked down and twiddled her thumbs. "Well, a little. See, this is the last time I'll arrive at Samphire for a new school year. So, you know, I suppose it is a bit sad." She turned her head just enough to peer at Sherry and smiled, this time for real. "But, sister, here you are! Starting your first year. I know I'm going to be so proud of you. It's just ... I've had a lot of great times here. I'm sad I won't be on the train with the other students arriving next year. But the place is still beautiful." She took Sherry's hand. "You'll understand one day."

Sherry smiled back at her.

Several minutes later, the train arrived at Samphire Station. Sherry disembarked with the other students, breathing deeply of the salty sea air, inhaling the sweet scent of seaweed. Only fifty yards away, magnificent waves lapped at the ivory sea walls, the ocean singing a welcome song in its watery voice. It was all so beautiful. She sighed in contentment and gratitude. What a gift from Hashem!

Her heart bubbled and spilled over in a *tefillah*. "Hashem, help me make good decisions. I want so much to make Ma proud ... and also Papa."

If only she could keep her mischievous nature in check.

2 Sherry Meets Mrs. Pepper

The Samphire school building was almost as magnificent on the inside as the scenery surrounding it. Sherry stared, open-mouthed, at the enormous foyer. Across the room, a grand staircase wide enough for four girls to climb without bumping into one another ascended to an impressive archway that disappeared into the bowels of the building. Gold swirls ran the length of the navy walls, adorned by a beige trim that lent an aristocratic air. It even smelled impressive, like old books and oiled wood and learning. Sherry stared in awe at the giant chandelier hanging from the ceiling, nearly bumping into a short, plump girl with frizzy hair.

"Excuse me," she murmured, sidestepping to get out of the way.

The girl grinned and stepped back, throwing her arms out to include Sherry with the rest of the students.

"Welcome, friends, to Samphire College! Lend your ears to new thoughts and knowledge."

"Bassy, more rhymes?" a girl groaned. With her straight, sleek hair, and tall slender frame, she looked so different from Bassy. A small oblong 110 camera hung by a strap from her arm. "I thought you'd given this up!"

"Sorry, Baila," Bassy said. "But rhyming's my game as sure as Bassy's my name."

Sherry grinned. Despite their teasing, she could sense they were friends. The tension in her gut eased slightly.

Dozens of girls soon milled about the entranceway. She felt somewhat lost and was grateful when Chava grabbed her elbow and shoved her along.

"Come on, Sherry, I'll show you to your dormitory."

Leaving the buzz of conversation behind them, they went upstairs. A "Second Form" sign was affixed to the door of the last room to their left. Chava led her inside, then wrapped an arm around her shoulder.

"I'm off to my floor now, but don't worry too much—you'll be just fine on your own. If you need me, I'll be around." She winked and left to join her classmates.

Sherry studied her dorm with great curiosity. Her classmates hadn't come up yet, and she wondered whether they were having tea and catching up with friends or if, like her, they were feeling a little apprehensive about the new school year and were taking things at a slower pace.

She took this time alone to have a good look around her new room. Freshly painted pale pink walls with pink gingham edging enveloped her like a comfy quilt. Two dozen beds lined the walls in two long rows. Pink curtains with matching tie-backs surrounded each bed, complemented by pink cushions edged with gingham ribbons. The night lamps next to every bed were pink, too. The room was at once welcoming and relaxing.

She chose a bed, near a window, and began to unpack.

"Hello," a girl said quietly. "What's your name?"

When Sherry turned, she saw the lanky girl from the train who had been so excited about Samphire School's history.

"Mine's Rivi. You're new here, aren't you? Isn't this place fabulous? It's always hard at first, but wait till you've been here a fortnight—you'll forget you were ever new!" She pushed her glasses up her narrow nose. "It's the same with all new things, I suppose."

Sherry just stared, and Rivi laughed. "Oh, there I go again, not letting you get a word in edgeways. I talk too much. Always did and always shall. My mother says I'm like a non-stop train, never pausing long enough to let people come on and catch up. Oh, well. So, let's hear, who are you?"

It took a moment for Sherry to conjure a response to this friendly yet blunt girl.

"I'm Sherry Spencer," she replied. She felt herself short of words, as if the other girl held a monopoly on them all.

"Oh, Chava's sister. I'm a bit in awe of her, you know." Rivi let out a whistle. "The sister of the head girl herself! Well, well, well. I had better mind my Ps and Qs with you around."

Sherry didn't know what to say. She certainly didn't want Rivi to feel uncomfortable around her. But when the girl saw her expression, she laughed.

"Just joking." She slipped her arm through Sherry's. "Come on, I'll show you around a bit."

Together, they went to explore the beautiful grounds, complete with netball courts, lush gardens, and a gently rippling pond surrounded by weeping willows and strategically placed benches, all to the tune of Rivi's lively prattle. Once back inside, they toured the classrooms, dining room, and spacious common room. Sherry expressed her admiration for it all.

Along one corridor was a wall lined almost completely with lockers. Sherry stopped and stared. Rivi chuckled. "Here's where you keep your personal belongings for class, such as stationery and files. Just make sure you're not caught here after the bell rings—unless you're the type who likes to get in trouble."

"I hope I'm not the type."

"That's good."

"But I'm afraid it may just be a faint hope."

Rivi didn't seem to hear that comment. She schlepped Sherry along with her, stopping at the library, music room, laboratory, gym, rehearsal room and more with dizzying speed and exorbitant chatter, leaving Sherry hardly any time to register anything.

"Thank you, Rivi. This place is huge. I would have gotten lost for sure."

Rivi smiled. "Nah, you would have been fine. We all get lost in here once in a while when we're new, but you'll learn this place like the back of your hand, lickety-split."

Sherry smiled back, thankful for Rivi's show of friendship. She had forgotten all about being nervous. Then she remembered that she was supposed to visit Mrs. Pepper, the headmistress, and all her butterflies returned. Chava had reminded her on the train that all new girls must report to her after they arrived. She mentioned this to Rivi, who offered to show her the way.

"Thanks," Sherry said, her voice tight.

They bumped into Bassy further down the hallway, and Sherry introduced herself.

"I know who you are," Bassy said. "Chava's sister. You look nearly identical." She grinned. "I bet your tour guide wasn't nearly as fine as the chickens that greeted me on my first day." She glanced at Rivi, hazel eyes twinkling. "No offense, Rivi."

Rivi laughed. "None taken. It's hard to beat a flock of hens, that's for sure."

"Chickens?" Sherry gaped, not sure she'd heard correctly.

Bassy turned to her to explain. "Apparently, someone left the coop open. Those hens wandered in here, pleased as punch with themselves, right down this hallway until Mrs. Cohen caught up with them and shooed them all back where they belonged." Bassy chuckled at the memory. "I kind of wish I'd thought of it myself."

Sherry grinned, and Bassy launched into another ditty.

"Sherry's checking the place out, Rivi is her own special scout."

"You make me want to scream and shout." Sherry added. Bassy's rhymes were getting on her nerves, and she had to go see Mrs. Pepper.

Bassy frowned. "Take it easy, you might as well—"

"Just be quiet or I'll really yell."

Sherry was joking, of course, but her nerves gave her tone an edge. Bassy waved and slipped away. While Sherry had been amused by Bassy's idiosyncrasies, she breathed a sigh of relief.

They reached Mrs. Pepper's office. Sherry stared at the closed door, her stomach performing flips.

"I'm going to do my duty now," she said. "Best to get it over and done with."

Rivi nodded. "Catch you later, yeah?"

"Sure," Sherry said.

Holding her breath, she approached the office. Sweat pricked at her palms, as she knocked on the door. A moment later, it opened to reveal a slender woman with lively blue eyes, a brown sheitel, and ramrod-straight posture.

Mrs. Pepper welcomed her in with a warm smile. "Ah, Sherry Spencer. I have heard so much about you. Perhaps one day you will be our head girl, just as Chava is now. It's a tremendous honor, you know."

"Oh, I don't know that I could be so grand as Chava!" Sherry exclaimed. "I'm too impatient and hot-headed. It would be—" She stopped short, aghast at her outburst. Her gaze drifted to the floor as she whispered an apology to the headmistress.

Mrs. Pepper smiled kindly. "We must all start somewhere, you know." Her wise eyes sparkled. "I'm sure you'll do your very best."

Sherry coughed politely into her hand and swallowed hard. "I'll try."

"Please, sit." Mrs. Pepper indicated the chair in front of her desk. Sherry did as she was told, and the headmistress took a seat on the other side.

Mrs. Pepper folded her hands and looked at her intently. Sherry felt as though the woman's gaze was boring right into her.

"Sherry, today is your first day at Samphire. You will learn many things here and will have many teachers to guide you. But, my dear, there is only one teacher with the power to train you in the ways that really count—and that teacher is you.

"Every student wants to be successful. To some, that means doing well in exams. For others, it's making friends—and these are both good things. But remember, it doesn't matter how others view you as much as how you view yourself. *Looking* successful is about popularity and accomplishment, but it is *being* successful that matters most. To be truly successful, you must teach yourself to act with integrity and courage, compassion and honor, at all times and in every situation."

Sherry's hands trembled. Had Mrs. Pepper talked to her teachers at her old school? She had *tried* to be a respectful student, but she'd received more than one reprimand for speaking out of turn and cracking jokes in class.

Mrs. Pepper bent closer, her eyes softening. "And you know what else, young lady? This may surprise you, but I believe that success can best be defined by how you make mistakes."

The headmistress became still. Sherry wasn't sure if she was inviting her to respond, so she remained silent. Mrs. Pepper straightened and glanced at the "*Shivisi Hashem*" poster on the wall.

"If you can admit your faults and work every day at fixing them"—her voice became a whisper—"ah, that's a fine success."

Sherry found herself nodding. Mrs. Pepper blinked at her, then gave her an encouraging smile.

"Knowing our faults sets us well on the way to correcting them, and judging from your little outburst earlier, you seem to know yours well enough."

Embarrassment warmed Sherry's cheeks and a tingle fluttered up her spine. She was filled with a burning desire to make a true success of herself by every one of Mrs. Pepper's definitions. She was sure the woman could see right into her heart.

"Yes, Mrs. Pepper."

Mrs. Pepper stood and came around the desk. "You will hear many inspirational talks and receive a lot of guidance, but the forming of your character lies in your own hands. And while today is the first day of school, it is also the first day of the rest of your life. Make good choices, Sherry."

The words sounded like a dismissal, so Sherry rose. But Mrs. Pepper wasn't done.

"Remember, young lady, I am always here for you. Look out for yourself. Be kind to yourself. And, Miss Sherry Spencer, look out for your friends, too."

Sherry shifted her weight, uncertain what to do next. Was the headmistress finished speaking? "Yes, Mrs. Pepper."

Sherry took a step toward the door, but Mrs. Pepper stepped forward and patted her shoulder. She stopped, her stomach clenching at the thought that she may have just acted disrespectfully.

Mrs. Pepper only smiled. "I hope that as you leave this room, your mind is full of ambition and your heart full of aspirations. Keep these alive and, *b'ezras Hashem*, you're going to go far."

"Thank you." The words were little more than a squeak. At last, Sherry made her escape, and the band around her chest loosened. She felt smaller and taller at the same time.

Outside in the corridor, a short girl with freckles and a ginger ponytail greeted her with a giggle. "You've been peppered, haven't you?"

She looked familiar, yet Sherry couldn't place her. "Huh?"

"Leah Felder, at your service," the girl said with a mock bow. "I can always spot a new girl who's gone to Mrs. Pepper. They come out all serious and proper, with perfect resolutions etched on their forehead. Didn't take long for mine to get rubbed off, though." She rocked on her heels, swinging her hands in front of her.

"Oh, so you're Suri's sister? I should say, 'forewarned is forearmed.'" Sherry winked. "And I guess it helps that you bumped into me not three yards from the headmistress's office."

"Well, tell me if I'm mistaken." Leah laughed good-naturedly. "Mrs. Pepper seems to have made a real impression on you."

"And so she has."

Sherry smiled as she continued down the corridor, chatting with Leah. In her heart, though, she still worried. Fun beckoned to her at every turn. Would she be able to squelch her impulses enough to actually perform well?

3

The First Day

At seven o'clock on Monday morning, Sherry awakened to the invasive clanging of a bell. She rolled over, too exhausted to budge from beneath her comfy duvet. She vaguely heard her name being called.

"Rise and shine, sleepy head. Get up and make your bed."

Bassy. But she wasn't good at mornings, so she simply ignored the call.

"Hey! Heed my warning: 'Tis time to make morning!"

Sherry groaned and waved a hand, and Bassy left her alone. She buried her head beneath her quilt, ignoring the commotion of the girls washing *negel vasser*, getting dressed, and brushing their teeth.

Ironically, it was the contrast of sudden silence that startled Sherry out of her slumber. She rolled out of bed and got up—it wouldn't do to be late on the first day of school.

As she rushed down the corridor toward the davening hall for Shacharis, she saw the girl who was last in line turn a corner ahead of her. Sherry raced to catch up and saw it was Rivi.

"Had a good night, did you?" Rivi asked.

Sherry opened her mouth to answer, but Rivi continued without a pause.

"I always think I'll find it impossible to fall asleep the first night. You know, homesickness and all that. But, somehow, the minute my head touches the pillow, I'm out like a light."

Sherry opened her mouth again, but Rivi prattled on.

"I say, what do you think of the dorm? Did you know we had bunk beds in Form One? Imagine that. Oh, the fights it caused. 'I want to be on top!' 'Stop moving about so much, I can't write like this.' 'Why do you have to block the light just as this story is finally getting exciting?' Oh well, I hope we've all grown up since then."

Sherry gave up trying to speak and just listened in amusement as Rivi filled the entire way to the Shacharis assembly with chatter.

"Ah, here we are," Rivi said, pointing through a dark oak door into a large room with rows of girls sitting and facing a small dais at the front. She led Sherry to the row where the other second form girls sat, and they eased past several pairs of legs to two empty chairs.

"What took you so long?" Leah whispered to Sherry as she settled in the seat next to her.

The girl beside Leah turned to look at Sherry. Sherry recognized her from the train. She had short black hair and wire-rimmed glasses, the kind of girl that the teachers liked to appoint as form captain, but Sherry wasn't dazzled. *The picture of goodness, all sweet and solemn.*

"Been up to some mischief, have you?" the girl asked. An impish smile transformed her face into one ripe for shenanigans.

"You'd better believe it," Sherry said, squaring her shoulders. "Some mischief indeed!"

"She seems a good sport," the girl said, nudging Leah.

"This is Nechama, my partner in crime," Leah said, gesturing to her friend with a cheeky grin. "She's enormously bright."

Sherry winked and laughed as Nechama sized her up.

"Think I might join in your fun from time to time?" Sherry said.

Bassy overheard and shook her head, unable to resist sharing her opinion in her inimitable way.

"Leah and Nechama, the infamous pair. I smell trouble brewing in the air."

"Oh, give it a rest, Bassy," Nechama said. "If anyone's ripe for troublemaking, it's you and Baila! We only ... *assist*, if required."

"Shh, the *tefillah* reps are here," Rivi whispered, silencing them all.

At seven-thirty, Shacharis began. At the front of the room, the *tefillah* reps led the davening. Never had Sherry been part of such a large *tefillah* gathering, and she couldn't help being swept along with the stirring tunes and beautiful songs. Samphire had an impressive Shacharis assembly indeed.

After davening, the girls walked to the breakfast hall. Sherry took a deep sniff of something heavenly wafting down the corridor.

"Is that fresh bread?"

Baila and Bassy, who were walking beside her, grinned widely, then led the way into the hall. When Sherry followed, her jaw dropped open.

Baskets of hot rolls and bread lined the tables, interspersed with delicious-looking spreads and fresh fruit salads. Jugs of orange juice with floating ice cubes were placed on every table. And, of course, there were side tables laden with coffee and tea alongside trays of muffins and buns. Although she usually skipped breakfast on many a late day, Sherry thought it would be fun to eat with such a large group of girls.

She settled herself on a bench next to Baila, who was buttering an onion roll.

"Is breakfast always as smashing as this?" Sherry helped herself to some fruit as a platter passed her by.

"Samphire serves delicious, wholesome food every day of the year," Baila answered in a deep, commanding voice, her manner prim. "Good food is the cure for many ailments of the body and spirit."

Sherry laughed at the clever imitation of the headmistress. "Yes, Mrs. Pepper."

"Oh, Baila. Mimic Mrs. Kirby!" Bassy urged. "I love that one best. You copy her so perfectly—the way she dramatically pitches her tone high and then brings it down so suddenly. Please, Baila!"

"Come on, Baila," the girls chorused.

"Sorry, friends," Baila said, "I don't do it on demand. It just doesn't work when I know you're all watching me—ready, set, go." When she saw the crestfallen faces around her, she chuckled. "Don't worry, though, I can never restrain myself for long."

Bassy grinned. "It's no gimmick. Baila will mimic."

She looked around for validation, and the girls returned her smile. As aggravating as her rhyming could sometimes be, they clearly enjoyed her succinct and comical way of putting things. Sherry guessed that Baila was as hooked on imitating others as Bassy was on rhyming. Then she noticed a brown-haired girl with a slight frown on her round face. She seemed ill at ease. Apparently, Baila noticed her as well.

"Don't worry, Becky," Baila said. "You can be sure I won't get carried away. Not like last year." She winced. "Well, that started innocently enough, but went too far, didn't it?"

Sherry's curiosity was piqued, but before she could ask for details, Becky rubbed her nose, pushed her glasses up, and looked straight at Baila.

"I'm all for harmless fun, as long as it doesn't hurt anyone along the way."

"You'll help me toe the line if I get out of hand, won't you?" Baila asked.

Becky's worried eyes softened. "Yes, you're good." She smiled kindly.

Sherry watched the exchange and wrapped a lock of hair around her finger, her remaining breakfast forgotten on her plate. *Who will help* me *toe the line?*

When the bell rang, Sherry walked briskly to the first class of the day, hoping to get a good seat next to a well-behaved student, maybe even Becky.

Please, Hashem. Let me find a friend like Becky. I need all the help I can get.

4 The First Lesson

Nechama walked out of the breakfast hall, Leah close behind her. She noticed Sherry slip into the classroom and take a seat in the middle row, at the double desk in the back. There was something about the way the girl moved, how she carried herself and, also, the unmissable twinkle in her eyes that compelled her to follow the newcomer. She gave Leah a sidelong glance, then eased herself into the vacant seat next to Sherry.

"Ahem." Someone cleared her throat beside her. It was Leah.

"Not sitting next to me?" Her eyes were wide.

Nechama's gaze darted around the room. For a fleeting moment, she thought about moving her things over to Leah's desk, but some gravitational pull held her back.

"I can't do it to her," she whispered, throwing a meaningful glance at Sherry.

Leah's eyes were sad, but they were also shooting sparks of anger. Nechama had to mollify her. Fast.

"We'll sit together in the common room. I'll save you a seat."

But Leah had already turned away. Nechama watched her take a seat by herself in the front corner. She tore a page from her notebook and scribbled a note.

Going to the Twilight Home during break. Joining?

She folded it into a paper airplane and aimed it at Leah. It landed squarely on the desk in front of her. Leah glanced at her with a cock of her eyebrow, then opened the note.

Becky ran to the door and peered through the window. "Shh, the teacher's coming!" She stood at attention near the door and waited, and the rest of the girls rose and stood respectfully behind their desks.

Leah read the note and gave Nechama a half-smile over her shoulder before tucking it into her book. She'd have to be happy with that for now.

Sherry leaned over. "Why is Becky going to the door?"

"It's one of her duties," Nechama whispered. "Becky Robinson was voted form captain at the end of last year."

Sherry nodded and flashed a charming smile, hinting to a streak of mischief that was lurking somewhere inside of her. Nechama could hardly wait to share with Sherry all the excitement they'd had with their teacher the previous year.

Mrs. Hampton, the form teacher, entered. Her charcoal-colored sheitel framed her no-nonsense face. The soft hair showed hints of brown when the sun's rays shone upon it. She looked around at her students and gave them a warm smile.

Nechama chuckled to herself.

"She's not all that formidable," she whispered. "Wait for all the fun we'll have."

Sherry wiggled her eyebrows. "Isn't it too soon to be plotting mischief?"

Her eyes twinkled, and Nechama grinned. She could hardly wait for the pranks they would plan together.

"Good morning, girls," Mrs. Hampton said.

Nechama faced forward, rearranging her features to resemble what she hoped was a model student. It was never good to cause teachers to be suspicious.

"I hope you've all had a good holiday. I'm sure you've welcomed the three new girls we have this year."

Bassy turned and whispered, "One new girl, two new girls, three—what fun and games, I guarantee!"

Mrs. Hampton cleared her throat but said nothing. She motioned to a petite girl with a neat auburn ponytail, sitting in the far-right corner. Her forehead was furrowed, and sadness glinted from her hazel eyes.

"Welcome, Michal Lempel. We are happy to have you join us this year."

Michal mumbled a reply that was barely audible.

Sherry tried to catch Michal's attention, an encouraging smile adorning her face. Her eyes wore an intent look as if she wished she could wipe all that melancholy away.

Nechama tugged at her sleeve, trying to yank Sherry's attention from the new girl.

"What is it?" Sherry asked.

"I just thought of the best thing. Why don't—"

But Sherry didn't take her focus off Michal. "I can almost feel her pain," she whispered. "I wonder—"

Mrs. Hampton's gaze stopped her mid-sentence.

"Sorry," Sherry said quietly.

The teacher moved on swiftly to the next new girl. "Mindy Gross, welcome to our class," she said, nodding to another girl who was sitting next to Michal.

Mindy smiled in response, her blonde hair dancing in front of cocoa-colored eyes. She had a friendly, open expression that made her instantly likeable.

"Here is Sherry Spencer, the last new girl," Nechama called, playfully poking Sherry with the tip of her pen.

"Welcome, Sherry." Mrs. Hampton smiled, a hint of rebuke in her eyes. "Nechama, you seem to have made her quite comfortable." Though she said no more, the warning in her voice came through loud and clear.

Undeterred, Nechama glanced at Sherry, who winked back. As Mrs. Hampton began the lesson, they dutifully looked forward, not wanting to stir the pot too soon.

The first day passed slowly. Each lesson began with an assessment test so teachers could determine the academic level of each girl. Finally, the last bell rang, signaling the end of the day's lessons. The girls remained in their seats for a few minutes, organizing their papers and books.

Nechama had been watching Sherry throughout the day. At lunch, she insisted that Sherry sit next to her at the end of the table, away from the other girls. Sherry punctuated the conversation with fun and wit, displaying a splendid sense of humor. *Hmm, we'll make a good pair.*

"Sizing me up, are you?" Sherry asked, giggling quietly. "It looks like we've got a lot to look forward to this year."

Nechama nodded, delighted. Her gaze swept around the room. "We've got a great bunch, but the two of us will be more than that. We can be the terrible twos." She laughed at her own joke. Then she noticed Michal, who was sitting very still, as though waiting for everyone else to leave before stirring. She hadn't spoken an unnecessary word to anyone all day.

"I don't know what's with *her*!" Nechama said. "I'm not sure why she bothered coming to this school at all. It's obvious that she wants nothing to do with any of us. Look at the way she sits with her back turned. And even the way she speaks to the teachers."

Sherry shifted in her seat, glancing at the auburn-haired girl. "I don't know. Maybe I should go over to her and make her feel welcome. She might be shy." She got up from her seat.

Nechama dragged her down. "Oh no, you don't!"

She was shocked at her own intensity. And, judging by Sherry's reaction, her new friend was none too pleased as well.

Nechama modified her voice. "Listen to me," she said softly. "Some people like their own company best, even when they're among a crowd. It's best not to make her feel uncomfortable."

Sherry raised an eyebrow.

Nechama put on her best smile. "Come, Sherry, let's go outside. I've just thought of the best trick we can play."

Sherry hesitated for just a moment as they passed Michal.

Nechama glanced at the smaller girl derisively. She, Nechama, was way more fun than a silent loner, and wasn't she actually trying to be Sherry's friend? She would make sure that Sherry soon forgot all about sad, quiet Michal.

"So, have you been to the gazebo beside the pond?" she said, catching Sherry's arm and tugging her forward. "There's a place beside the steps where you can hide in the bushes and no one can see a thing."

"Oh?" Sherry said, her face lighting up. She tore her gaze from Michal and gave Nechama her full attention, following her outside.

Nechama smiled. *This will be easy.*

5 Shabbos at Samphire

On Friday afternoon, the sweet melody of *Shabbos, Heilige Shabbos* flowed through the sound system, signaling a mere twenty minutes left until candle lighting. Michal ran her fingers through her freshly washed hair, the smell of Pantene tickling her nose. She opened her closet wide.

So, what should I wear?

Her favorite white cardigan, the one her mother had bought for her, beckoned. She slipped on an elegant light-blue skirt, then buttoned up the delicate cardigan, admiring its fine embroidery and pearl detailing.

Mummy! Why aren't you here? I need you. She covered her face with her hands, breathing deeply, willing the dull heaviness in her chest to disappear. Then pulling herself out of her bitter musings, she readjusted her features, steeling herself to join her class.

Right, time to go down.

"*Gut Shabbos*, Michal," Mrs. Pepper said, smiling at her as she entered the dining room.

Michal was startled. Mrs. Pepper looked so special in her Shabbos finery, with a layered pearl choker framing the neckline of her navy knitted dress. She looked almost ... almost like Mummy.

Michal gave her a shy "*Gut Shabbos*" and rushed to her seat.

The tables looked regal, bedecked with white lace tablecloths, fine china, and gleaming silverware. Finally, the last girl entered the room and the clock chimed six. With slow, dignified steps, Mrs. Pepper walked to the head table. She struck a match and lit the tall white candles. Then she moved her hands gracefully in a welcoming motion to usher in the Shabbos. Michal watched, transfixed. Mrs. Pepper covered her face with her hands, swaying softly as she made the *brachah* and, no doubt, offered up a *tefillah*, too.

She's davening for all of us.

Michal stared, unable to take her eyes off the scene. There was something so touching about the way Mrs. Pepper bent over the flames, she had to suck in her breath to hold back her tears.

Someone patted her shoulder. She turned to see happy-go-lucky Sherry Spencer sitting between Nechama and Baila. Even though they'd only been here for a few days, Sherry was already one of the bunch. Sherry leaned toward her. Nechama cast a wary glance at them through her round spectacles, but said nothing.

"It's special, isn't it?" Sherry whispered.

Michal nodded. "It makes me miss my mother."

"I miss mine, too."

Goosebumps spread over Michal's arms, tingling all the way to the nape of her neck. *What are you thinking, Sherry? Do you even know what it means to miss someone? To really miss someone?*

Sherry turned away and continued watching Mrs. Pepper.

Oh no! She must've sensed my skepticism. I've got to get better at hiding my feelings.

A form six girl passed around *siddurim*, and *Kabbalas Shabbos* began. Michal took a *siddur* and opened it to *Lechu Neranenah*. She was once again transported home. As she lifted her voice, she could almost hear her mother singing next to her as though this were an ordinary Shabbos with her family. Her heart warmed and she was overwhelmed by a fierce longing. She stretched her neck and took a deep breath.

I'm okay.

After Maariv, the singing began. The beautiful, stirring tunes created something magical in the air and she closed her eyes, no longer in the davening hall at Samphire but back in their small dining room at home. Her mother was sitting next to her as Tatty sang the *zemiros* in his sweet baritone voice. Michal felt safe, calm and protected. She didn't want the moment to end, but then Kiddush was announced and a hush fell upon the hall.

She opened her eyes to see Rabbi Pepper making his way to the front of the room, his head bent. He poured wine into an ornate silver *kos*, raised it high, and recited Kiddush, his voice ringing loud and clear. Several sixth formers went around the room, filling each girl's cup. Michal took a sip of the wine, and made a face at its tartness.

She coughed and looked around, wondering if anyone had noticed her moment of indiscretion. Sherry caught her eye again and flashed her a smile. She didn't seem bothered by Michal's reaction at all. If anything, she was laughing with her, not at her.

Should I ask her to come with me to wash for Hamotzi? *No, Nechama has already asked her. Never mind.*

Michal watched the two girls traipse to the sinks, laughing and talking to each other, and ignored the familiar ache in her chest. She returned from washing and was handed a fluffy piece of challah. *Delicious!* But as she sat down, she wished there was someone she could share it with, someone who would laugh and talk with *her*.

She stared at her plate. Usually, every part of the *seudah* seemed charged with a special atmosphere. She had always loved this meal—it used to be her favorite time of the week. But since Mummy was gone, it had been a source of pain, a reminder of what used to be.

Even tonight, the dignity and peace that filled the room were bittersweet. She tried to take it all in—the singing, the grandeur, the inspirational thoughts being shared, even the taste of the golden chicken soup. She longed for what was, but also yearned to savor what she had now. The conflicting emotions played tug of war in her heart, and it took all her energy to focus on the here and now. *There's nothing like Shabbos.* Faint whispers of happiness crept into her heart, so quietly she was hardly aware.

Mrs. Pepper stood up to share an insight on the *parshah*, a well-used *sefer* in her hand. A stillness descended upon the room. The headmistress cleared her throat and began to talk about the *bikkurim*—the mitzvah of bringing the first of the *shivas haminim* up to Yerushalayim to present to the *kohen*.

"I want to read to you how the Mishnah describes the annual parade," Mrs. Pepper said, and bent her head to read from the *sefer* in her hands. "An ox with horns bedecked with gold and an olive crown on its head led the way. The flute was played before them ... When they arrived close to Yerushalayim, they ornamentally arranged their *bikkurim*. The governors and chiefs and treasurers went out to meet them ... All the skilled artisans of Yerushalayim would stand up before them and greet them, saying, 'Our brothers, men of such-and-such place, we welcome you in peace.'" Mrs. Pepper looked up. "Quite a commotion—and all for a little olive or dried fig?" She raised an eyebrow and looked around the room.

Michal tilted her head. She hadn't considered this. *Why indeed?*

Mrs. Pepper closed the *sefer* and clasped it in front of her with both hands.

"There are many beautiful commentaries to explain this. But today, I want to leave you with just one small nugget. The *bikkurim* were given from the first fruits. And the first is something very special. We are all attached to firsts—a mother to her baby's first smile, a businessman to his first deal, an author to the first book published. Firsts are precious. Hashem says, 'Take that first fruit you labored over and give it to Me.' This is something else entirely! It elevates all the farmer's produce from the simple to the sublime."

Mrs. Pepper put down the *sefer* on a nearby table and paced a little. The candlelight glowing on her face gave her a mysterious aura as she spoke, lending weight to her words.

"Today is your first Shabbos here. Use it well. Dedicate it to Hashem. Control your anger. Watch your speech. Smile at a friend. Think of anything you can do to make this day extra special. It's a *bikkurim*, if you will, to Hashem."

Michal glanced down. She wanted to follow the headmistress's words, but she didn't know how to make this day special when her heart was so heavy *every* day. Even the wonder she'd felt earlier in the evening was beginning to fade as she thought of all those firsts she would never again have with Mummy. She blinked back tears, and when she glanced up, Sherry's eyes met hers, shining in the candlelight. When Sherry saw her looking, she quickly glanced back at Mrs. Pepper.

The headmistress's next words sliced through the stillness.

"There's one other thing I want to say." She looked around at the girls and gave a rueful smile. "It's something you've all heard before: Today is the first day of the rest of your life!"

A hushed giggle rippled through the room, and Mrs. Pepper smiled.

"Girls, make each day a worthwhile first. *Gut Shabbos!*"

As the girls left the hall and tromped up the stairs to their rooms, Michal found Sherry Spencer walking next to her. She looked up in alarm, wondering what she could possibly want from her now.

"Here." Sherry thrust a small pouch of pistachio nuts into Michal's hands. "I noticed you enjoyed this. I want you to have mine."

Michal started, reflexively accepting the gift. "Thanks," she murmured. "Don't you like them?"

"They're my favorite." Sherry flashed a smile, then hurried to catch up with Nechama.

Michal's eyes stung. The speech from Mrs. Pepper still rang in her ears and the quiet majesty that had permeated the Shabbos table still whispered, promising to soothe her heart if she would only let it. She looked at the nuts in her hands, and a bubble of hope expanded inside her chest.

For so long, she'd been stuck in final moments. Tonight she had been reminded that she still had some wonderful firsts to experience, too.

If only some firsts could last forever.

Sherry Gets Up to Mischief

It was the second week of school, and Sherry was making her way to the classroom for the last period of the day—geography—thinking about how hard she'd been working. *Too hard, and it just won't do. Preparatory work, assignments, tests, readings ... a never-ending wheel of boredom.*

She continued down the hallway, quietly singing, "All work and no play makes Sherry sad and dull."

"Hey, Sherry, watch out," Chava said, bumping into her. She smiled. "You being good, sis?"

Chava's expression was earnest. Sherry smiled back. *She really wants to be proud of me here.*

"Of course!" she said.

"Good."

"Chava, hurry or we'll be late," said an older girl walking down the hallway.

"Coming, Naomi." Chava glanced at Sherry. "See you at supper.

Keep up the good work." She hurried after her friend.

But Chava's words had the opposite effect on Sherry. Without understanding why, she had the urge to do something really naughty, like putting fish in water bottles or locking the teachers into the staffroom.

Oh, but I couldn't do that. It would be taking mischief too far. But, hey, who says I can't lock away the workbooks? As it is, Miss Stern gives us far too much work to do.

She flipped her hair behind her shoulder.

Yes, geography would be the perfect lesson for some fun. Hah, that will save me dollops of time.

"Why should I do some silly assignment when I could be having fun instead?"

"What are you up to?" a girl asked from behind her.

She jumped, startled. She hadn't realized she'd said the last sentence out loud. When she turned, she faced a student she hadn't yet met, a pretty girl with a strong chin and iridescent amber eyes. She was only a smidge taller than Sherry.

The girl chuckled. "I'm Mali Atkins. Who are you?"

"Sherry Spencer. And here I thought I already knew everyone. What class are you in?"

"Oh, so you must be a first former. I was quite sure you were in second form, like me."

"What? You're also in second form?"

Mali frowned. For a moment, she seemed puzzled. But then her eyes lit up. "So you're also a new girl?"

Sherry gasped. "Are you a mind reader?"

"Maybe I am." Mali's voice was neutral, but she couldn't disguise the playful twinkle in her eyes. "Well, who else wouldn't know another student if not a first former or a new girl?"

Sherry laughed. "Yeah, I realized that by now. You're starting school a little late, no?"

She leaned forward to share something with her new friend, but Mali looked behind Sherry and drew away, her eyes wide.

"Are you both prepared for your next class?" Mrs. Pepper asked.

The girls straightened their backs. Sherry stole a glance at Mali. The girl's face was perfectly respectful and obedient as she smiled up at the headmistress.

"Yes, Mrs. Pepper."

"Well, then, run along, girls. You wouldn't want to keep your teacher waiting."

Sherry rushed to class, but Mali was faster. By the time she entered the room, the new girl was already seated at a desk that had mysteriously been added to their classroom that morning.

A moment later, the door opened and Miss Stern stepped in, surveying the class with a sharp gaze through her wire-framed spectacles. Everything about Miss Stern was sharp—her nose, her piercing green eyes, even her bony shoulders.

"Good morning, girls," Miss Stern said, placing her books and a key on the desk.

Sherry peered at the key. Yes, that was the key to the cupboard where the workbooks were kept. She recognized its unusual shape. She glanced back at the teacher before she had a chance to become suspicious.

"And good afternoon, Mali," Miss Stern continued. "I hope the girls have made you feel welcome. I'm sure they will help you catch up on the work you have missed."

"Yes, Miss Stern," Mali answered, the picture of obedience.

As Miss Stern handed out worksheets to the first girl in each row to pass behind her, Sherry marveled at the transformation in Mali.

All traces of the mischief she'd seen in the girl's face when they'd met in the hallway were now safely hidden behind her round amber eyes. She wondered how Mali would react to a homework-free night if Sherry took Miss Stern's key. Would she be happy or upset? It was hard to make sense of the girl's reactions.

And how does she know Miss Stern's name?

Sherry didn't have time to ponder for long. Miss Stern walked up and down the aisles, checking that each girl was doing her work. Sherry pretended to fill in her paper, but kept an eye on the teacher's progress. Miss Stern stopped by Rivi's desk in the corner to help her, her back to the rest of the room.

It's now or never.

Sherry eased out of her seat and tiptoed to the front of the class and Miss Stern's desk. In a flash, the key to the cupboard was in her hand. She stole a peek behind her. Mali was watching her. She bent back over her work, her face betraying nothing.

Brilliant, Miss Stern is still at Rivi's desk. It didn't take more than a split second for her to pocket the key and return to her seat.

From the corner of her eye, she saw Nechama flash her a thumbs-up. Every other girl was conscientiously doing her assignment and hadn't noticed a thing. Mali didn't look up again. *Good, the fewer in the know, the better.*

Footsteps approached her desk. She lowered her head and wrote faster. It wouldn't do for the teacher to see she was behind in her work.

"Good, good," Miss Stern said as she passed her desk.

Sherry smiled inwardly. *She wouldn't be praising me if she knew what was hiding in my pocket.*

Soon there were only ten minutes left until the end of the lesson. Miss Stern looked down at her desk and began lifting random items and putting them down again.

"Is something the matter?" Nechama called out with a cheeky grin.

Becky raced to the front of the room. "Let me help you look. Here, are you missing this pen?"

Miss Stern glared at her. But before she could gather her wits, three other girls—Nechama, Baila, and Sherry—joined in the search, sharing in the fun. It was only Sherry and Nechama who knew precisely what Miss Stern was missing, though.

"Are you missing your ruler?" Baila held it up.

"Or maybe this notebook?" Sherry asked, holding out a pretty spiral book.

"Or this piece of chalk?" Nechama said.

"No!" Their teacher shook her head in exasperation and, as if on cue, every girl in the room let out a loud sigh as they commiserated with her, though not without expressions of amusement.

Well, every girl but one. Sherry noticed that Mali's face looked strained, but she was certain the girl was doing everything she could to stifle her laughter. Mali didn't seem the goody-goody type at all. Then she remembered that it was Mali's first day. That explained it. She was sure the girl would have participated in the fun otherwise—perhaps she was still just a tad intimidated.

"The key to the cupboard seems to have vanished into thin air," Miss Stern said, checking beneath her briefcase for the third time. "I distinctly remember putting it down on the desk as soon as I walked in." She shrugged. "Oh well, I'm sure Miss Bentley has another one. But there's no point in you doing preparatory work if I haven't explained it beforehand." She shook her head and tsk-tsked. "That's just too bad."

Bassy whistled. "That's too bad, and just so sad."

Sherry restrained herself from grinning. Things couldn't have gone better if she'd tried.

While Miss Stern stood by the door to dismiss the class, Sherry slipped the key into the pocket of the teacher's blue cardigan, which was draped over the back of her desk chair. Then she hid behind a pillar in the hallway near the door and waited. Nechama pressed against her, merriment in her eyes.

Sure enough, a few minutes later, Miss Stern left the classroom wearing her cardigan. There was a puzzled look on her face as she checked her pocket and pulled the key out. Sherry and Nechama clapped their hands to their mouths to stifle their giggles.

Behind them, Baila whisked a camera out of her pocket and focused on the teacher through the viewfinder. She pressed the shutter all the way down. Click.

"Good shot." She whistled and turned the advancing wheel clockwise, ready for her next shot.

Sherry chuckled. "You like taking risks, don't you?"

Baila giggled. "Not such a risk, taking a shot from this far away. And luckily, mine hasn't got a built-in flash, so the light can't even give me away."

She slipped her camera back into her bulging pocket and patted it. "No one's the wiser," she said, grinning.

But of course Bassy noticed. "Baila, Baila, you're a scream and a half, just make sure to keep it hidden from the staff!"

"And in years to come, you bet we'll share a laugh," Sherry added, giggling.

The class, obviously pleased as punch, was wise enough to mask their joy until they were safely in the common room. Then pandemonium broke loose. Who would have believed it? No geography prep work! It was too good to be true.

"An evening to ourselves—yippee!" Sherry shouted. "I vote we play a good game of Pictionary."

"Yes, let's," said Baila, and went to the games cupboard to retrieve it.

Sherry couldn't hold back her smile. She was positively beaming at how well her trick had played out.

Mali sat on a sofa and looked up at her. "You're a naughty little thing."

Though Mali kept a straight face, she had a gleam in her eyes. Sherry knew her secret was safe.

"You're getting to be a real pro," Nechama said. "I knew you'd be a good sport from the moment I saw you."

Sherry smiled back. She should have been pleased by that comment, but for some reason, she felt a pit in her stomach.

Oblivious to her discomfort, Nechama took her hand and whispered her latest plan—switching the sugar in the sixth form common room for salt.

"Just picture their faces at tea time!" Nechama broke into a fit of giggles.

Sherry nodded eagerly, already anticipating the reaction of the older girls.

"We'll have to be careful that Chava doesn't notice," Nechama added. "As head girl, she'd report us for sure."

That gave Sherry pause, but only for a moment. Even if Chava found out who did it, she was sure she'd see the joke.

After all, it was only a little harmless fun. Wasn't it?

7 Trouble

Sherry sat on the garden bench, her shoulders slumped. The student copy of her first month's progress report lay in her hands. Ma had received the original by post. Sherry rubbed her shoes against the pebbles.

The sound of someone running interrupted her dismal musings, and she looked up to see Mali approaching. When she saw Sherry sitting there, she jogged over and paced in place.

"What you doing here on your own?"

Sherry handed the report to her classmate. "My mother will be so disappointed." Her gaze shifted to the ground. "I don't like upsetting her."

Mali was silent. She opened her mouth, then closed it again.

Sherry sighed. "Say it already—well deserved!"

Mali handed back the report. "I won't read it," she said, her voice low. "It would be wrong of me." She shivered and rubbed her arms. "I'm the wrong person to tell you anything."

Sherry looked at her. *What did that mean?* But Mali didn't offer any explanation.

"Did you not know about the report?" Mali asked.

Sherry shook her head. "This must be a new thing. I can't recall Chava ever receiving a report card so early in the year." She smiled. "Anyway, good for you, you clever thing. It was smart of you not to join in all my cuckoo acts." A quiet chuckle escaped her throat. She'd had a good time in too many classes. She winked. "I'm not sure they weren't worth the trouble."

When Mali remained silent, Sherry looked at her again. "You seem the fun type. How do you manage to control yourself so well?"

Mali blushed a bright crimson but retained her taciturn demeanor, and Sherry didn't press her. Instead, she read aloud the comment that Mrs. Pepper had written at the bottom of her report:

"Sherry has it in her to be a true asset. She's thoughtful, cheerful, and honest—all fine traits. What a shame that she's using her intelligence and charm to stir up trouble. I sincerely hope she'll come to realize that while mischief may earn her a chuckle or two, it will never earn her respect."

Mali nodded. "Strong words, huh?"

"Nicely coated, I'd say."

"She's a smart woman to see through your pranks."

"You're too kind." Sherry twisted her mouth. "I've got to try and buckle down. I just don't see how I'll manage. The class will be looking at me to rustle up some fun. And with Nechama egging me on, how will I be able to refuse?"

"I'm ... I'm the wrong person to say anything. By the way, thanks for the custard biscuits. They were delicious. Your mother is kind."

"I'll tell her you liked them. She baked them just for you, you know. She sent me two cellophane packages, one for me and one for my friend."

"Generous!"

From the corner of her eye, Sherry noticed Nechama and Leah coming toward them. She stuffed the report in her blazer before they arrived. Nechama leaned down and whispered in her ear.

"I have the most splendid idea. During maths, every time Miss Bentley turns her back, you should stand up and count to ten. It will be a hoot!"

Sherry gave a weak smile in return.

Leah, standing behind Nechama, glared at Sherry, animosity radiating from her eyes. Sherry couldn't fathom why. *What on earth has she got against me?*

The bell rang for lessons, and she and the other girls rushed to be on time.

"*Hatzlachah*," Mali whispered as she took her seat.

Miss Bentley, the maths teacher, came into class. She pushed her glasses up her nose and began teaching.

The lesson was so boring, Sherry found herself dozing off. She had already learned all the stuff Miss Bentley was droning on about at her previous school.

Nechama poked her with a pen and arched an eyebrow, looking meaningfully at her. Sherry didn't know what to do. She wanted to commit to changing her behavior. On the other hand, she didn't want to let Nechama down.

Miss Bentley handed out a worksheet.

Sherry wanted to roll her eyes, but saw Miss Bentley glance sharply at her. She stopped herself at the last second. *This is too much. I can't be expected to learn this math all over again.*

Nechama poked her again. "Come on," she whispered.

Miss Bentley turned to the blackboard to write up examples of the algebraic techniques she'd just been explaining. Sherry didn't think she could survive the boredom.

You know what? I'll accept Nechama's dare this one last time. But as soon as this lesson is finished, I'm going to tell her it's over for me. I'm ditching this mischief-making, whatever it takes.

Glancing at Nechama, she got to her feet and counted to ten. Nechama gave her a gleeful grin. Mali bit her lip and tried to concentrate on the examples on the board. Leah was still glaring at her. The rest of the class giggled quietly as they watched Sherry's antics.

"What is going on with you today, class?" their teacher asked, letting out an exasperated sigh. "I'm teaching an important and complex concept, and none of you are focusing."

The reprimand was met with a few giggles. Even more annoyed, Miss Bentley frowned and looked around the classroom, pausing here and there but not focusing on any one girl in particular. Sherry thought nothing of it and planned her next move. To her consternation, when Miss Bentley was about to write another example on the board, she swung around and caught Sherry rising out of her chair. Sherry's heart nearly stopped, and she froze.

"Sherry, must you disturb our lesson? Take your books and leave the room."

Cheeks burning, Sherry headed toward the door.

"Don't worry," quiet, almost-too-good Michal whispered as she passed her desk.

Sherry did a double take. *Michal risking getting into trouble?* Miss Bentley never allowed whispering. Sherry wanted to respond kindly but was too afraid, and too ashamed. To add to her humiliation, Mrs. Pepper was walking down the corridor and noticed her leaving the classroom. The headmistress searched her face for answers.

Sherry didn't know if she could stand the mortification. She glanced nervously at Mrs. Pepper, even as her gaze kept returning to the floor. Her throat scratchy, she barely managed to whisper, "I'm sorry."

Mrs. Pepper gave her a long, harsh look, then went on her way. Sherry wished she had given her a telling-off, or at least had said a few words. It was almost as though the headmistress thought she wasn't worth the bother.

She stood outside the classroom for twenty minutes. The time crawled by and was more than enough for her to think about her actions. It wasn't pleasant, but she considered herself an honest girl and admitted that she had misbehaved.

I must change my behavior. The dare seemed like a good laugh, but now it's not so funny. She let out a deep sigh. *If only I had Esther here with me—I miss her support.*

The end-of-lesson bell rang. Miss Bentley came out and handed Sherry a long worksheet.

"This must be completed and handed in tomorrow, along with the rest of the class's worksheets. You may find it difficult as we've learnt something new today, which you've missed. But you only have yourself to blame." Then, as she looked at Sherry's abashed face, her expression softened. "Sherry, I know you can do better. Show me that."

"I will try," Sherry said, and she meant it.

When Miss Bentley walked away, Rivi came over. "How was it?"

Sherry sighed. "Being sent out of class in disgrace, having to stand outside, bored, and on top of that, having Mrs. Pepper find me here ... I'm not sure what you'd call that. Certainly not enjoyable."

"Don't take it to heart," Nechama said, patting her shoulder. "It was so much fun!"

"Not when you're the one getting in trouble," Michal said, giving Nechama a pointed look.

Sherry glanced at her. Michal met her gaze and gave her a small smile.

Nechama noticed and grabbed Sherry by the arm, casting a malicious look at Michal.

"C'mon, Sherry. Even if you don't want to play pranks, I still have some ideas for fun. Why don't we walk to the cliffs and get some fresh air?"

Sherry studied the worksheet in her hand. "I don't know. I should probably start working on this."

"Oh, this won't take long," Nechama said. "You'll have plenty of time to finish your homework."

Sherry thought about it. Michal eyed her with a hint of reproachful concern. Sherry turned to Mali for support, but the taller girl averted her gaze.

"I don't think so, Nechama. I'll come another time. I need to start behaving, starting now. No more mischief for me."

She pulled her arm away from Nechama's and headed down the hall to the common room. When she glanced over her shoulder, Nechama was still staring at her, her eyes round and disappointed through her thick lenses. She noticed Sherry looking and turned away, frowning.

Sherry's spirits sank. If she was doing the right thing, why was it so hard?

8 More Trouble

When Sherry arrived at breakfast the next morning, Nechama was already there with an empty spot on the bench beside her.

"I saved you a seat," she said, patting it.

On Nechama's other side, Leah noticed Sherry standing there and huffed. There was also an empty seat next to Michal, but though she looked invitingly at Sherry, she said nothing. Sherry thought it might be nice to sit with Michal, but she already felt like she'd let Nechama down the night before. She put her tray down beside Nechama.

"You look happy this morning," Nechama said, handing her the milk.

"I got my maths worksheet done with time to spare last night. I want to surprise Miss Bentley by handing it in early."

Nechama chucked her on the shoulder. "See? We would have had time to walk to the cliffs. You missed out on some good fun. Leah and I went, and we had a blast, didn't we, Leah?"

Leah frowned.

Sherry pursed her lips. "I'm sorry, Nechama. I just can't afford any more bad marks. I have to focus on my schoolwork if I want to turn around this year."

Nechama snorted. "Okay. We'll see how long this lasts."

Sherry ignored the snide remark. She could be good. She had to be.

The girls were all seated around their tables and tucking in with enthusiasm. At the head of the room, not far from the second form table, their teachers were enjoying their food with a little more dignity.

"Anyone care for a cup of coffee?" Mrs. Cohen asked her colleagues.

"Who can resist a shot of caffeine?" Mrs. Davis responded. Most of the other staff members smiled and nodded.

Mali was sitting on Sherry's other side. She watched as Mali stared at the teachers' table. Every now and then, Mali would turn away and try to rearrange her features in a nonchalant expression. Soon, Mrs. Cohen returned, carrying a tray with cups of coffee and a jug of milk.

"It's just coffee, you know?" Sherry said to Mali, giving her a puzzled look.

Mali nodded. "I know." She bent her head to her oatmeal, but still kept glancing up at the teachers' table.

That's when distraught, muffled sounds started emanating from the teachers' table, and Mali looked as if she might burst at any moment.

What is going on with her?

Sherry looked up to see what was happening to the teachers. Several of them, including Mrs. Davis, the perfectionist Chava had warned her about before school began, were holding paper coffee cups close to their faces—and they couldn't pull them away. The cups were firmly attached to their lips!

"It's stuck!" Mrs. Lee stammered, trying to pull the cup away without burning herself with the hot coffee.

"What a mean trick," Mrs. Davis said, but the cup attached to her lip muffled her words.

By now, the students had figured out what was happening, and many of them were giggling behind their hands. However, watching the teachers struggling to remove the cups from their faces, some of them getting burned from the coffee, had the opposite effect on Mali. She stared at the chaos, turning white as a sheet.

Nechama glanced around, then walked over to the side table where the food was laid out. She picked up a discarded bottle of food-safe glue from the wastebasket. She met Sherry's eyes.

"Was that you?" she asked, her head jerking toward the commotion at the teachers' table.

Sherry shook her head, horrified that Nechama could think such a thing after she'd made the decision to reform her behavior.

"No? Well, that's a shame, it was a really good prank!"

Nechama let out an enormous roar of laughter, which was all the girls needed to let loose with howls of delight. By then, most of the teachers had left the room.

Sherry turned to Mali, still laughing. "That was a good joke, wasn't it? But I'm glad it wasn't me this time. Did you see those teacher's faces? Whoever did this is going to be in so much trouble."

Then she noticed Mali's expression. The girl looked as though she might cry.

"Did you see Mrs. Pepper? She's furious. And Mrs. Hampton spilled coffee on her white blouse. I hope they have an easy time removing those cups."

Sherry put a hand on Mali's shoulder. "At least whoever swapped the glue for the milk didn't use a strong type of glue. So fret not, dear friend. The teachers will be back in their classrooms before the bell rings."

Mali shook her head.

"Know something I don't?" Sherry asked, wiggling her eyebrows.

Mali blanched. "I think I'm going to be sick." She jumped up and fled the room.

Sherry watched her go. *That's strange. Could Mali have ...? No. She's too straight-laced to do something so outrageous. She just feels bad for the teachers.*

The bell rang. Without the teachers to direct them, the girls left the room in a mad scramble as they rushed to class. As Sherry made a beeline for her desk, she was glad to see Mali already seated. She winked at her friend, but Mali didn't seem to notice.

The clock dinged as it hit the hour: nine o'clock. The girls looked around at each other. Something was wrong. Where was Mrs. Hampton, their form teacher, who was supposed to teach them for first period? She was never late.

"Perhaps it's taking a long time to remove the cups," Rivi said.

Bassy shook her head. "Come on, it's just a little glue. I wonder who gets the thank you."

"It could have been a girl from any form," Baila said.

Bassy looked around the class. "Well, well, it wasn't me, and Sherry says it wasn't she. Nechama and Leah have ruled themselves out, and you others are far too mature, no doubt."

Sherry blinked at Bassy. "Whoa. A double couplet. How do you come up with those so fast?"

Bassy grinned, her freckles stretching across her round face. "It's a family talent. My grandfather was a famous *badchan*."

The school bell rang again, but it wasn't the ordinary ring indicating the beginning of lessons. It was a sound that summoned the girls to the assembly room.

"What's happened?" Rivi shrieked. "Is there a fire?"

Bassy giggled and glanced at Sherry, as though to say, *Watch this.* "What do you think it is, Rivi? It's Mrs. Pepper, don't you see? Surely with something so amiss, she wants to get straight to the bottom of this."

Becky stood, taking command. "Well, don't just sit there. Pack up. It's time to go." She glared accusingly at Sherry.

Does she think I *did this?*

The girls got up from their seats and gathered their things. Sherry took her time as she put her things away, thankful that Becky didn't wait for her. She thought she was the last person to leave, but as she headed through the open door, she noticed Mali crouching behind it.

Mali tugged at Sherry's blouse. "Wait for me." Her voice wobbled like jelly.

Sherry helped her stand up. "Whatever's the matter, Mali?"

"I'm going to be expelled!" she cried, her voice mounting in hysteria. She said many things, but because she was sobbing, Sherry could only make out the words, "I'm here on trial."

She wrapped her arm around Mali and encouraged her to breathe slowly to calm herself. Then, noticing how pale her friend appeared, she ordered her to sit in the nearest chair.

"Wait here until you feel better, okay? I'll tell Mrs. Pepper that you aren't feeling well if she asks about your absence. Now, Mali, listen here—I've got to run, but you need to take yourself in hand. I'm telling you that you're safe. Got that?"

Mali responded with a meek nod, then laid her head on the desk and tried to steady her breathing. Sherry did her best to comfort her for a couple of minutes, then left the room to make her way to the assembly hall.

Michal was waiting for her outside the room. "Sherry?"

"What is it?" She hurried with Michal down the corridor.

"I ... I just want to say ... be careful. It's okay for you to get yourself into trouble ... but I think you may have encouraged Mali too much."

"What are you talking about?"

"Well, it's obvious, isn't it? Mali is the culprit."

Sherry stopped. All of a sudden, she was filled with admiration for this quiet girl who was worrying about Mali. But even more, she was filled with humiliation. She had done what she had promised she would never do again. She felt sick.

"You're right, Michal," she said at last.

Michal looked intently at her. "Sherry, you don't have to get into mischief all the time."

Sherry nodded slowly. "I'm so sorry," she said, her voice catching in her throat. "My Papa always said that one day, my love for adventure would get another person into trouble. And I'm afraid it just did."

"Don't apologize to me. I think you need to apologize to Mali."

Sherry looked at Michal, stricken. "I know," she said quietly. "I just hope it's not too late. Mali didn't just play any trick! This was a doozie. I wonder what Mrs. Pepper will say to her."

They had reached the assembly hall, but the rest of the girls were already piling out. They were a subdued group—quite a contrast to the carefree laughter of earlier.

Someone grasped her hand. Bassy was too serious to speak in rhyme for once. "You and your tardiness. What are you thinking of, turning up now?" She leaned closer. "The glue wasn't the end of it. Can you believe that someone actually went and spread charcoal all over the back door to the teachers' room? They've had to contend with more than just the cups sticking to their lips—their hands are totally coated in black, too."

Sherry shook her head in disbelief as Bassy pulled her along. She had *never* done anything so extreme. What had Mali been thinking?

"Mrs. Pepper said that the perpetrator better own up by ten o'clock or she'll have to cancel visiting day for the entire school."

"But she can't do that!" Sherry cried. "I've been waiting for visiting day ever since I boarded the train to get here."

She missed Ma more than she had imagined she would. The promise of visiting day was the only thing keeping her going. *I can't imagine not seeing Ma for so long.*

But she knew she wasn't the only one. What about her friends? What about the poor first form girls, so young and away from home for the first time? They would be devastated.

"Are you okay, Sherry?" Bassy asked.

"Huh? Oh, um ... yes, I think so."

Bassy frowned. "You look worried."

Sherry stared at her as if seeing her for the first time. Bassy stared back in confusion.

Then it came to Sherry in a flash.

If I go and own up to Mrs. Pepper, she'll never need to find out that it was Mali. Poor Mali. She's really nice, and I like her a lot, and I can see that she's so shaken up by her behavior that she wouldn't dare play such a trick again. I can't let her be sent home in disgrace. Especially if ... I ... I was the cause of it all.

Her breath hitched at the possible consequences, but she knew she probably deserved whatever they may be. With firm, bold steps, she made her way to Mrs. Pepper's office. Before she knew it, she was looking into the stern face of the headmistress. Almost instantly, her boldness left her.

"I ... I ... um, I did it," she stammered, her gaze dropping to the floor.

A long, taunting silence ensued.

"Sherry," Mrs. Pepper said finally, "I am deeply, deeply disappointed. I thought you were made of better stuff."

Another excruciating silence followed.

"I don't trust myself to talk to you right now. Wait in the room next door."

Sherry wiped sweat from her brow with a trembling hand as she left the room, her heart pounding. Though she knew she was innocent, she felt so small. Then terror filled her, leaving her gasping for breath.

Is there a chance Mrs. Pepper will expel me? What will Ma say?

Large tears rolled down her cheeks, and her whole body shook as she awaited the awful punishment she was sure Mrs. Pepper would mete out. But more than anything, her heart ached at the thought that she had once again let down Ma, and Papa, too.

Sorry, Papa. I tried.

9 Mrs. Pepper Is Shocked

Mrs. Pepper sat in her office with Sherry seated across from her. The headmistress was clearly pondering the situation.

"Sherry, I am absolutely shocked that you would have done such a thing. I would never think that you, of all the girls, would bear responsibility for these horrible tricks."

Sherry clasped her hands in her lap and listened as Mrs. Pepper went on.

"Now, I know you're a bit prone to mischief, but this ..." She inhaled deeply, gathering her thoughts. "This crosses a line, one that I was certain you would not step over. You are a jolly, brilliant girl. Why?" She shook her head in disbelief.

Sherry couldn't look at the headmistress. She was too ashamed. She recalled the high hopes Mrs. Pepper had held for her on her first day and wondered if she was now thinking how different she was from Chava.

Someone knocked on the door—a frantic rapping that indicated trouble. Sherry hoped the urgency of the matter would offer her a reprieve.

"Come in," Mrs. Pepper called, her voice still infused with disappointment.

The door inched open and in walked Mali Atkins, her eyes red and swollen.

"Mrs. Pepper," she sobbed, rubbing her nose on her sleeve. "It was me." Her bottom lip trembled. "I ... I did it!"

Then she broke down, her shoulders shaking with loud, racking sobs.

"I've let ... I've let everyone down. Mummy and Daddy are going to be so ... so ashamed of me. And I know I'll be ... expelled. Expelled from Samphire, no less!" She sniffled and straightened, tears dripping from her wet cheeks. "I ... I didn't deserve a chance. I didn't!"

Sherry sat frozen. She stared at the headmistress, who looked back at her, head tilted.

Finally, after what felt like an eternity, Mrs. Pepper's intimidating voice broke the silence.

"What on earth is going on?" she asked. "Were you both in it together?"

Sherry caught her breath. What would she say now?

Before she could gather her wits, Mali spoke, her voice barely audible.

"I guess Sherry was trying to protect me. I told her I would be expelled if you were to find out."

Mrs. Pepper looked from Sherry to Mali and back again. Then she shook her head, her expression one of sadness and disappointment.

"Sherry, I'll have to deal with you later. This is not the type of behavior I expect from a Samphire girl."

Sherry coughed out a shaky sob that had been lingering for far too long. "S-sorry."

Mrs. Pepper then looked at Mali. "Mali, I've been hearing glowing reports about you. What suddenly made you plot these ridiculous and, dare I say, cruel tricks?"

Mali opened her mouth, then closed it.

"Do you remember the deal we made before you came here?" Mrs. Pepper arched a brow.

Mali gave a sad nod.

"You were here on trial. You promised that you would give as much as you could to the school, instead of ..."

She glanced at Sherry, as if only now remembering she was there.

"I apologize, Mali," Mrs. Pepper said. "I shouldn't have said these things in front of Sherry."

Mali shook her head and sniffled. "It's okay." Her voice sounded tiny. "She knows." She looked straight at her friend. "I was here on a trial basis due to Mrs. Pepper's kindness and a special arrangement to pay my fees in installments."

Sherry couldn't prevent the question from popping out of her mouth. "Why a trial basis?"

"All my older sisters were here at Samphire and loved it. But then my father was cheated by a so-called friend and his business went downhill. He couldn't afford to pay for me to go to school here ... and so my parents sent me to a local day school."

Her face turned a bright crimson and Sherry threw her a sympathetic look.

"I'm embarrassed to tell you," Mali continued. "But I couldn't bear the disappointment and didn't do even half as well as I could have. And then I thought of this wonderful idea—a brainwave, I called it. I phoned Mrs. Pepper and asked if she would accept me—without fees."

She glanced at Mrs. Pepper, who folded her hands in front of her and patiently waited for Mali to continue. Sherry sat quietly, too fearful to ask questions. But Mali took a deep breath and shivered.

"My mother was shocked after I told her I had called. But then she said that she was taking on a new job and would be able to save up enough to cover the fees if Mrs. Pepper would allow installments." She looked down at the floor. "I knew the reports Mrs. Pepper would receive about me might be far from glowing, and I promised her I would do my best if she accepted me. She kindly allowed me to come but said it was for a trial period. My trial is meant to end tomorrow." Her voice shook. "But I guess now it's goodbye for good!"

Mali sat with her shoulders hunched, crushed by the weight of her impending expulsion. She threw a pained glance at Sherry, and Sherry startled: the twinkle in her eyes had dulled. Her amber irises were paler than ever, her raw sense of failure transparent through them. Sherry took Mali's icy hands in her own. And then, she realized something.

"Mali, you did this purposely before the trial period ended. Am I right? Something compelled you to do it. I'm quite sure about that. Why? Why did you do it?"

Mali's face turned white.

Mrs. Pepper stared at Sherry, as if surprised at the girl's intuition. She turned to Mali. "Young lady, please tell me why you didn't wait until your trial was over before pulling such silly pranks."

"You see, Mrs. Pepper," Mali responded, her voice quivering, "I have been on my best behavior, but it doesn't come easy to me. I was so worried that you would tell me tomorrow that I could stay, but you wouldn't actually mean *me*. You would mean the person I've been pretending to be. I think everything just built up inside me and came out this morning."

She hiccupped as tears streamed down her cheeks. "It's like I had to warn you who I really am. I didn't want to be allowed to stay on false pretenses."

Mrs. Pepper stared at her, open-mouthed, then caught herself and straightened.

"I see." She took a long, deep breath, pursed her lips, and exhaled through her nose. "I've got a good many things to tell you, but not when Sherry is here, of course. One thing I'll say right now—and you know I am not happy with your behavior. But you can stay at Samphire."

Mali's face glowed and her tears glistened. "Really?" For a moment, it seemed as though she was about to give the headmistress a hug, but then she glanced at Sherry and held back. "I promise, Mrs. Pepper, I won't let you down. I won't!"

Mrs. Pepper patted her shoulder.

She then turned to Sherry. "And now, I must ask you to leave so that I can deal with other school issues." She looked up at the clock. "Hurry to class, Sherry. I expect to see you back here in my office at one o'clock so we can settle the matter of your little ... dishonesty, shall we say?"

Sherry's eyes burned. "Yes, Mrs. Pepper." She glanced at Mali, then opened the door and eased it shut behind her.

Dishonesty, Mrs. Pepper said. Oh, how did I manage to get it so awfully wrong?

10 Trouble Calls Again

Sherry thought the incident with Mrs. Pepper would have brought Mali and her closer, but somehow the opposite seemed to have happened. Mali was more than glad to spend time with her, but whenever the conversation turned to anything more meaningful, she would deftly change the topic.

Perhaps she's ashamed of what I know. Maybe she doesn't want me to know that her parents aren't well off? Well, never mind, I've got other people to hang out with. I just wish I could make a special friend. I'd quite hoped it would be Mali.

Sherry seemed to be going from one bout of trouble to another. Having hardly settled the issue with Mrs. Pepper, giving her firm word that she would really do her best, she was summoned by Miss Bentley. She had been on her best behavior since the disgrace of being sent out and couldn't imagine why the teacher would want to speak with her.

Mali had been summoned by Mrs. Pepper, so they walked up the stairs together before parting ways.

"*Hatzlachah*," Sherry said as her friend headed toward the headmistress's office.

"Good luck to you, as well," Mali called back. The door to the student-teacher room opened and Miss Bentley ushered Sherry inside.

"Sherry, a cheat cannot be tolerated," the teacher said in a low voice that was tight with suppressed anger. "At Samphire, cheating is taken very seriously."

Sherry was too stunned to even open her mouth. Miss Bentley held in front of her the worksheet she had filled in and stared at her for what seemed like forever. Sherry feared her silence was being taken as an admission of guilt. Except she wasn't guilty.

The teacher cleared her throat, her gaze firm and stern. "You will not be allowed to sit in the common room during prep time this week. All preparatory work will have to be completed under supervision." Her frown deepened. "I am disappointed in you, Sherry."

Sherry trembled, on the verge of tears, and her face turned cold. Miss Bentley took no pity on her and dismissed her from the room.

Someone ran off as she left the room, and she caught sight of Leah disappearing down the corridor. *Oh no! If she overheard Miss Bentley calling me a cheat, soon the whole form will be talking about me.*

She wouldn't stand for it. "I am not a cheat!" she declared quietly to herself, lifting her chin and squaring her shoulders. "I have never cheated in my life."

As she walked toward her dorm, she met Leah and Nechama whispering in the hallway.

"I am not a cheat," she said again. She turned to Nechama for support, but the girl she thought was her friend looked away.

"Nechama, let's go study in the garden, shall we?" Leah said. She gave Sherry a sidelong glance.

"Yes, let's," Nechama said. "It's less crowded there."

She deliberately put her arm through Leah's and led her away. It seemed as if they were once again back to being chummy-chummy.

My friends at my old school would never have believed such a ridiculous accusation. She pressed at her eyelids—they were swollen and sore. Longing for Esther welled up inside her.

She ran to her bed, where she tried in vain to stop the flow of tears. That's where Michal found her.

"Sherry, what's happened?"

Sherry wiped her eyes and nose with a handkerchief and regarded the other girl. While Sherry might have preferred that Mali or Bassy had been the one to find her, neither one was in sight, and Michal seemed genuinely concerned. Before long, Sherry poured out the whole story.

Michal listened intently, rubbing her lips in thought.

"It seems to me that someone copied your worksheet—someone smart—and Miss Bentley thought it was *you* who'd done the copying." She stood very straight and pointed to the door. "You have to go to Miss Bentley and sort this out."

Sherry stared at her. "You're right, Michal. It's so obvious when you put it that way. Ugh, why did this have to happen to me?" Another thought flashed through her mind. "I suppose Miss Bentley didn't expect me to know the answers after having been sent out of class. When she saw two identical worksheets, she assumed I was the one who cheated. She couldn't have known that I'd already learned quadratic equations at my previous school."

"That makes sense," Michal said. She vaulted over to sit on the bed and smiled, her eyes round with sympathy.

A heavy sense of gloom swept over Sherry and she let out a long, heavy sigh. "It's awful to be thought of as a cheat."

"I can only imagine." Michal still bore an expression of anxious sympathy. *When has this loner become so likeable?*

It occurred to Sherry that Michal spent an awful lot of time on her own. She cast her mind back to the times she'd seen Michal sitting by herself at break and lunch, or outside on the grass. *I assumed she just liked her own company, but maybe there's more to it.*

"Why are you here?" Sherry asked.

Michal's face froze. Her mouth opened, but nothing came out.

"What I mean is, why are you here being nice to me?"

Michal shrugged. "Why wouldn't I? You're nice to me."

Sherry nodded. "Of course."

But a burning shame niggled at her—shame that she hadn't made a better effort to get to know Michal. She'd been too caught up in being popular to spend time getting to know the quiet, reserved girl who was sitting with her.

"You'd better go down," Michal said. "Otherwise, the girls will think you must have cheated and now you're too embarrassed to face them."

Sherry swallowed. She *was* too embarrassed to face them.

Michal seemed to sense her hesitation and jumped to her feet. "Come on, we'll go together."

Sherry smiled, hope filling her. She wasn't alone.

"You're a good sort, Michal," she said, gratitude filling her. She made up her mind to be a real friend to Michal from now on.

Michal said nothing, but gave her a shy smile in return.

They found their classmates in the common room. The entire second form was there, except Mali. *She must still be with Mrs. Pepper.* When Sherry walked in, they stopped talking and turned to her with accusing eyes.

Sherry and Michal stopped short. Sherry stared at her classmates, her tongue thick in her mouth. Michal, usually so quiet, spoke first.

"I know Sherry wouldn't cheat," she said fiercely.

The girls, however, weren't so easily persuaded. No one said a word.

"Sherry has a kind heart," Michal said, her tone resolute. "She's also brilliant. Anyone can see that. Surely some of you have seen how well she answers questions in class without even a book to look through. She doesn't need to cheat. She knows the subjects. You *know* she knows them. Every time she did something wrong, she admitted to it. So, if Sherry says she didn't cheat, well, I believe her." She locked eyes with the other girls.

Sherry opened her mouth a few times before she could speak. Her heart was warmed by Michal's defense, and the positive attributes Michal had seen in her.

"I didn't do it," she said. "I … I would never."

Leah folded her arms. Nechama frowned.

Her other classmates looked uncertain. They glanced back and forth between Leah, Michal, and Sherry. Michal's mouth was set in a staunch line.

"Michal believes you," Becky said at last. "I believe you, too."

"So do I," a few more girls chorused. Sherry smiled at them, grateful for their support. Only Nechama and Leah remained huddled together, steadfastly ignoring her, but she was determined not to care.

"So then, who's the real cheat?" Michal wondered aloud. "Who can it be?"

The girls looked at each other, but no one offered an answer.

"Well, it wasn't me," Michal said. She turned to Sherry. "Say, would you like to study with me tonight? I could use some help with maths."

Sherry brightened. "Sure, I'd love to."

As she and Michal pulled out their preparatory books, Sherry couldn't help but wonder if this was payback time. Mrs. Pepper had called her dishonest, and, well, she *had* been dishonest when she'd tried to save Mali. Only she hadn't meant to be. But good intentions were never enough.

She shook her head sadly. She remembered a story Papa had told her about a boy who lied rather than face up to his troubles, and eventually all his friends deserted him. Her eyes started to tear. *I wish Papa could be right here with me now. He would have good advice. I seem to be heading from one trouble to another. Hashem, please, please help me. They say a* middah *takes a lifetime to conquer. But I don't have the luxury to wait that long. I need to conquer it now. Please?*

If she'd expected a lightning bolt from heaven to solve her problem, she was quickly disillusioned. Her classmates had all dispersed to chat with each other, and no one came to her to confess.

She sighed. *I suppose that would have been too easy.*

She glanced at Michal, who looked at her from over her workbooks, her eyes kind and understanding. Sherry winked back. At the beginning of the year, she'd prayed for a true friend who would help her. It seemed Hashem had answered her.

She closed her eyes. "Thank You," she whispered.

11 A Brave Decision

Michal put her pencil down and looked around at the girls in the common room. She leaned forward and whispered so the others couldn't overhear.

"So, are you going to talk to Miss Bentley?"

Sherry shook her head. "She won't believe me. It's my word against the cheat's, and I haven't exactly been a model pupil recently."

Michal frowned. "Then we need to find a way to get the real cheat to own up."

She glanced around at the groups of girls in the common room. They could overhear snippets of conversation that made it clear the mystery cheater was still a hot topic, but how could they find out who the culprit was?

Mali was one of the last to find out about the incident. She came into the room and looked around in consternation. She came to sit with Michal and Sherry.

"What's going on?" She gestured to their classmates, who were talking heatedly.

Michal filled her in. Mali was outraged and sympathetic. Sherry felt like she had her friend back.

"I'm so upset, Sherry," she said. "You bet that if I had been in the room instead of Mrs. Pepper's office, I would've stopped this nonsense right away, before it could escalate."

Sherry gave her an appreciative smile as the three girls slipped outside the room. She wanted to say more, about how she felt she was being punished for her other acts of dishonesty, but something held her back. She was about to head to the dining room with Michal and the rest of her class when Mali grabbed her hand.

"I've got something important to tell you. I'll be going home next month."

The news stopped her in her tracks, right there in the corridor. Several paces ahead, Michal turned around and gave a slight wave to show she was going ahead. Sherry's stomach grumbled, but she couldn't even think about food.

"Not in disgrace, though," she added, and Sherry let out a sigh of relief.

"My mother told me a while ago that we might move to the States," Mali continued, dragging her back into the now empty common room. "My uncle has a business in New York, and he's offered my father a partnership." She looked down and sighed. "My father took his business failure very much to heart. He's of the firm belief that it's his duty to provide for his family. My mother said that she thought this opportunity would give him back his pride. Maybe she's right. Either way, we're going."

Sherry was glad about Mali's family, but worried for her friend. "And are you happy?"

"Yes and no. I'm pleased my parents are happy, but I would have liked to stay here. In fact, when I sensed they were seriously contemplating the move, I didn't want to talk about it." She smiled shyly. "Even with you, Sherry. I was afraid that if we became too close, saying goodbye would be so much harder."

Sherry didn't know what to make of all this. Mali's distance now made sense. She realized that Hashem had already answered her *tefillah* for a friend, even before she and Michal became close.

"You're just the type of friend I would have loved to have during my years here," Sherry said. "But I'm sure you'll make new friends easily. You're such a likeable person."

"Oh, that's such a kind thing to say."

"I'll miss you, Mali."

"I'll miss you, too." Mali laughed a little and shook her head as if shaking off a thought. "Oh, and one more thing—please don't tell anyone. It would be just like you to arrange some sort of farewell party."

Sherry's cheeks burned. Somehow Mali had read her mind.

"If you're sure ... The girls would probably love a chance to have a party."

"I would really rather not tell anyone, okay?" Mali leaned closer. "The two of us will keep in touch, but no one else can know until I've gone. Got that?"

"Your wish is my command," Sherry said, winking. But when Mali looked away, she bowed her head. Making friends at Samphire was harder than she'd thought. She'd miss Mali a great deal.

They must have spent a while talking, for before she knew it, her classmates were returning. When they entered the room, they broke off into small groups, still discussing the cheating incident. The mood was sour.

Michal made her way toward them and pointed to the fireplace. "Shall we sit there?"

There was an empty couch in front of the fireplace, and though there were groups of girls crowded around it, it beckoned like a safe haven in a storm. Sherry nodded gratefully. The three girls made their way between the others and sat down. Bassy and Baila came in, spotted the three of them, and sat on the coffee table in front of them.

"I'm so rattled," Bassy said, seething. "To think there is someone in this form who could cheat and then allow another girl to take the blame! It's unheard of!" She shook her head. "In due course, the cheat will appear. If she doesn't own up, she'll be dragged by her ear."

Becky stood up in front of the fireplace, glancing around at the gossiping girls. She cleared her throat loudly.

"I don't like what's going on here," Becky said. "Girls are being accused, and others are looking on, distrustful. I wish this whole thing would just blow over and be done with."

Although most of the form agreed with her, there were a few faces that weren't as open. Behind her, Sherry could hear Leah's voice carrying as she talked to her friend Keren.

"I never liked Sherry," Leah fumed, obviously unaware that Sherry was nearby. "First, she cheats me by taking away my friend, and then she cheats on her schoolwork."

Understanding struck Sherry. *Oh, so that's what she has against me. Well, she can keep Nechama. A fine friend she turned out to be.*

Michal leaned close to Sherry's ear. "Leah might have done this to spite you," she whispered.

"Huh?" Sherry said.

Michal averted her gaze guiltily. "Nothing." She toyed with her hair ribbon. "Forget I ever said anything."

Sherry let the matter drop. She looked around at the girls, divided into little cliques. *Look at what that cheat has done!* Not only had she upset Sherry, she had upset the entire form, turning them against each other, resulting in lashon hora and other hurtful talk. And still, she wouldn't come forward.

Sherry couldn't force the cheat to own up, she knew that. So what could she do?

At once, the answer became clear. She took a deep breath to subdue her fury, then made a firm decision. Ignoring the whispers, she stood up next to Becky and faced her classmates, her heart thumping against her ribs.

The girls fell silent, watching her curiously.

"Since it's me who's been unjustly accused, I feel I should be the one to decide what should be done about it." Her voice was a little hoarse, and she coughed to clear her throat. "Like most of you, I cannot stand what's going on. I vote that we stop. As far as I'm concerned, it's all forgiven and forgotten!"

"Hear, hear," Baila cried.

"Well done," Rivi said.

Mali smiled widely, and Bassy gave her a thumbs-up. Many of the girls sighed with relief and Sherry heard several "thank yous" thrown her way. Nechama stared at her with wide, uncertain eyes, as she nervously smoothed her short black hair behind her ears. Only Leah looked upset. She folded her arms and stared around the room, snorting.

Maybe Leah is the cheat. Sherry stared at the girl for a moment, and a small worm of resentment squirmed into her heart. She didn't know for sure, though. It could have been anyone, she reminded herself, and either way, she had to be *dan l'kaf zechus*. But as she sat back down with Michal, Mali, and the others, she kept a wary eye on Leah Felder.

After a few moments of chatter, Bassy got up and turned on the tape recorder. Several girls turned their heads toward the source of the music, and soon smiles could be seen throughout the room. Many girls even sang and danced. Sherry was relieved and, even more so, comforted by the way her classmates had reacted. Their camaraderie was amazing. The bitter feelings of only moments before had dissipated as though an eraser had rubbed them out. She finally understood why Chava had always considered this place to be so special.

Mali grinned at her classmates. "Well, that's sorted. Nicely done, Sherry. I'm not sure I would have had the guts to do that."

Baila nodded. "Or to forgive someone who made me look like a cheat. You are truly wonderful, Miss Spencer."

Sherry smiled weakly. "Truth be told, I'd half-hoped my speech would make the cheat feel so guilty that she'd 'fess up."

She sighed. That's what had happened in Papa's stories, but it hadn't happened now. The worm wiggled, and her face grew hot.

She turned to Michal. "I could do with a bit of fresh air. Care to join me?"

The girl's face brightened with a flash of joy that lifted Sherry's spirits a little. A smile like that from Michal Lempel was a precious and rare thing. In her mind, Sherry snapped a photograph.

Look how glad she is. Oh, why didn't I think of reaching out to her earlier?

She walked down the pathway with Michal skipping at her side. A rush of wind whipped Sherry's cheeks, lashing hair about her face. She snuggled into her scarf and pulled her jacket tighter.

Michal laughed and Sherry looked at her.

That smile! She couldn't help smiling despite herself, marveling at the transformation in Michal. The sullen girl who had seemed to simply be going through the motions looked so alive now.

"I love the wind," Michal said. "It's so chaotic and wild." She pulled up her collar to cover her ears. “Erratic. It can be anything, from a faint rustle to a thunderous howl.”

Sherry glanced at her. The girl’s words reminded her of something Papa would have read to her. Or of something that she would have read because of Papa.

“That’s deep.”

Michal stopped, as did Sherry, hoping she hadn’t offended her new friend.

Michal’s eyes had a faraway look. “That was so something my mother would say. I guess we’re even more similar than I thought.” She grabbed Sherry’s hand. “Come, let’s run to the Cliff Promenade. I bet the waves are climbing right up the wall.”

Her excitement was contagious, and soon Sherry was marveling at the water. The sea was a mass of giant waves. And Michal was right—the waves *were* crashing over the sea wall. Sherry squinted as she drank in the sight of the surging white foam and felt the cool spray on her face. Her own problems seemed so insignificant in the face of this power and majesty. *Let it go*, the waves seemed to say. *None of it will matter in the end.*

“What’s the matter?” Michal asked, noticing the expression on her face.

Sherry peered at her. “You’re an intuitive one, aren’t you?”

Michal blushed. “I notice people. But you’re easy to read. You wear your emotions on your face.”

“Do I?” Sherry started. She stared at the waves a moment longer and sighed. “I know I said all was forgiven and forgotten. I wanted the girls to stop accusing each other. But I’m having a really hard time not being angry with Leah. How could she do such a thing?”

Michal’s face paled, and Sherry covered her mouth. *Oh no! Michal hadn’t wanted me to hear what she said about Leah. I know I should be dan l'kaf zechus, only I'm finding it so hard now.*

Michal studied the floor, pondering the situation, her hands deep in her pockets. Abruptly, she looked up. "I spent most of the first term without any friends, and it was hard not having someone to talk to. But I didn't know anyone, so it's not like I was missing a friend I used to have. Nechama wanted you all to herself, and when she chose you as her friend, she snubbed Leah. I can't imagine how hard it was for Leah to be ignored like that. I'm not saying that what she did was right—if it was even her—but I am saying that maybe all she wanted was to not feel so lonely."

Sherry stared at her in amazement. "I think the real hero of this story is you, Michal Lempel. How did you become so wise?"

Michal shrugged off Sherry's comment, blushing. "That's another thing my mother would say. She noticed people, too."

As the two girls stood staring at the sea, the wind blowing around them, Sherry realized that she, too, had done bad things in order to not feel lonely and get the other girls to like her. Could she really judge Leah for doing the same, if it even *was* her? And even while Sherry had made mistakes and been dishonest, Hashem had blessed her with not one, but two good friends. Could she let go of her resentment and forgive whoever had done this? She wasn't sure. But she was willing to try.

Hashem, help me forgive.

She exchanged smiles with Michal, feeling the wind pull them together in a tight bond. Happiness rippled inside her heart.

It started to rain, and they dashed back toward the school. As they walked up the path together, Sherry noticed Mali coming toward them. She hoped her friend wasn't upset that she hadn't been invited along.

"Hi, Sherry. Hi, Michal. You're brave, going out in this weather."

Michal shivered. "It *is* cold. Come, let's go inside and warm ourselves with a cup of hot cocoa."

After taking off their coats, they made their way to the common room, where the rest of the girls were still relaxing. The atmosphere in the room was very different than it had been earlier. Sherry smiled happily. It was amazing what forgiveness could do. She spotted Leah and Nechama reading together in the corner. Leah cast her a sullen look, and Sherry pressed her lips together. She would try, she really would.

While Michal prepared the drinks, Sherry turned to Mali. "Shame you didn't join us," she whispered.

"Oh, but I'm pleased I didn't."

Sherry was shocked. "Why? You're not upset with me, I hope."

"Quite the opposite."

"Huh?"

"Listen, Sherry, how do you think I'd feel, knowing I'd left for the States without you having a special friend? Michal is a great choice. She'll be a wonderful friend for you."

Sherry's heart fluttered. "Wow! You really are something." She looked Mali in the eye. "You'll always be the first friend I made at Samphire."

Mali chuckled. "And thanks to the Royal Mail, our friendship will go on."

Michal returned with a tray loaded with hot drinks. Sherry stood up to help her.

"These look so good!"

The smell was tantalizing, and soon most of the form had joined them. Sherry wiggled her eyebrows as she watched everyone add their unique flavor to their cups. Baila threw in a bunch of small marshmallows and watched as they floated to the top before melting like little snowmen. Becky dropped in a piece of dark chocolate, and Mali popped in a Belgian truffle.

Bassy topped hers with a swirling mound of whipped cream, then drizzled hot fudge sauce around the edges. She caught Sherry's eye. "The expert at hot chocolate, that's me. I'm the winner of this, Sherry."

Sherry winked. "Gotta hand it to you, Bassy!"

Becky put down her empty cup. "Ah, that was good! Thanks, Michal."

As the rest of the girls finished their drinks with free time to spare before bedtime, Sherry got up from her seat. "Let's play a game. I vote for a round of Balderdash."

"Yes, let's!" Rivi said, and most of the other girls echoed her sentiment.

To Sherry's delight, the girls grabbed pencils, eager to get started. They had a fine time, with some girls making up definitions while others tried to guess the right one. The common room echoed with laughs and jokes as the whole form got in on the action.

Well, almost the whole form. Leah and Nechama stood apart and watched, refusing to participate. Leah rocked on her heels, swinging her hands. She leaned over and whispered something to Nechama, who giggled and glanced at Sherry.

Sherry smoothed back some stray hairs and shrugged. Now that she'd discovered the true meaning of friendship, she wasn't going to let herself be bothered by fake friends. Michal was good for her—she needed friends who brought out her best, not her worst. And she hoped she could do the same for Michal. Maybe she could help her shake off the miserable veneer she carried at times. She could help her find happiness.

I can, can't I?

12 Michal Tries to Help

The rainy weather continued without let-up for days, and the girls were becoming impatient at being cooped up inside for so long. Michal had already read every book she'd brought with her to school twice, and even board games no longer held any appeal.

"I'm so bored," Sherry lamented one day during the lunch break. She was lying on one end of the couch in the common room, across from Michal, who was doodling in her notebook.

"My father says that boredom is the sign of an inactive mind," Michal said absently.

"Yeah?" Sherry challenged. Then she sat up, brightening. "You know what? He's right, Michal. My mother says there's always something to be done to cheer up the gloomiest day. We just need to be creative."

Sherry jumped off the couch and grabbed some markers and cardboard from the cupboard. She glanced at Michal. "Come with me. I have an idea."

Michal set aside her notebook and followed her friend out of the common room. "What have you got up your sleeve?"

"You'll see. We're going to have some fun and shake away the boredom once and for all."

Sherry sat on the stairs and bent over the cardboard. She drew a row of pairs of eyes with different expressions. Then she drew a variety of noses, and finally, mouths that varied from smiling to alarmed.

Michal giggled. "Is that Mrs. Pepper you're trying to draw?"

She took a marker and lent a hand. With quick, deft strokes, she added life to the eyes and mouths until anyone seeing them would've guessed at once whose features they represented.

Sherry's eyes widened. "That's some talent you have!"

She dashed back to the common room while Michal finished up and returned with a pair of scissors. "Now for the fun part."

In no time, there was a pile of cut-out facial features was in Sherry's hand.

Michal examined their work. "Not half bad, I say."

"We make a good team." Sherry grinned, and Michal warmed. It was lovely to have a friend at last, especially one as fun and brilliant as Sherry Spencer.

Michal stooped to pick up the supplies, and Sherry put the trash in the wastebasket.

"All ready now? Let's go." Sherry gathered everything together.

They raced back to the common room and took in the scene.

The mood in the room was dull and dreary, just like the weather outside. Even Bassy, ever cheerful, was slumped against the window, looking glumly at the rain. Michal hadn't heard a couplet from her in two days.

The twosome went to stand at the front of the room. Michal

spread the paper features on the table.

"Come on, girls," Sherry called. "It's time for a good game."

The girls were slow to get up, but as soon as they saw the papers, the mood brightened and Bassy's twinkle returned.

"Sherry's come to shoo boring away. Trust her to come and save the day!"

"Come on, pals, it's time to play!" Sherry added.

She produced a pile of scarves she had gathered from the lost and found and invited her friends to come forward one by one. When they were blindfolded, she instructed them to form a face using the cut-out features, and then take off the blindfold to see how they did. Soon, whoops of delight rang around the room.

"I got all eyes!" Mindy Gross exclaimed.

"That's nothing. Check mine out." Bassy pointed to her face, which was a mishmash of mouths and eyes, all of which seemed upset in some way. "Mrs. Pepper seems to be having a very bad day."

Michal watched, pleased. She'd helped bring joy to her classmates, thanks to Sherry. She was right—they were a good team.

Nechama got up from her seat, dragging Leah behind her. "We're not in kindergarten," she said, sneering at the game. She opened the door, pulled Leah through, and slammed it shut.

Michal shook her head. She'd thought that the situation with Nechama and Leah had been resolved. Now that Leah had Nechama back, why were they being so mean? *For some odd reason, they have something against Sherry. And it's got to stop.*

"Don't bother with them," Sherry whispered. She straightened Michal's collar and winked. "We're having fun, anyway."

Michal tried to shrug away the pair's behavior, but found it too difficult.

Sherry doesn't deserve this!

But soon, even she got lost in the game. The faces the girls put together were getting funnier by the minute.

Outside, the rain was finally petering out to a rhythmic pitter-patter, the soothing sound as comforting as the lullabies Michal's mother used to sing. Michal pressed her face against the window and stared at the vague shapes becoming clearer in the distance.

Sherry touched her shoulder. "Are you okay?"

Michal shook off her sudden melancholy. "Yeah. I'm just sad the rain is stopping."

"Is it?" Sherry peered out the window. "Happy day! But why would you be sad about that? We've all been going mad from boredom!"

Michal glanced at her friend. She wasn't yet ready to share her secret with anyone at school ... not even Sherry. "Well, we were just starting to have some fun. Now everyone will go back to what they were doing before."

Sherry laughed. "I'm sure we'll still find something fun to do. Never fret."

The school bell rang for afternoon lessons. The girls scrambled to pick up the pieces of their game and gather their books and supplies for class.

Michal stopped short at the door, seeing Sherry scrambling through her locker. "Come, Sherry, let's get to class."

Sherry looked frazzled. "I can't find my maths book. You run up; I'll join you in a minute."

Michal hesitated. She didn't want to leave her friend alone. Or, perhaps, she was the one who didn't want to be left alone. But Sherry wouldn't let up.

"Go," she said when she saw Michal still standing there. "It's bad enough if I'm late. I can't get you in trouble, too."

So Michal hurried to class, hoping her friend would make it in time.

Alas, it wasn't to be. When Miss Bentley came into class, Sherry still hadn't arrived, and Michal's heart dropped. But a minute later, someone knocked at the door.

Miss Bentley opened it to find Sherry standing there. "What is this? Been playing around again?" Her voice was hard.

Sherry stammered out an apology, but the teacher just shut the door behind her.

Michal couldn't believe it. *Why is Miss Bentley always so harsh on Sherry? Yesterday, Rivi came to class even later and Miss Bentley just let her come in.* She clenched her hands. *I bet she's still bothered about the "cheating." She's so straight herself, and she probably can't imagine that anyone would ever cheat. But Sherry didn't do it!* She bit her lower lip, and then it came to her. *I know what I'll do. Why didn't I think of it before?*

Now that she had a plan of action, she opened her book and got down to work. Her plan meant she would risk getting herself into Miss Bentley's bad books too, but, for Sherry, it was a risk worth taking.

The bell rang for the end of the lesson and Miss Bentley left the room. Michal raced after her.

"Miss Bentley!"

The teacher turned around. "Yes?"

"I wanted to tell you ... uh ... about Sherry."

"I do not discuss one student with another. Ever." Miss Bentley clicked her heels and turned around, her footsteps echoing down the corridor.

Michal let out a long sigh, her shoulders slumping. *That went down well.* Dejected, she walked back into class. *Now, the only thing is to hope that the culprit finds the courage to own up and clear Sherry's name.*

The days extended into weeks and, between schoolwork and projects, Michal found herself too busy to give the issue more thought. In particular, the Shabbos competition was keeping her occupied. Mrs. Hampton had given the class a range of topics to choose from, and the students had to research their topic and produce a model along with an accompanying report. Points would be awarded for accuracy, detail, and presentation.

Michal, of course, paired up with Sherry, and together they worked on a model that would demonstrate the connection between Shabbos and the Mishkan. Using bits and pieces they'd found in the stockroom, they were kept busy making a replica of the Mishkan with all its vessels. It was coming along nicely and had impressive features. Michal was especially proud of the *keruvim*, which could turn one hundred and eighty degrees, and the imitation fire on the *mizbei'ach*. The flames were really a piece of cloth, but when they were lit up by a lightbulb and blown by a fan, they shone brightly and blew in the air, resembling a real fire.

"This model is magnificent," Rivi said, admiring the fine details.

Michal spent ages on the phone with her father, who ensured the girls' research was thorough and accurate, so the accompanying report was every bit as special as the model. Both she and Sherry really enjoyed working on the project and spent every spare minute perfecting it.

"This is such fun," Sherry told her one evening. "Not least because I get to do it with you."

"It is! It is!" Michal agreed. "I feel like we're sisters, slogging away on our favorite project together." She did see Sherry as a sister, of sorts. "At least, I think this is what it would be like to have a sister. I'm an only child, but I always wanted one."

Sherry laughed, tapping her friend's shoulder. "Nice to see you, long-lost sis."

From then on, the nickname "Sis" stuck, and they volleyed it back and forth.

As the two spent many long hours refining their miniature Mishkan, their classmates looked on with amazement.

As usual, it was up to Bassy to say aloud what they were all thinking. Pretending to hold a microphone, she announced dramatically, "First place honor, La Royale, awarded to Sherry and Michal."

Oddly, Bassy's silly rhymes had a way of hitting the nail on the head. But Michal couldn't fail to notice Leah's reaction—the girl's green eyes, hard as marbles, glinted with enmity.

This, she feared, would not end well.

13 Secret Competition

Nechama zipped up her jacket as she jogged down the path with Leah. The cold wind blew against her cheeks, but she didn't mind. She found it bracing.

Leah thrust her hands deep in her pockets and buried her face in her scarf. She was not nearly as fond of cold as her friend was. "Nechama, we have to win this competition, you hear?"

Nechama turned. "Whoo-hoo, since when do you care so much about such things?"

The determination in Leah's voice didn't falter. "We're going to win this thing."

"Thought of an idea yet?"

"Oh yes! But this is going to be our secret. Like a surprise competition." Leah gave a small laugh.

Understanding flashed. "Oh, I get it!" Nechama nodded. "Yes, I'm with you."

"There's no way we're going to let a cheat of a girl get away with winning."

"Uh-huh." Nechama nodded, biting her nails. An unfamiliar feeling gnawed at her. "So, what's your big idea?"

Leah rocked on her heels on the tarmac. She lowered her voice. "Listen to this. We're going to make a model of each one of the thirty-nine *melachos*. And we'll explain next to each one how it's relevant today. It's going to be massive. There's no way it won't win."

Nechama cocked her head. "Leah. This is a ton of work. Who has the patience for it?"

Leah's enthusiasm didn't wane. "But it will be worth it. We'll win."

"And?"

"And ... we *need* to win!"

Nechama pursed her lips tightly together. "Leah, why are you doing this?"

Leah's eyes blazed. "Because Sherry can't win. She took my friend from me. Can you think for a moment what it felt like to have no real friend to talk to?"

Nechama shook her head. *Leah doesn't know half of it. Sherry is not to blame.* Seeing Leah's anger rocked her insides. She *had* chosen Sherry over Leah, enamored as she was by the new girl. She felt bad now. She wanted to apologize, to tell Leah she hadn't meant any harm. But she couldn't. Apologies admitted weakness. And she wasn't weak. No, not her.

Her friend didn't seem to care for her inner musings. "Are you in this with me, Nechama? There's no way I can do it without you."

Nechama wanted to shake her head. But the fire in Leah's eyes bored right through her. So, instead, she found herself nodding. "Yes, we'll do this. We'll do it together."

Leah gave a deep chuckle. "Like the good ol' times."

Nechama nodded again. "Like the good ol' times," she echoed.

Her heart felt hollow as they planned the project together. They would have to put in a lot of early-morning and late-evening hours if they wanted it completed in time, and with no one else knowing. However, as their ideas took shape, Nechama became more excited. As Leah had said, there was no way they would lose the competition with their grand plans.

A few weeks later, Leah surveyed their model with pride. They already had little clay figures demonstrating all the farming activities, and had made a good start on the weaving and fabric-making figures. "I can't wait to see Sherry's expression when she sees what we pulled off."

Nechama smiled, but her heart wasn't in it. It was a tremendous amount of work. And more than that, she wasn't even sure she wanted to take away Sherry's chance. A vision of Sherry's dejected face in the common room swam before her eyes. *Shame on you, Nechama.*

14

A Day Off

In due course, Mali left for the United States. Sherry kept the secret right until the end, but Mrs. Pepper spoiled the surprise with a cake on Mali's last night. That had been over a month ago, and Sherry was feeling her absence.

Of course, they'd agreed to keep in touch, but it wasn't the same as having her around. Sherry found it puzzling that the rest of the class seemed less bothered about her friend's absence. But then again, not many of them had gotten to know Mali the same way she had.

"Don't worry," Michal said, linking arms, "you'll exchange letters. For all you know, your friendship will become stronger."

"You're right. Come on, let's write her a letter now. Won't she be glad to receive it before she's even had a chance to miss us?"

Michal chuckled. "Don't tell me you're ditching your tardiness, too. Soon you really will be Little Miss Perfect."

Sherry giggled. "I don't think that's happening any time soon."

As it happened, all the second formers had been working so

diligently that Mrs. Hampton decided to reward them. With the approval of Mrs. Pepper, she gave them a day off for a group activity of their choice. Most of the girls wanted to go to the nearby beach. Miss Bentley and Mrs. Lee, the history teacher, agreed to accompany them.

When they arrived, Rivi exclaimed, "I know the perfect place to go." She pointed to her far right. "If you walk in that direction, you can see the South Foreland Lighthouse—you know, the one that was built in 1843, well over a hundred years ago. It's a beautiful spot, perched up on the White Cliffs, overlooking the Strait of Dover. And there's an amazing view from there."

Leah rolled her eyes. "I mean, who *doesn't* know it was built in 1843? I did. Didn't you, Nechama?"

Nechama snorted in agreement. "I didn't know we had a walking encyclopedia in our midst."

Rivi gabbled on, as she tended to do when she was excited, undeterred by their snide remarks. The rest of the girls had grown used to her chatter and weren't usually inclined to take her seriously. They started to wander, some of them going to admire the view of the ocean while others sat on the grass and chatted.

Rivi noticed that no one was paying her words any heed, and the excitement shining in her eyes began to dull into disappointment. Sherry looked around at the other girls. This wasn't right. Rivi knew what she was talking about, and Sherry remembered how much the girl loved old buildings. If anyone would make a good tour guide of the area, it was Rivi.

"That sounds super," she cried with enough gusto for the others to hear. "Come on, Rivi, show us the way."

And so the girls gathered around Rivi and walked on. The weather was at its best—beautiful, clear, and cold, the perfect winter day—and it was exhilarating to walk along the cliff tops and marvel at the stunning views beyond the Channel. At the water's edge, ferocious waves marched on to their own unchanging beat. With a blue sky overhead offering a perfect backdrop to this lovely panorama, the girls were quite taken by the stunning *nifla'os haBorei.* In great spirits, they skipped along the path, humming as they went.

"Here it is," Rivi said at last. "This is the cliff I was talking about. Can you see that coast over there? That's France. Four hundred commercial vessels use the Dover Strait every day, with some as long as 318 meters. I say, that's massive, isn't it?" She spoke at a mile a minute, but it was clear she knew what she was talking about.

The secluded area was an oasis of serenity, which lent itself to deep and meaningful discussion. Sherry and Michal were talking about all sorts of things when Michal suddenly fell silent, the miserable mask she'd worn at the start of the year falling over her face.

"What's the matter, Sis?" Sherry asked, concerned. But it was obvious that Michal didn't hear her. She was gazing at a far-off point as if her mind was in a faraway place—one that was obviously filled with pain.

"Michal, what is it?" Sherry tried again.

Michal snapped back to the present, as if nothing had happened. "Sherry, look at that massive ship." She pointed out to sea, ignoring her friend's question, but her voice was tight.

Sherry was having none of it.

"Michal, what were you just thinking about? Why did you look so sad?"

Michal whirled around, torment written on her face. "Stop this, Sherry! Stop this right now!"

Sherry stared at her, dumbfounded. *Why is she shouting? Why is she so angry? I've never seen her behave like this.*

A few girls turned around, and Sherry nudged her. "The others are looking. It's okay, Michal. You can tell me another time, when you're ready. Just know that I'm here when you need me."

Michal's fists unclenched, and she nodded.

Sherry's stomach knotted. She deeply cared for Michal, and the pain in her friend's eyes was all too familiar. She wished there were something she could do to help the other girl.

"Girls, gather round!" Miss Bentley called from the lawn near the lighthouse. "Time to eat!"

Sherry gave Michal a questioning look, as if to say, *Are you ready to be with the others?*

Michal nodded, and they made their way to where the other girls were gathered around a delicious spread of scones, cream, and lemonade.

"Oh, this looks good!" Becky exclaimed.

"Yeah," Nechama agreed. "We should do this more often."

"I dare you to earn this reward again," Miss Bentley said. She winked at Nechama, well aware of her student's notorious dares.

Michal's melancholy pulled at Sherry's good mood, but she was determined to have a nice time regardless. She surveyed the table that Miss Bentley had prepared.

"Doesn't this look smashing?" Her mouth began to water. "I vote we daven Minchah before it's too late, and then we can tuck in."

"That's a good idea, Sherry." Swept up by the girls' giddiness, Miss Bentley was clearly in a generous mood, even with Sherry. She smiled. "Everyone to the alcove, and Sherry will lead the davening."

Stirred by the stunning surroundings, Sherry's heartfelt *tefillah* was made even more beautiful by her melodious voice. All the girls were moved and inspired, and their Minchah that day was more poignant than any *tefillah* they had davened in a long time. The atmosphere was charged with a wholesome Elul-like feeling of purity and yearning, and all ill feelings were instantly purged. Sherry lovingly kissed her *siddur* and silently thanked Hashem for helping her rid herself of her resentment.

Nechama stood with her eyes closed, listening to Sherry's voice carry over the Channel in a stirring, soulful melody. The words sank in. "*Ana beko'ach gedulas Yemincha,*" *We beg You with the strength of the greatness of Your right hand,* "*tatir tzerurah,*" *untie the bundle of sins,* "*kabeil rinas amcha,*" *accept the prayerful song of Your people,* "*sagveinu, tahareinu*" *strengthen us, purify us.*

She looked at Sherry, who had borne the accusation of cheating with so much humility and goodness. *And what about me? Am I tied by a bundle of sins?* She trembled, overwhelmed with shame. She felt like her secret was strangling her. The time had come to put things straight. She glanced around to make sure Sherry wasn't nearby, then took a deep, steadying breath.

"Miss Bentley, please come here," she said, beckoning her maths teacher over, trying to keep her voice as natural as possible. "I ... I want to tell you something."

At the urgency in Nechama's voice, the teacher straightened and frowned, then made her way to the back of the alcove.

"What is it, Nechama? Is something the matter?"

Light from the setting sun glinted off Miss Bentley's glasses like an extra pair of eyes glaring at her.

Nechama turned her back so the girls wouldn't see her talking to the teacher. "Miss Bentley, I ... I have a confession to make." Her words came out in a breathless rush. "I took Sherry's worksheet and copied it."

Miss Bentley placed her hand over her mouth. "Nechama, *you?*" Her eyes were very wide.

Nechama squirmed as the silence stretched. What would Miss Bentley do?

"But you would have known the answers without help. Why would you copy someone else's?"

Nechama forced herself to look her teacher in the eye, though she was terribly afraid. "I didn't have time to do the work, and I saw Sherry spending hours on it, so I assumed her answers were correct."

Miss Bentley shook her head. She glanced over at Sherry, and Nechama guessed she was disappointed with herself for having wrongly accused her. "I'm pleased to know that Sherry didn't cheat, but..."

The teacher blinked a few times, as if seeing something clearly for the first time, and leaned closer to Nechama.

"But how did you know I had accused Sherry?"

And so the whole story came out—how the conversation between Miss Bentley and Sherry had been overheard and spread through the form, and how Sherry had courageously ended the controversy. Miss Bentley nodded and glanced again at Sherry with wide eyes, visibly impressed.

"Thank you for coming forward, Nechama. Everyone makes mistakes—even me. The important thing is to learn from those mistakes. I think you ought to own up to the other girls."

Nechama swallowed. "You mean apologize?"

Miss Bentley nodded gravely. "Absolutely. When we wrong another, we must make it right." She put a finger to her lips, thinking. "I suppose we both owe someone an apology. Why don't we do it together?"

Nechama blinked in surprise. Straight-laced and strict Miss

Bentley was going to apologize publicly? She'd always viewed apologies as a sign of weakness, but Miss Bentley was one of the strongest, most forceful people she knew.

She glanced at her classmates, who were milling around the food table chatting. Her throat closed at the thought of facing them and she looked down at her shoes.

"I don't know if I can."

Miss Bentley smiled gently. "Of course you can. If you really want to, you can do anything. Even something as difficult as owning up to your mistakes."

Nechama took a shaky breath and nodded to the teacher. If apologizing was this difficult, it could not be a sign of weakness. It showed strength.

"What punishment are you going to give me?" she mumbled.

Miss Bentley tilted her head. "I will have to think about that. But I think the misery of carrying this secret has been punishment enough. Hasn't it?"

Nechama's eyes watered. If Sherry had felt half as bad as Nechama felt now, Sherry must have been miserable indeed. Nechama told herself that she would never again allow someone else to be punished for her wrongdoing.

"Okay," she said. "I'm ready."

Miss Bentley smiled and gave her shoulder a squeeze. Then she stepped forward and clapped her hands to call the girls to order.

"Girls," she said. "Nechama has told me something important, and I think she wants to share it with the class."

Nechama took a deep breath, closed her eyes, and exhaled slowly. When she opened her mouth to speak, the words remained lodged in her throat—she couldn't bring herself to say that she'd cheated. She knew that the girls didn't take kindly to deceit of any sort, and allowing another girl to take the blame would be simply unacceptable to them.

"What is it, Nechama?" Leah asked, growing impatient.

Nechama swallowed, looking at her friend. Leah really didn't like cheats. What would she say when she found out it had been Nechama all along? Would she lose Leah as a friend, too? Nechama hadn't thought she would care so much, but she suddenly realized she would care a great deal. Fear paralyzed her.

Bassy came up to up her and took hold of her arms with both hands. She spoke in a gentle yet firm tone. "No reason to be coated red with guilt—nothing's so broken it can't be rebuilt."

Nechama shook all over. She looked Sherry straight in the eye. She owed her this. Before she could lose her nerve again, she spit the words out.

"I was the cheat. Not Sherry. I'm terribly sorry." She turned in Sherry's direction, though she was too frightened to meet her gaze.

Sherry stared at her in open-mouthed shock, then looked at Leah. "But I thought ..." She shook her head. "Never mind. It's not important." She came over and patted Nechama's shoulder with a kind smile. "I accept your apology. Like I said in the common room before, all is forgiven."

Nechama blinked. "Just like that?"

"It's wrong to hold onto a grudge, and besides, I want to be friends with you. We're friends again, aren't we?"

Nechama swallowed the lump in her throat. "I'd like to be."

Sherry beamed. "Perfect." She looked around at their classmates. "And now, how about we eat some of the food Miss Bentley has so kindly prepared?"

The girls stared at Nechama. One by one, the expressions on their faces went from denial and anger to calm acceptance.

Becky spoke up. "Sherry's right. It's water under the bridge. Don't you all agree?"

The girls nodded and started to head toward the food.

Nechama relaxed. It had been harder to apologize than she'd ever imagined, but the results had been worth it. Sherry was her friend again, and the other girls weren't even angry.

Then she caught sight of Leah, standing in the corner with her arms folded over her chest and a thundercloud on her face. She sighed and went to make another apology. She wondered if this was the sort of thing that got easier with practice.

She hoped she wouldn't make enough mistakes to have to find out.

Miss Bentley cleared her throat. "I also have an apology to make." She gave Sherry a meaningful glance and opened her mouth to continue, but Sherry pre-empted her.

"It's okay, Miss Bentley. You wouldn't have accused me if I hadn't caused my share of trouble. And, anyway, let's not ruin such a perfectly gorgeous day." She clapped once and gave a little jump. "Want to race me down the cliff, Miss Bentley?"

"First one down gets an extra dollop of cream," Miss Bentley declared.

And the race began. Sherry easily took the lead, but Miss Bentley didn't seem to mind at all.

~

On the way back to school, everyone was in top form. Sherry couldn't stop smiling. She was glad it hadn't been Leah, and would of course, make up for having thought *and* spoken badly about her. Yes, in all, it had been a great day. Only one thing marred it.

What had made Michal so upset? And why won't she share it with me?

15 A Letter from Home

Michal lay on her bed, fingering the trimming on her quilt. Around her, everyone was still asleep. It was quiet, the sun just peeking above the horizon.

The dream had visited her again. She placed a hand on her heart. It was still beating wildly. If only there was someone she could talk to. Someone she could share her fears with. She turned over to her right. Sherry was there. Should she confide in her? Sherry was her friend. Surely, she was loyal enough to hear her out and remain her friend, despite everything ...

Feeling suddenly hot, she bent over to wash *negel vasser*.

Oops! The letter she had stashed under her pillow the previous night fell into the bowl. She quickly retrieved it and placed it on the bed, hoping the letter hadn't gotten too soggy, then washed her hands and got dressed. Before leaving the dorm room, she stuffed the letter in her pocket.

It had arrived yesterday, but she hadn't found a solitary moment to read it last night, and a letter from Tatty was a too-precious occurrence for anyone to see her reading it. She couldn't risk someone barging in on her. It was best to read it outside, where no one was around.

She put on her jacket and pushed open the front door of the school. A rush of wind greeted her. It was colder than she'd realized. Still, an early-morning walk never harmed anyone.

She made her way along the lane between the school and the cottages at the edge of the nearby village. She had always enjoyed solitary walks. In fact, growing up as an only child, she'd managed to find enjoyment in doing most things alone. That was much easier before her mother had passed away. Since Mummy had been *niftar* last year, Michal had felt truly alone for the first time.

Now that she and Sherry had become friends, that loneliness had eased somewhat. Sherry was fun, and every moment spent in her company seemed to sparkle with life and energy. But Michal needed something more. She needed someone to care, someone to listen, someone to understand. But who?

She'd reached the end of the lane and found herself at the top of the cliffs. She peered at the foaming grey sea far below, its depth seemingly endless. Several boulders sticking out of the water looked like mere pebbles from this height.

That's how far away Mummy seems. And Tatty is at home in Kent, too far away to tell him when I'm upset by a bad dream or missing Mummy so badly. Maybe I can share my pain with ... Sherry. She shook her head and dismissed the thought. *Sherry, with her perfect family. Sherry, with the too-jolly disposition. Can she ever really understand me?*

When she stuck her hand in her pocket, the soggy letter brushed against her fingers. She was all alone here—she may as well read it now. She went and sat on a nearby bench, sheltered from the wind by some scrubby bushes.

She appreciated that Tatty bothered to write to her at all, knowing how he hated letter-writing. Not like Mummy, who had always relished it. Alas, the words were blurred, for the most part. She was just able to make out the words *happy*, *get on well*, and *sis* between the runny splotches of ink covering the page.

She rubbed her nose. *What? What on earth is written here? I can't make heads or tails of this. I wish I could ask Tatty, but then he would know that the letter he wrote so painstakingly got ruined. I can't do it to him.*

Someone came running toward her. *Ah, it's Sherry. I wonder why she's up so early.* Absently, she caressed the letter.

Sherry sat beside her on the bench and smiled. "Hi, Michal. A letter from home? That's nice. What's Mum got to say?"

Michal startled. "Uh ... actually, it's from my father." She stopped. "He doesn't ... often write."

Sherry's eyes widened. "Whew, that's something!"

"It's no big deal."

"Uh ... okay."

A seagull glided above them and instinctively, they both looked up.

"You're up early," Sherry said.

Michal opened her mouth to respond, gripped by a sudden urge to release the feelings she kept bottled inside her. As she debated with herself, silence stretched between them.

"Tell me a bit about your family," Sherry said. "I feel like you can't really know someone well until you understand where they're coming from. Know what I mean?"

"Wh-what?" Michal spluttered.

Sherry stopped walking. "What's your mother like?"

Michal's head buzzed. Before she knew it, she was talking about Mummy for the first time in ages.

"She's wonderful. Beautiful, artistic, gentle. You know, this one time ..."

The words came as if on autopilot. There was so much to say. She spoke about their shared love of nature and passion for art and about her mother's soft, gentle ways. Soon, tears were streaming down her cheeks.

Sherry gasped. "What's the matter?" Her voice was as soft as a cotton bandage on a raw wound.

Michal averted her gaze. "Sorry, I'm just thinking about someone I know ... Her mother passed away." She pressed her lips together. "It's hard for her. Very hard."

Sherry nodded and Michal was taken by the empathy in her eyes. She wanted to say more, but she couldn't. Fear gripped her. She didn't want to lose Sherry, as she had lost countless other friends. She shook her head. No, it wasn't worth it. She rubbed her fingers on the letter. Ah, the perfect escape. She giggled. "My father is something else."

Sherry looked at her, eyes filled with genuine interest. "Tell me about him."

"He's very different from yours. Not as young, but still ..."

Sherry's jaw dropped. "Huh? How do you know my father?"

"I saw him when he dropped you off at the train station when we left to school."

"Oh. You live in Kent? I can't recall ever seeing you."

Michal nodded. "My father is a pediatrician there. We've lived in Kent for seven years now."

Sherry beamed. "So we've been neighbors all this time and never knew it? What are the chances?"

Michal nodded, glancing at the ocean. "I suppose we are."

Sherry broke the awkward silence that followed. "Uh, what is your father like?"

"As I said, he's not as young, but you wouldn't know it. He's so full of life. He's the kindest man, of course, but I would say that, wouldn't I? Just to give you an example, I once had an urge to paint a sunset, and he drove me every night for a few weeks to the spot I chose. He doesn't love the cold, but he did it for me. He huddled in his coat, and took his small pocket *gemara* with him to learn while I lost myself in painting. Once, I painted there for two whole hours, engrossed as I was in the scenery. And when I turned, I saw he had fallen asleep, using a few rocks as a cushion. He was so tired, but he hadn't wanted me to know."

Sherry listened with rapt attention. "Wow, that's really something!"

The two spoke together for a while, then headed back to school, walking briskly so they would be on time for davening. Every now and then, Michal stole a glance at Sherry, wondering if she should tell her friend her secret. Finally, they reached the school building. Sherry opened the door for her and they went in together. As Sherry headed toward the davening hall, Michal sighed inwardly.

I'm glad my secret is safe. Sherry is marvelous, but she could never understand.

16 Troublesome Spats

The outing had done the girls a world of good. Not only did they come back refreshed and eager to work, but, to Sherry's delight, they were now more united than ever. Nechama seemed particularly keen to rekindle their friendship.

"Care for a quick stroll?" she asked one day during the break. Sherry was happy to comply. She ran to fetch her raincoat, and Michal joined them as they headed outdoors.

Leah, standing at the main exit, seemed alarmed as the small group passed her. Her gaze traveled from Sherry to Nechama, and Sherry shuddered.

Leah doesn't like this new friendship one bit. She's going to be more jealous than ever. The last thing she needed, after everything had turned out so well, was Leah bothering her. Indeed, she was getting quite fed up with the girl's snide remarks.

Leah's voice dripped with sarcasm. "How do you do, Queen Sherry? Got yourself another maid?"

"I think I may jolly well have to teach Leah a thing or two," Sherry said quietly, unfamiliar irritation surging through her.

"Don't take any notice of her," Michal advised. "If you do, you'll just be putting yourself in the wrong."

Sherry looked at Leah, about to retaliate with a sharp comment, but instead bit her lip and did her best to control her urge to lash out. She cast a rueful gaze at Michal, grateful for her calming support,

More girls had joined the group. Bassy giggled as she watched Sherry swallow her words.

"What's gone on with dear old Sherry? Her eyes are really much too glary, and her temper's risen very, very!"

Sherry wrinkled her nose at Bassy, who only grinned back.

"How do *you* manage to stay cool and collected no matter how much we badger you about your rhymes?" Sherry said brusquely.

Bassy folded her arms, amusement on her face. "Getting angry ruins the fun, but calmness calms down everyone."

Sherry thought there might be some wisdom in Bassy's rhyme, but that only made her more annoyed. She didn't want to be calm right now. Leah had done nothing but goad her since the beginning of the year. Didn't she have a right to be upset? She kicked a pebble on the cobblestones.

What had Papa always said? "Understanding another's shortcomings is difficult when it contradicts one's own strength."

She pressed her lips together.

A smiling Rivi bounded up to her form mates. "Sherry, you're wanted. The head girl asked for you."

She was clearly waiting for a response, but none came. Sherry was too stunned at having been officially summoned to her sister's dorm. This was quite a rare occurrence. She saw Chava often, mostly in the halls, and they'd spoken frequently during holidays, but this was quite unusual. She worried that something was wrong. The last time she was summoned to a family meeting with such a sense of urgency ... No, she wouldn't think of it. Not now.

"I say, what's going on here?" Rivi asked. "Sherry, you look like a blown-up balloon, ready to pop. It's not—"

"Thanks for the message," Sherry snapped, effectively silencing Rivi before rushing back to the school. So desperate was she to get away from Leah, she hardly looked where she was going as she raced down the corridor, up the stairs, and then ... *smack*! She crashed into Mrs. Winter, the Tehillim teacher, who teetered, almost losing her balance.

"Sherry! What's with you? Where are you rushing to?" the woman asked, her voice shaky. "This is not the way you should be using the corridors."

"Sorry," Sherry mumbled, hoping she would be excused.

Mrs. Winter was having none of it. "Come with me," she commanded and led Sherry back down the stairs and into the teachers' room.

Oh no! Mrs. Winter was known for her long lectures. And things were about to get worse. As she followed Mrs. Winter into the office, Mrs. Pepper rounded the corner.

No, no, no! Now the headmistress will think I've returned to my mischief-making. Sherry scratched her ear. *Well, I did almost lash out at Leah. That's not a good thing.* Her head throbbed. *Why am I finding it so hard to put myself in her shoes?*

17 A Game with Leah

Visiting day drew closer and the girls were busy preparing the school for their families' arrival. Walls were decorated and artwork was displayed. For the second form, their Shabbos models would be the highlight of the occasion.

Thinking of a clever addition for the Mishkan, which had become somewhat of an obsession, Sherry raced to her dorm. She was surprised to find Leah hovering over the model.

As soon as she saw her, she remembered what Michal had said some time ago, about Leah being upset over losing her friend. She did some fast thinking. *If I were Leah, what would I want me to say right now?*

"Leah, I'm so glad you're here."

Leah jumped and whirled to face Sherry, looking stricken.

"Sherry! I thought you were in the dining room."

"I was, but I'm trying to figure out something for our model, and I could really use your help—you're so creative with these things. I want to add flames to the *menorah*, and I thought I could do it like the fire on the *mizbei'ach*, but on a smaller scale. The thing is, the batteries will be too big. What do you think?"

The girl soon recovered from her alarm, and Sherry reckoned she was astute enough to see through her request. Leah's face twisted, and for a moment, Sherry thought the other girl would toss another snide remark her way and stomp off as she'd done so many times before. But then something changed in Leah's demeanor—her eyes softened and her shoulders slumped.

"I am so embarrassed," she whispered, her bottom lip trembling. "But even more, I'm ashamed of myself."

Sherry stepped forward, about to touch her shoulder. "Leah, it's—"

"No, don't!" Leah snapped, stepping back. "Don't comfort me. I am horrible. I am just so mean. I was going to break your project. I am just—"

"Leah, listen," Sherry said firmly, concern softening her tone.

Leah looked at her, tears glistening in her eyes.

Sherry swallowed hard, hoping she could draw on the strength her Papa had imbued her with. She had made so many mistakes this year, and surely hadn't made him proud, but maybe just this one time she could get it right. Maybe she could step beyond her own feelings and put herself in the shoes of her nemesis. She would try. She turned so she was facing Leah.

"Listen, when I'm upset, I become capable of things I never thought I could do. Last year, there was a girl in my form who always put her muddy shoes on top of mine. Every time it rained, there was mud inside my shoes. I finally got so upset that I took both her gym shoes and threw them out the window." She blushed at the memory. "It was not one of my finer moments."

Leah frowned. "You did that? You?"

Sherry held up her hands, palms forward. "Honest."

Leah wiped an eye with the back of her hand. "I *have* been upset." She sniffled. "I was afraid you were taking away my friendship with Nechama. It made me feel so ... so ... unimportant."

"I understand you, Leah, I really do."

Leah nodded, but kept her gaze on the floor. "I've been so upset with myself for thinking such awful things. I never thought I was malicious but, suddenly, there I was, full of spite."

"But don't you see? It wasn't the real you. Your real character was buried beneath all that worry and fear."

Leah looked at her for a long moment. "How do you do it? How are you so kind, even when others are mean to you?"

Sherry winced. "I'm not always so kind. I threw a girl's shoes out the window, remember?"

Leah giggled through her tears, and Sherry smiled.

"But it's something I've been working on for a long time." She swallowed. "I wish I could be more like my father and not get ruffled. Ever."

Leah fidgeted with her sleeve. "I'm sorrier than you can imagine." Gazing at the floor, she flicked a timid glance at Sherry. "Can ... can we be friends?"

Sherry looked deep into her marble eyes, which sparkled with a curious mix of shame and admiration. "We *are* friends," she declared. "Care for a game of Scrabble?"

Leah bobbed her head, a grin adorning her face. She ran to fetch the game and they got ready to play.

A knock on the door startled them, and Sherry went to open it, only to find Chava outside.

Chava's face held a worried expression, and Sherry suddenly remembered that she had called her the other day. Her run-in with

Mrs. Winter, quite literally, had made her forget all about it.

"What is it, Chava?" she asked, fear pounding in her ears.

Leah approached them, having finished setting up the game.

Chava stared, her gaze traveling to the game of Scrabble. "Were you two just playing?" she asked, incredulous.

"We were just going to," Leah said.

"Okay, then I'll leave you to it."

Sherry's nerves couldn't be stilled. "But what about... what about what you wanted to tell me? What is it?"

Chava smiled. "Nothing. Nothing at all." She leaned toward Sherry and lowered her voice. "You go back to your game. I see I wasn't needed after all."

"Okay, then." Sherry waved her sister off.

She drew in a deep breath through her nose and exhaled slowly. Then she settled back next to Leah. It was good to have an older sister who cared so much about you, and it was even better to have a papa whose influence would never cease.

Her heart whispered a thank You to Hashem.

The door rattled again, and Michal entered the room, a worried frown on her face. "Oh, so there you are. I've been looking for you all over the building. I need your help with this booklet." She held up the small stack of papers they'd been working on together for their Shabbos project.

"I'll be along shortly." Sherry glanced at the game board, then held up a hand to catch Michal's attention before she left. "Hey, why don't you join us for Scrabble first?"

Only then did Michal notice Leah sitting there, laying out the game—a sight anyone would have thought extraordinary a short time earlier. Michal's jaw dropped.

"Uh ... sure."

She came over and plopped on the bed, which messed up the game.

"Sorry, Leah. Here, let me help." Michal began to reposition the tile trays.

"Thanks," Leah said, smiling.

Sherry smiled, too, until she caught something odd in Michal's eyes. It didn't seem like Michal had a problem with Leah being here—on the contrary. But she kept looking at Sherry as though she intended to say something and then kept stopping herself.

What is it? Has she something to share? Something to tell me?

Whatever it was, it would have to wait. Obviously, Michal didn't want to say it in front of Leah.

The girls chatted and laughed as they played. All three were good with words, which made for a challenging game. Finally, the last tile was laid down and Leah won by a small margin.

"Good game," Sherry said, and Michal agreed. "To the victor, the spoils." Sherry handed Leah a sweet from a recent care package Ma had sent. Leah took it shyly.

"Thanks." She looked happy. Her eyes radiated a light from within, which Sherry suspected didn't come from winning the game. "By the way, you should be able to get hold of mini batteries for the flames of the *menorah*. I'm sure I've seen some in the lab. Ask Mrs. Frank."

Sherry clapped. "Yes, you're right, Leah. Thank you."

Michal blinked in pleased surprise as she watched Leah slip out the door.

"I'm so excited," Sherry said to Michal once Leah had left the room.

"Because you're friends with Leah now?"

"Well, yes. But also because my mother's coming. I can't wait to show her around the building and the gardens and have her meet you and all the teachers. Oh, I'm so happy this business with Miss

Bentley was sorted before she comes."

"Good for you," Michal said, looking down. Sherry, ever intuitive, saw she had touched a raw nerve.

"Michal, something's bothering you." She rubbed the floor with her shoe. "I wish you would share it with me. What else are best friends for?"

Michal seemed about to speak, but then changed her mind. "It's nothing you would understand, anyway. Your life is so perfect."

She walked out of the room, leaving Sherry to wonder how Michal had ever come to believe that.

18 Visiting Day

A few days later, Mrs. Pepper came into the second form room before lunch to announce the winners of the Shabbos competition.

"I am proud of this class," she said. "Each one of you has surpassed yourself with your projects. The panelists had a hard time selecting a winner, but at last . . ."

She let the sentence hang in the air and looked around the room. The air was heavy with excited anticipation. Unable to wait, girls started calling out their guesses.

"Sherry and Michal!"

"The Mishkan!"

"Michal's!"

"Sherry's!"

Mrs. Pepper nodded proudly. "Yes, the model Mishkan is superb. And the accompanying book is simply wonderful. Such detail! Amazing! Michal and Sherry, I am very proud of you both. But though it was exceptional, there was one other project that had even finer attention to detail."

She turned to Leah and Nechama. The other girls looked around in confusion.

"Leah and Nechama's project about the thirty-nine *melachos* was one of the finest works I've ever seen. So while the Mishkan wins an honorable mention, the *melachos* win first place. Well done, girls. Both awards are well deserved." She lifted her hands and clapped. Mrs. Hampton joined her, beaming warmly at the girls from beneath her chin-length *sheitel*.

Sherry's heart leaped. She hadn't even known what Leah and Nechama were working on. She looked at them, as the shock on their faces gave way to delight. The rest of their classmates began to applaud them, too.

"Well done," Sherry whispered across the aisle as she clapped.

Nechama's cheeks were as red as tomatoes. "Thanks. It was mostly Leah," she admitted.

Michal looked at Leah with wide eyes. "I had no idea you were so creative, Leah. I can't wait to see your project."

Leah only smiled. She looked as if she might burst from pride.

Later, on the way to the exhibition display, Sherry met Mrs. Pepper in the corridor. The headmistress gave her a long, meaningful look.

"Sherry, you have made me so proud."

Sherry smiled, and her heart fluttered. She knew Mrs. Pepper wasn't only referring to the Shabbos project.

With joy bubbling up inside, Sherry practically danced all the way to the hall. She stood in front of the *melachos* model and admired the fine stitching on a farmer's robe. She could see why Mrs. Pepper had chosen this model over hers and Michal's. Though it stung a bit to have their model outshone, she was pleased that it was still displayed in pride of place in the second-year form room alongside the winning model. She also couldn't be happier for Leah and Nechama—they had obviously put in a lot of work, and she couldn't begrudge them one ounce for coming out on top. Papa used to say that "being happy for the winner means true winning." *That makes me a winner of sorts too, doesn't it?*

Over the next few days, all the other classes came to admire the models. Sherry tried not to show how eager she was to see their reactions, but they were effusive in their praise, which she found gratifying.

Of course, Baila took pictures of the models from every angle, causing Bassy to playfully poke fun at her.

"Baila is at it again; nothing can escape her one to ten."

"But these models are prize winners," Baila protested, pretending to be miffed. "Surely they're worth a shot or two."

"Or three, or four or five," Bassy added drily.

Sherry giggled.

She'd thought Michal would be as excited as she was about receiving such high honors—but she was wrong.

"I wish everyone would stop talking about the model," Michal complained. "Who cares if we got an honorable mention or not?"

Visiting day arrived bright and clear, unusual for February. Sherry shivered with anticipation. She stood outside, bundled against the chill, to see if she could spot the family car arriving. Finally, her patience paid off when it came around the bend with Moshe in the driver's seat. Sherry hoped that he would get to see some of the original manuscripts of the Rambam that were supposedly housed at the Dover library, just a few streets away from the school.

She leaped with joy and clapped as he parked the car and her mother's door opened. She raced over and hugged her mother tightly. Out of the corner of her eye, she noticed Michal watching her, clearly upset. She wanted to introduce Ma to Michal, but the expression on Michal's face made her change her mind. She decided to introduce Ma later, after Michal had a chance to calm down. Maybe her friend would finally be ready to talk about what was bothering her.

The Spencer family walked into the school and met Chava as soon as they entered the building. Chava's welcome was as joyous as Sherry's, if a little more dignified. With her two daughters in tow, Mrs. Spencer took a tour of the school, stopping every now and then to revel in their handiwork. She admired Chava's silk painting, marveled at Sherry's needlework, and was blown away by the award-winning model Sherry and Michal had made.

Rivi approached. "Mrs. Spencer, isn't this model amazing? You should have seen how many hours Sherry put into it. Look at the fire and the *menorah*. We all knew that she and Michal would be winners. And we were so happy! Because, Mrs. Spencer, Sherry is—"

"Rivi!" Sherry cut in, speaking in a mock-serious tone. "There is no need to go on and on."

"Yes, Miss Spencer," Rivi said. Her expression was so perfectly respectful and obedient, the Spencers couldn't help laughing.

At two o'clock, Mrs. Spencer was scheduled to meet with her daughters' teachers. Parents were given a time slot to speak with the staff, and the students were free to spend that time as they wished.

"Let's go for a walk," Chava suggested to Sherry. "It will be a while till Ma's finished."

Sherry was proud to be walking with Chava, enjoying some bonding time together, something their busy schedules hadn't afforded them much of that year. Giving her sister a sidelong glance, she noticed that she must have grown a little since the fall. She was nearly eye level with her sister.

As they approached the pond, Chava stopped. "What's Michal doing on her own?" She nodded at the girl sitting alone by the water's edge.

Where were Michal's parents? Why wasn't she with them? Sherry remembered how upset Michal had been earlier. Seeing her alone now, it all made sense. At once, Sherry felt guilty and ran over to her. How could she have been so selfish?

"Michal, I'm sorry your parents couldn't make it. Come, join us."

But Michal refused. "No." She sighed as she pulled blades of grass from the ground beside her. "You go to your family. You don't need me tagging along."

Sherry looked at Chava, who gestured for her to sit with her friend and take her time.

Without waiting for an invitation, Sherry sat next to Michal. "Try me," she said at last. "Tell me what's bothering you."

Sherry's concern and compassion hit their mark, and Michal let out a long sigh. "Promise me first it won't ruin our friendship."

"Ruin our friendship?" Sherry asked, confused.

"I know you won't leave me," Michal said. "I'm just worried you'll start to pity me, and I don't want that. My mother always said that pity and respect are exclusive. You can't have both."

"Michal, nothing could make me stop respecting you." She touched her friend's arm. "Nothing!"

"It's just that everything about you seems so perfect."

"There's nothing perfect in this world," Sherry said. "The more perfect things seem, the more cracks they may be concealing. My mother taught me that." She put her arm around Michal and looked at her, eyebrows raised slightly.

The words came tumbling out as Michal shared her secret. "That girl I told you about the other day... the one who lost her mother? That girl is me."

"Oh."

Michal continued to talk. She described how much she had loved her mother, all the more so because she was an only child, and how her mother had fallen ill. Although they had fought for her health, she had passed away so quickly. Sherry learned how the girls at Michal's previous school had pitied her, so she had chosen to go away to a new school where no one knew her, in the hope that she would be able to make true friends. She talked and talked until she fell back on the grass, spent.

"I had hoped that a change of environment could help me forget my pain," she said, propping herself up on her elbows. "But I found out that a change of scenery can't change a broken heart."

Sherry nodded. "I know what you mean."

Michal continued as though she hadn't heard, staring over the water. "The sea always brings back memories of Mummy. It was our favorite place. We would often go to the seaside for a special treat."

"I'm glad you have so many good memories of her," Sherry said. "I know it's not the same, though."

Michal frowned. "No, it's not. But it's all I have now."

Sherry took a slow, deep breath and released it slowly. The pain Michal carried was a pain that she, too, carried. A pain she could not fix, but one she could share.

Michal pointed to some distant cliffs beyond the area they were allowed to walk without a staff member. "I hope to paint these one day. My mother was an artist ..." Her voice faltered. "I think it's one of the things she may have passed on to me." She gulped. "I miss her so much! If only she were here."

Sherry didn't say anything. Michal looked at her and saw her own anxiety mirrored in Sherry's eyes.

"Michal, I get you, I really do," Sherry said finally. "I understand you so well. Far better than you can ever imagine." A few tears escaped and slid down her cheeks.

Michal gave a wan smile, and then her tears began to flow. They wouldn't stop. Eventually, the sobs eased, and soon, the gentle sound of the rippling water overtook the sound of grief. She turned again to the cliffs.

Sherry followed her gaze. "They're magnificent, aren't they?" she whispered. "Imagine what they look like illuminated with the soft-hued rays of sunrise."

Michal closed her eyes, sketching the scene against the black stillness of her eyelids.

"I've painted a sunset," she mused. "Maybe it's time I did a sunrise." The words made her heart rustle. *Hadn't Mummy said something similar? Oh yes, that's it.* "Because the longest sunset is always followed by the brightest sunrise," she said aloud.

Sherry smiled. "I like that." She took Michal's hands in her own and their eyes locked.

"Thank you, Sherry," she said at last. "You do understand." She stared at the calm pond. "I feel better now that I've talked to you. You're the only person here I've told, and keeping it all inside almost killed me. It's as if it was all waiting to be said, and now that I've told you, I can be more like myself again. You know, sort of like after one throws up, the nauseous feeling goes away and a sense of wellness settles in."

Sherry nodded, then looked down, fidgeting with her cardigan. She decided to take the plunge. "Michal, I ... I wanted to tell you ..."

Michal's eyes opened wide. But before Sherry could continue, she was distracted by Mindy running toward them.

"Sherry, Mrs. Pepper is calling for you." She took a deep breath. "Where have you been all this time?"

Sherry looked around and realized that Chava was no longer waiting for her. The familiar dread returned. *Oh no! How long have we been sitting here?*

"Go, Sherry," Michal said, getting up. The wind had long dried the tears on her cheeks, but streaks remained. Sherry rubbed at the salty tracks on her own cheeks, but they were too crusty to be wiped away.

"I'm exhausted," Michal continued. "I think I need a nap." She smiled. "Call me when they serve supper."

Sherry went to Mrs. Pepper's office, wondering why she'd been summoned. Had Mrs. Pepper decided to chasten her for all her mishaps that year in front of her mother?

When she opened the door, her worst fears were confirmed. Her mother and Chava were waiting for her there. But instead of looking stern, Mrs. Pepper was smiling.

Sherry stepped hesitantly into the room, burning with curiosity. "You called for me, Mrs. Pepper?"

"Your mother drove a long way to be with you today," Mrs. Pepper said, her eyes twinkling. "I think it's only fair that you give her some of your time."

Chava grinned, but the smile faded as she studied her sister's face. "Sherry! Whatever is the matter? Have you been crying?"

Their mother looked concerned as well. Sherry shrugged. "It's nothing. I was talking to my friend, and she told me something sad that made me cry. I'm fine."

The two seemed to accept this answer. Sherry then asked why

she had been rushed to the room in such a panic.

"It was the only way I could think of getting a hold of you." Chava's grin returned.

"You frightened me," Sherry said, but then she grinned back. "I couldn't think what I'd done wrong this time."

"You've done a lot of things," Mrs. Pepper said in mock admonition. "Most of which I am very, very ... proud of!"

Sherry gave a doubtful smile, but inside, her heart sang.

As they left the office, Chava waved at Ma and Sherry. "I've got to run. I'll be back shortly."

Sherry smiled and nodded in understanding. This was Chava's way of giving her some quality time alone with her mother. She couldn't be gladder. There was so much she wanted to talk about. No one could understand her like Ma could. And the more they spoke, the happier she became.

"Thank you, Ma," she said, jumping for joy. "I'm so glad you've come! Oh, it's just so good to be with you."

A burst of delight radiated throughout her body. And the look in Ma's eyes told her that she, too, was overjoyed at how things had developed, especially the drastic change in her behavior since the first report card.

The bell rang for supper and Sherry scrunched up her mouth. "I think I'd better go wake Michal."

Ma glanced sideways at her. "Michal ... as in Michal Lempel?"

Sherry nodded. "Yes. Do you know her? I found out that she lives in our town, but I'd never met her before coming here."

Ma looked away.

Sherry noticed a faint tinge of pink in her cheek that hadn't been there before. Was Ma blushing?

Her mother passed her hand over her face as if to erase the color and smiled at Sherry. "Have you two become friends?"

Sherry grinned. "The best of friends! We're like sisters, almost."

For some curious reason, Ma looked inordinately pleased. She patted her daughter on the back. "You go, Sherry. I'm sure Chava will be here shortly to keep me company, and as soon as you're ready, you'll join us." She paused. "Bring Michal over, too. I'd love to meet her. But if she's had a stressful day, don't press her, and I won't mind if you stay with her to keep her company."

Sherry stood. "Okay, I'll ask her."

With a tingling heart, Sherry ran to the dormitory, where she found her friend wide awake and content.

"Ready for supper, Sis?"

Michal nodded, looking sheepish and straightening her ponytail. "Sorry for taking up your time earlier. But thank you for listening."

Sherry gave her a hug. "That's what friends are for. Listen ..." She looked at Michal and closed her mouth, not wanting to dampen her friend's mood again. Besides, the tantalizing aroma of freshly baked buns wafted up the stairs, and her stomach rumbled.

"What is it?" Michal looked curiously at her.

Sherry shook her head. "Nothing. Only my mother would like to meet you. Would you like to sit with us at supper?"

Michal's forehead furrowed. "I don't know. I'll feel out of place sitting there with you and your sister and mother ..."

"Nonsense," Sherry said. "You're my sister, too. It will be a family table."

Michal looked at her with wide hazel eyes. "Are you sure?"

Sherry grinned. "I was never surer, Sis."

19 A Glorious Beginning

"Purim is coming, Purim is here. It's time for fun, gladness, and cheer," Bassy sang as she sauntered into the common room where the rest of the form was already assembled for a brainstorming session. She sat in the empty seat between Sherry and Baila.

Sherry grinned at her. Bassy's rhymes were starting to grow on her.

"So, what are we planning to do this year?" Becky asked, looking at her friends. A clipboard was poised on her lap, ready to take down ideas.

Baila snorted and clapped a hand over her mouth.

"What? What did I say?" asked Becky, who obviously had no idea that she'd just completed Bassy's rhyme.

"Never mind," Baila said with a dismissive wave. The other girls giggled.

Every year, the classes were allowed to choose a theme for decorating their common rooms. The girls had fun working together and making their ideas come to life. They especially enjoyed seeing all the different rooms decorated in creative ways.

But before the second formers could come up with any suggestions, the secretary, Mrs. Hayley, poked her head through the door. Then spotting Sherry, she motioned to her.

"Sherry, there's a phone call for you."

"Won't be a moment," Sherry whispered to Michal, before hurrying out of the room. Chava was standing outside, waiting for her.

"What's up?" Sherry asked.

Chava's face was white and her chin quivered ever so slightly.

Sherry felt suddenly cold. "What is it, Chava?"

Without a word, Chava led her to the office and closed the door behind them.

"Ma's on the phone. She wants to talk to you."

Sherry's heart sank, unable to bear the suspense any longer. She grabbed the phone. "Ma, what is it?"

"Sherry, dear. I've got news I want to share with you—"

"Okay." She bit her lip and listened.

"You know how much you and Chava and Moshe mean to me. Probably even more so since Papa passed away. You three are my whole world. But now, my darling, there is someone I want to share that world with. Will you let me?"

Sherry dropped the receiver, prickly beads of dread crawling all over her skin.

I can't! A new father? But what about Papa?

With trembling hands, she covered her face and shook her head. *Papa, it can't be happening. It can't!*

Chava put her arm around her shoulders and picked up the dangling receiver, making sure Sherry could hear.

"Ma?"

"Oh, Chava, darling," their mother said. "I would have loved to share this news in person, but Hashem obviously wanted it otherwise. I just couldn't work it out."

"Uh-huh," Chava whispered.

"Chava, are you happy?" Their mother's voice cracked. "Chava," she tried again, "I want you to be happy for me. But I want you to feel at peace, too."

"Ma, I'm happy," Chava said at last.

"You don't know how much that pleases me. Tell Sherry I love her, and I'll talk to you both soon."

After hanging up, Chava rubbed Sherry's back, trying to rouse her from her dismal thoughts. Just then, someone tapped on the door. Michal entered and looked at Sherry, who couldn't stop the tears from falling.

"Sherry, what is it?" Michal looked to Chava. "I had a feeling something was going on and came to see if I could help."

Chava filled her in on the news. Michal was shocked. "What?" she cried. "Sherry, I didn't know you'd lost your father. Why didn't you tell me?"

Chava slipped out to give them some privacy.

"Why didn't you tell me?" Michal repeated, looking wounded, betrayed. Sherry opened her mouth to say something, but her lips shut, as if of their own accord. It was tough. She hadn't told anyone about Papa.

"Michal … I … I am sorry. I wanted to share it with you the other day, before Mrs. Pepper called for me."

Michal's eyes softened. "It's okay, Sherry. Don't feel you have to say anything you don't want to."

Sherry nodded. Then she looked into Michal's eyes, which were full of warmth, empathy, and genuine understanding. "Your mother," she continued, her voice barely a whisper. "The beautiful memories you shared, the way you painted them for me. Yes, I, too, know that loss, and I know those memories. My paintings are becoming a bit faded, but the words are there. The words and the feelings they bring are stronger than ever."

Michal sat up straight, staring at Sherry, who averted her gaze to look out the window. She could just about see the edge of the cliffs.

She reached for Michal's hand. Michal returned the grasp, her fingers firm.

When Michal eased open the window, a blast of fresh air blew against their cheeks. "Tell me, Sherry, tell me about him."

"My Papa ..." Sherry started. Her voice cracked and tears pooled in her eyes. Michal's cheeks were now streaked with tears.

"It was so sudden. We didn't even know he was ill. The shock. The paralyzing dread." The tears rolled down, soaking the collar of her shirt. "But Papa, he was gone. Like that. Just gone. Hashem had taken him away, and it was so sudden."

The two sat in silence.

Sherry shook her head. "But you see, he's not really gone. He always read stories to me. Stories of *emunah*, stories of kindness, stories filled with empathy and *ahavas habrios*. He sat me on his lap and taught me so much. And his messages, they penetrated deep inside me. He told me ... He told me that I could never really understand anyone else until I had seen the world through their eyes. He told me that stories were the way to see the world. To really see them. And eventually, he taught me how to tell my own stories."

She sniffed and smiled. "We would often write stories together. And I would write my own. He told me how powerful words were because they were the vehicle through which we expressed ourselves, and through which we could understand others. And much like you feel that your mother is still with you, through art and nature, I feel as though Papa is still with me. With every word I write. I write them for him, and I write them for me. Because I know he'd want me to."

Her bottom lip trembled. "How can Ma remarry? Papa is still here." She pointed to her heart and took a steadying breath. "Uh, and ... I know that very soon ... we'll see him for real. It's what keeps me going, when the pain gets too tough. *Achakeh lo b'chol yom sheyavo.*"

Michal didn't answer, and the silence stretched between them. Sherry swallowed, finding Michal's presence comforting. Her tears retreated. Maybe the breeze had whisked them away.

"Tell me, what are you most worried about?" Michal asked.

Sherry considered. She thought about Ma, and what she meant to her. "I just hope he's a good and kind man. If I know he will make my mother happy and treat her well, I'll relax. I'm just so worried. My father was a very special man. My mother deserves nothing but the best."

"If Hashem helped your mother find such a husband once, I'm sure she will find one again," Michal said.

Sherry pondered this. "That's very true. And Ma has been raising us alone for a long time now. She does everything for us, working hard to pay the bills and our tuition and still finding time for us whenever we need it. You know what? I'm happy for her. She deserves to be happy."

Michal smiled encouragingly. "It sounds like you're right."

"But I didn't congratulate her! I'm calling her back right now." Sherry dialed her home number. As the phone rang, she eyed her friend. "You're a great comfort, Michal. I'm so glad you followed me here."

"You did the same for me."

Sherry and Michal exchanged understanding glances. This time, Sherry knew it was true.

She heard a click on the line, but the answering machine picked up, so she quietly hung up.

Maybe it's better to wait until I'm feeling more myself.

Chava returned and they spent a few minutes speculating about who their "new father" might be. Then a knock on the door silenced the trio.

Mrs. Pepper walked in. "Michal, your father is here to speak to you."

Michal gasped and brought her hands to her mouth.

Chava and Sherry got up to leave, but Mr. Lempel stepped into the room and held up a hand to stop them.

Sherry was taken by his regal and calming appearance. She was thankful that her friend had such a strong and noble father.

"Michal, it's *hashgachah pratis* that the Spencers are here," he began, looking at the sisters. "I see your mother has already spoken to you." He smiled at them, and Sherry wondered how he knew that. Then he placed a hand on Michal's shoulder. "I'm here to fit the other pieces of the puzzle into place." He looked at Sherry and Chava. "Your mother couldn't be here, so she called, but I was able to come in person."

Sherry couldn't quite grasp what she'd just heard. Michal looked bewildered, too, but then something seemed to click and her friend gazed at her, wide-eyed. Sherry turned to Chava, whose mouth was agape. All three girls turned shocked faces to Michal's father.

"Tatty, is this really happening?" Michal asked.

Mr. Lempel smiled as he nodded. "Yes, my dear children. The Lempel family is growing."

Michal hugged Sherry. "This is not the news I was expecting!

And I never would've thought I would be so happy to hear it."

Sherry smiled through happy tears, and a few sad ones. But she was grateful for this beginning. "Oh, Michal, we're really going to be sisters after all. How amazing. How beautifully Hashem arranges our lives, like in a good book."

"Or a beautiful painting," Michal said.

"A beautiful painting," Sherry echoed softly. "One blushing with dawning sunshine." She winked at her through wet eyes, allowing rays of the nascent sunrise to illuminate a path of ascent and change—one that she would try to follow.

Michal returned the wink, a similar happy and wistful smile on her face. Chava hugged them both.

The girls finally stood back and laughed, joy swelling in each of their hearts—a wonderful start to a new beginning.

PART II

Stormy Winds

1 Back to School

Sherry finished wrapping her last book and set it on the pile on the dining room table. She pushed a stray lock of dark-brown hair out of her eyes and back into her half-pony. She glanced at Michal to gauge her progress. Her new stepsister was still putting the final touches on her own book covers, carefully tucking in the edges of the paper as her thick auburn ponytail slid over her shoulder.

Sherry had finished first. But Michal's books looked like pieces of fine art.

Sherry grinned. "Trust you to make your books look like they came that way from the shop."

Michal looked up, an anxious look in her hazel eyes. "What do you mean?"

"Don't worry," Sherry said quickly. "I like them. They're beautiful."

Relief flooded Michal's face. Sherry's mother and Michal's father had put widowhood behind them and gotten married a month ago. Since the Spencer house was bigger, the Lempels had moved in there. Ever since, Michal had been tripping over herself not to offend anyone. She had barely even redecorated her new bedroom yet—the one Sherry's brother, Moshe, had vacated two years ago when he'd left for yeshivah in northern England. At least the view from it was as beautiful as ever, with the Thames and Medway canal visible from a distance away. The dazzling waters in ever-changing hues reflected the sun's rays as it made its rise and descent, accompanied at night by the moon's glow. From deep blue and turquoise to orange and purple, it was a gorgeous palette of color—a true artist's delight and one that Michal could revel in.

Sherry chastised herself quietly. She should have known better than to tease. As annoying as Michal's sensitivity could be, it couldn't be easy having to adjust to a whole new house and a new family. Sherry was having a hard enough time adjusting to her new name.

Lempel. Lem-pel. Sherry Lempel.

Nope. It was still weird. Still, she had offered to change her last name to Lempel as a gift to Ma so she would know that Sherry was pleased about the remarriage—particularly after her initial less-than-gracious reaction. Michal was glad too, and that made Sherry doubly happy.

From the kitchen, Ma called, "Sherry, you have a phone call." She entered the dining room and stopped short, her brown eyes widening in surprise. "What's this? You're almost done with all your book wraps? Is that Michal's doing?"

Michal's neatly covered books were piled in a perfect stack. Sherry felt herself blush. However, she was strangely gratified to note that Michal's face would make an almost perfect match for the shade her own face had just turned.

"Don't these look lovely?" Ma said, leafing through Michal's pile.

Sherry grinned. Ma must have also observed Michal walking

on eggshells. Sherry was glad she was trying to make Michal feel at home.

Michal gave a shy smile. "Uh, thank you, uh ... Ma."

Sherry couldn't help but notice how her friend-turned-sister still stuttered when she said "Ma."

Will she ever really consider Ma as her own? I know that Ma loves her just the same as Chava or me. Well, maybe not just the same, but almost. I would love for Michal to really feel it so we can be a real family.

Sherry stretched her neck and took a deep breath. Bringing a father into their home was nowhere near enough to make their family complete. They would not be a true blended unit until Michal felt like a sister instead of being one only in name.

Sherry scratched the back of her neck. Noticing Michal's discomfort, she offered her a smile, but her new sister didn't return it. Michal's pink cheeks turned even redder as she glanced away.

Someone patted Sherry's shoulder. Ma.

"Sherry, what's taking you so long? Your friend is waiting for you on the phone."

Sherry brought her hand to her mouth so fast, she almost slapped herself. "Oh no! I hope the line hasn't been disconnected."

She rushed to the kitchen and picked up the phone. The cord was tangled and she had to unloop it several times before she put it up to her ear.

"Hello?" She twisted the cord around her fingers.

"Hello, Sherry!" came a girl's cheerful greeting.

Sherry blinked. She knew that voice! "Oh, Mali! So good to hear from you. It's not every day I get an important international phone call."

"Yes, isn't it exciting? Speaking of which, are you excited about going into third form?"

Sherry nodded. "What do you think? We're looking forward to Samphire, big time—"

A noise muffled Mali's next words.

"Sorry, Mali, did you say you're planning to join us next week?"

"Ah ... you never know. It would be smashing if I could!"

"Ooh, it would!" Sherry clenched the phone cord in excitement. "So, should I save you a good bed in the dorm?"

"Nah, I'm just pulling your leg. I wish I could come, though!"

Sherry laughed. "I wish you were coming too!"

"How's Mich—"

Someone cleared her throat, and she looked up to see Michal.

"Sorry, Mali, what was that?" There was no response. "Hello ...?"

Sherry held out the receiver and stared at it.

Michal cocked her head. "Anything up?"

"That's odd. The line went dead before we got to say goodbye. Oh, well." She placed the receiver on the cradle and shrugged.

"Mali, huh? Is she planning to join us at Samphire again?"

Sherry wasn't expecting the sharpness in Michal's voice. When she looked up, her friend's expression matched her voice.

"Would that be a problem?"

"I thought we ... never mind. So, when's she coming?"

"She's not."

Michal exhaled, almost like a growl.

Sherry squinted. "What's that for? Is Mali not in your good books or something?"

Michal shrank away. "Don't be silly. I like Mali, just the same as you do. She's fun. She's kind. She's ... great. It's just that I ... I don't want ... okay, you know what, let's just drop this." She drew her mouth into a tight line, but then produced a bright smile. "I can't wait! It's so exciting to start school with you."

Sherry winked back. “The feeling’s mutual.” She looked Michal squarely in the eye. “You know, last year I was terribly anxious about going to school. I wasn’t sure that I’d fit in, make friends, or even understand the schoolwork. This year is different. I’m so glad to have you with me. I’m not worried at all.”

Michal nodded, more to herself than Sherry. “I ... I’m . . .” She pulled the bow of her ponytail, releasing some of her soft copper-brown hair, then had to retie the ribbon. “I’m not sure I can take the place of your American pal ...”

“What are you talking about? You know Mali isn’t my best friend.” Sherry scratched her ear. “Well, yeah, we were pretty close, but how can we be now that she lives on the other side of the ocean? I mean, we’ve only exchanged three or four letters since she left last year. And, now I’ve spoken to her for, like, twenty seconds, before we were cut off. I mean, honestly, Michal, can’t a person have more than one friend?”

Sherry shook her head but maintained eye contact. Her voice had risen nearly an octave. She took a deep breath to calm down.

“Besides,” she added, “for your information, she is not American.”

Michal’s petite face deflated as if it had been punctured. “Okay, okay. Forget I ever said anything.”

Sherry was puzzled. *What has gotten into this girl? Why does she have to be so touchy? She seems to have dumped all her friendliness and kindliness somewhere else. Somewhere far away.* She looked at Michal and sighed. *If only I could rip off that melancholy mask and talk to the real Michal.*

All of a sudden, she felt sick. The shame made her nauseous. How could she be so cruel? She knew Michal hadn’t gotten over the agony of losing her mother. They had been so close. She shook her head as if to release the horrible thoughts from her mind. *Am I really that merciless?*

She wrapped her arms around her best friend. “Mich, we’re not just friends, we’re sisters.”

Michal stared back, wetting the corners of her lips with the tip of her tongue. She didn’t say a word.

After a few moments, Sherry couldn’t take it any longer. “What are you thinking, sis?”

“Uh, just about last year.” Michal let out a long sigh, her shoulders drooping.

Sherry gave what she hoped was an encouraging smile to prod her on.

Michal gave a half-smile in return. “Isn’t it a marvel how much has changed? When I first joined the form two class, I thought I had made a dreadful mistake. I had come to school a year late and was very lonely until you and I became friends. After that, everything seemed a little brighter.” She chuckled quietly. “It’s funny that I called you ‘Sis,’ and now we really are sisters. Unbelievable, isn’t it, how Hashem has shaped our lives?”

“Yes, it was an amazing year.”

Sherry had been almost in the same boat as Michal at the beginning of last year, going into a new school in second form. Unlike Michal, though, she had quickly made several friends—Mali, who was also a newcomer; Bassy and Baila, the precocious pair; and the mischievous Nechama, who had gotten her into a fair share of trouble.

But that wasn’t the only trouble Nechama had caused her. The cheating incident flashed into Sherry’s mind. Desperate to shove the memory aside, she put on her brightest smile, hoping her angst wouldn’t show on her face.

“I know what you’re thinking about,” Michal said. She bit her lower lip. “But, hey, all’s well that ends well, right?” She offered an encouraging smile of her own.

Sherry chuckled. It was thanks to Michal's perceptive nature and support that she had handled the situation as well as she had, managing to restore harmony to her suspicious classmates before the finger-pointing had gotten out of hand.

"You know me too well. Oh, but it was awful to be accused of cheating." Sherry took another deep breath, then blinked and smiled. "But you believed me. You knew I hadn't done it. I don't know what I'd have done without you. You saved me a world of trouble."

Her heart warmed with the same gratitude she'd felt at the time. The culprit had ended up being Nechama, who had eventually come forward and apologized—but that didn't make what had happened seem less awful.

"Yes, and now we're returning as sisters. What could be better?"

"Nothing," Sherry declared. "And I'm Sherry Spencer no more. Instead, I'll be known as Sherry Lempel."

She gave an involuntary shudder, but maintained her smile. If Michal noticed, she said nothing.

Sherry's older sister, Chava, walked in, a stack of worksheets in her hand. She glanced at Michal's stack of books, which was wrapped in yellow and navy tartan paper, and chortled. "Oh, Michal! Trust you to choose wrapping paper that perfectly matches your uniform."

"Anything wrong with mine?" Sherry asked, pouting.

Chava held up one of Sherry's books. It sported random stripes in vivid green, orange, and yellow, but when she peered closer, she smiled.

"Hey, this is cool. The yellow lines are formed out of words."

She read one and burst out laughing. "'I can't figure out why I can't do maths.' But you're great at maths, Sherry."

Sherry laughed. "But it was too funny not to buy it. Look at the grammar one."

Chava bent to squint at the other books, her wavy dark brown hair—so like Sherry's—falling elegantly over her shoulder. "There it is." She picked it up. "'Grammar can't stress me anymore—I'm past tense.' Oh, Sherry."

"This one's my favorite," Michal said, picking up the art book and handing it to Chava.

"'I drew a blank.' Well, that wouldn't apply to you, would it, Michal? Your art is beautiful, and your ideas seem endless."

Michal giggled, her face glowing pink.

Chava set the book down and read the others. "'Geography means the world to me.' Hmm. And what's this one?" She frowned at a book that read "Why get stuck in the past?"

Sherry grinned. "History, of course."

Chava laughed, her eyes twinkling just like Ma's had when she'd read them.

"Sherry, Sherry, Sherry. If you had told me that you designed these yourself, I would've believed you. These are so you."

"Just like Michal's are so her."

Chava chuckled. "Michal, the artist, and Sherry, the trou—"

"The terrific one," Michal cut in.

Chava arched a brow and smirked.

Michal shifted her weight, then brightened. "I can't believe that we're off next week."

Sherry grinned at her. "I guess we'd best finish with these supplies, huh?"

"And I've got to go finish preparing these worksheets," Chava said, and headed toward the stairs, undoubtedly to get everything ready for her first year as a Junior Three *Kodesh* teacher at Kent Primary School.

The girls started to pack their remaining school supplies into their new school satchels. As Sherry organized her stationery, a swarm of thoughts ran through her head. She hoped Michal's insecurity would fade as soon as they arrived at school. She flicked back her hair. Of course, she was grateful to have such a special friend. Still, she didn't want their relationship to stifle her. It would be strange enough returning as "Sherry Lempel" without having to worry about Michal's diffidence.

Michal looked up from flipping through her books, a big smile on her face. "I can't wait for school."

Sherry's heart lifted as Michal's smile elbowed away any worries she may have felt. Last year, she'd been so nervous before school began. This year, she could hardly wait for it.

"If only tomorrow were Monday."

"Yeah." Michal sighed wistfully. "We can't get to school soon enough. It feels so different this year, now that I'm not going alone. I've got you. My friend."

"Your sister." Sherry nodded for emphasis, pushing aside her remaining doubts. They were family now, after all. It was time for her to act like it, to prove to Michal that she belonged here.

Ma bustled into the room again and cocked her head at the piles of pencils, erasers, and other supplies yet to be labeled.

"If tomorrow *were* Monday, you'd be very behind. Hop to it, girls. You still have your uniforms to press."

Sherry and Michal exchanged glances and grinned.

They had each other, and they'd soon be seeing all their friends again. It was going to be the best school year ever.

2

Grand Arrival

Despite their anxious anticipation, Monday came quickly enough.

Last year, Sherry had spent nearly the entire journey sitting silently next to Chava, a rock-hard bundle of nerves in the pit of her stomach. This year, Chava wasn't with her, but Michal was. Sherry laughed and teased the girls who took the train from Maidstone in the heart of Kent down to Samphire near the Port of Dover, while Michal read a book beside her.

When the majestic white stone walls of Samphire came into view through the train window, Rivi—the tall, lanky girl who adored architecture—stopped prattling about her summer in the Lake District to let out a gasp. She wasn't the only girl who reacted that way. Even Michal looked up from her book and admired the view.

The beauty, the atmosphere, it was like a piece of heaven. Sherry soared on the wings of joy, her hopes and aspirations loftier than ever.

Hashem, please help me scale the heights of perfection. She knew she had a long way to go. But at that moment, she had a fierce longing to really make something out of herself, to become a person worthy of the title *bas Melech.*

As soon as they walked into the grand foyer of the school, someone called over the crowd, "Sherry, Michal, I'm glad you're here! I was waiting for you two to appear."

Michal groaned. "Oh, that has to be Bassy. She's still at it with her rhymes."

Sherry clapped. "Aw, Bassy. How does she always know exactly when the girls who travel by train are arriving?"

Girls in double-breasted navy blazers and pleated skirts, yellow tartan shirts, and smart-looking navy berets milled about Samphire's enormous stately entrance hall. Sherry looked over their heads and soon spotted Bassy, a short, plump girl with frizzy yellow hair, standing on the stairs across from them. Baila, Bassy's friend and partner-in-mischief, stood next to her and waved them over. With Baila's tall, slender frame and straight, sleek nutbrown hair, the two girls couldn't look more different—but they were practically inseparable.

As Sherry and Michal approached, Baila gave them a huge, open grin.

"Bassy has her ways. Now come along, friends, have something to eat and drink, and then we can help you unpack."

Sherry and Michal exchanged glances, and fell into step behind Baila as she and Bassy forged a path through the crowd toward the refreshments set up on the other side of the hall. Sherry was thrilled to once more hear Bassy's rhymes. The giggling of the girls passing by reminded her that she was no longer in the awkward position of being the new girl at Samphire. Even the unfamiliar voices of first form girls staring at the hall in wonder brought her comfort.

"It's lovely to be one of the bunch," Michal whispered, echoing Sherry's feelings.

After a quick tea, the girls went upstairs to their dormitories, which were opposite the library. It didn't take them long to unpack their belongings. Everyone in the third form had already arrived—all twenty-three students—and with some time to spare, they decided to go to the netball field for a game.

The sky was a crisp blue and a fresh wind brushed their faces as they raced. Tomorrow, lessons would begin, but for now, it was fun to relish the luxury of free time.

Sherry gratefully accepted the red vest thrown to her. She scanned the court to see who she would be playing against. "Hey, Rivi, we're opponents. That should be fun."

Rivi laughed, tucking wisps of black hair under her navy beret to keep it out of her eyes. "Watch out. I won't be giving you an easy time."

Leah Felder arrived just then, her blue goal-defense bib neatly pulled over her shirt. Sherry stopped short, staring at the ginger-haired girl as she hurried to her position. Leah had spent most of last year giving Sherry the cold shoulder, jealous of Nechama's attention toward her. They'd patched things up by the end of the year, but would Leah still hold a grudge? Cautiously, Sherry made her way to the center of the field, resting the rubber ball on her hip.

When Leah saw her, her expression changed to dismay, and Sherry's heart sank.

"Oh no," Leah said, "I see you're playing on the opposing team. It would've been fun to have you on ours."

Sherry gave a hesitant smile. Leah seemed sincere. Perhaps bygones were truly bygones.

"Totally." Sherry nodded, then grinned. "Well, at least having you on the other team makes for a more challenging game."

Bassy caught Sherry's eye and grinned. "All is well that ends in smiles. Red will win this game by miles."

Sherry laughed, but then noticed Michal's expression. Her sister caught her watching and dipped her chin, smoothing her red goal attack bib, but it was too late. Sherry had seen the jealousy in her frown, too similar to the sullen pout Leah had worn most of last year.

Her heart fell. *I hope I'm misreading her.*

With a blow of the whistle from Becky Robinson, the game began. Both teams played their best, attempting to score goals by passing the ball down the court to their team's goal shoot for her to hurl through their goal ring. The warm weather urged them on, and soon the game was in full swing. The blue team was ahead by two goals, but then the red team shot two goals in quick succession and leveled the score, with Michal and Bassy each scoring one. In mere minutes, the match would be over. Both sides upped their efforts, eager to shoot the winning goal.

The ball came to Sherry. Michal stood at the edge of the court and waved her arms to indicate that Sherry should throw it to her. Out of the corner of her eye, Sherry saw a blue bib dashing to block the throw and Bassy standing on the other side of the pole.

"Sherry!" Michal shouted, still waving her arms.

"Bassy, here!" Sherry threw her teammate the ball, but fumbled it. The ball went to the side.

Bassy ran for the ball. Leah, her opponent, loomed ahead and tried to stop her, but Bassy was swift. She caught the ball and eyed the post. Sherry swallowed and glanced at her watch—time was moving fast. They only had thirty seconds left. Michal stood near the post, ready to catch the ball if Bassy should miss.

Bassy held up the ball in front of her face. "Listen, ball, you score a goal. Go neatly through the net pole."

"Shoot!" Sherry shouted. "Score the goal!"

Although Bassy was short, she was a sharpshooter. She kept a firm hold on the ball, focused on the net, and aimed. The ball slipped through the hoop.

Everyone on the team cheered. Sherry breathed a sigh of relief. Michal stood on the sidelines, offering half-hearted applause and casting hurt glances at Sherry.

Becky blew the whistle. "Time's up," she called. "Well done, Bassy! You get better every year. Keep it up and you'll be in the matches, no doubt!"

Bassy's naturally pink cheeks became pinker still—most likely as much from pleasure as from the heat of the game. She cupped her hands around her mouth. "Hear, hear! Is the games captain about? Holler for her, tell her to check me out."

"Yeah, you're almost as good at netball as you are at rhyming," Baila teased as she pulled off her bib.

"Thanks, form captain," Bassy said, tipping her beret at Becky and giving Baila a mock salute.

Becky pushed her glasses up her nose and chuckled. "Not anymore. We're in Form Three now, and that means we get a new form captain." She threw the whistle to her. "Who knows, maybe it'll be you."

Bassy rolled her eyes, then nodded solemnly. "You've got that, Becky," she deadpanned. She placed her hand over her heart. "Form captain of Form Three—none other than troublesome Bassy!"

The girls standing nearby chuckled.

Michal tapped her lips with her index finger. "I actually think you'd make a really good form captain," she said, turning to Bassy.

Her expression was so serious, Sherry wondered if she was joking. She nudged Bassy. "I wish you would be too," she said, then shook her head. "Now, how do I know that the teachers would never make such a wise choice?"

"You're hilarious!" Bassy laughed.

The players settled themselves on the grass in the field nearby, the breeze cooling their ruddy cheeks while they relaxed. Sherry sat near Bassy and noticed Michal hanging back, looking uncertain.

"Michal, sit here!" She patted the empty spot next to her.

Michal brightened a little and sat. "Thanks," she said. Some of the hurt left her eyes.

Sherry gave her a big smile, hoping she would realize that her choices during the game were nothing personal. "No problem, sis."

Michal smiled shyly, and Sherry relaxed. If Michal needed constant reassurance that Sherry could still be her friend even if she had other friends, then Sherry was up to the challenge. Michal wasn't as adaptable as Sherry. That meant Sherry had to be the one to make the best of their new situation and help Michal to do the same.

Becky turned up with a jug of lemonade and poured the drink into cups. Sherry gratefully accepted a cup of the sweet, refreshing liquid. Rivi passed around packets of crisps, along with a running commentary on which flavors were the best. Cheese and onion were by far the most popular, and they were gone in no time. The flavor tingled on their tongues, getting the girls thirsty all over again.

Sherry dashed to the third form common room to prepare a fresh jug of lemonade. While she was there, she couldn't resist sliding her fingers over the keys of the grand piano. But the thought of her thirsty friends had her rushing off the stool. She had to refill the jug twice to satisfy her friends. When she returned for the second time, she noted with satisfaction that Becky and Michal were having a quiet conversation. Michal was sitting with her arms clasped behind her neck and smiling.

Good for you, Michal.

"By the way, gals," Nechama said, "did you know we're getting another new girl this year? Her name is Rayla, and she's coming all the way from New York."

"From the States?" Michal asked, looking pointedly at Sherry.

Sherry drummed her fingers, remembering her telephone conversation with Mali the previous week. "Are you sure? That's barmy! Could she not find a school nearer to home?"

"A school as good as Samphire?" Nechama teased. "No, this Rayla is related to Mrs. Pepper somehow—if that means anything."

Sherry caught her bottom lip between her teeth. She found the prospect of a new American student intriguing, but was hesitant to believe it. Why would an American girl come all the way to Samphire? On the other hand, Nechama always knew what was going on at Samphire. Sherry could scarcely remember a time when her information had been wrong.

"That sounds very interesting. I wonder what she's like," Sherry said.

She was trying to envision the new girl when she felt Michal's gaze on her, and a flash of irritation rushed through her. If Michal was going to be jealous just because Sherry showed interest in another girl, they needed to have a serious conversation, and soon.

The other girls chimed in with questions, wanting to know when the new girl would be arriving and any other juicy details.

Nechama tittered, clearly reveling in all the attention. "I don't know much more than I already told you. But I did hear that she'll turn up in a limousine."

"A schoolgirl who arrives in a limousine? Now that's a sight fit for a queen," Bassy said dramatically. Or, rather, as dramatically as her rhyme scheme would allow.

"Oh, Nechama's just pulling your leg," Michal said darkly. "I bet this Rayla will turn up in a regular black taxi. And, anyway, who cares what she arrives in?"

Sherry stifled her annoyance. She jumped up and clapped her hands.

"Let's go greet her! I'm itching to see this limo—and what she looks like."

Before Michal could even get to her feet, Sherry flew down the field and rushed to the front of the building, the other girls racing after her.

"I don't know why we couldn't relax a little longer," Michal said when she caught up with her best friend. She groaned and pulled at her ponytail.

Sherry restrained herself from rolling her eyes and forced a cheery smile. "We'll have plenty of time to relax later. For now, we have to welcome Rayla. It can't be easy being a newcomer in Form Three. It was hard enough for us last year."

"I suppose," Michal grumbled. She wrapped her arms around herself and said nothing else. Behind her, Nechama stood with an expression of mingled smugness and curiosity.

They could hear an engine, and Sherry turned to face the gate, straining to see if the rumors were true.

A minute later, there were quiet gasps. To Sherry's astonishment, a white limousine purred as it came up the driveway and glided to a halt. A gloved chauffeur got out and opened the back door, and a tall, composed girl emerged, her soft hair falling over her shoulders in graceful golden curls. *This is Rayla?*

Sherry was about to step forward and greet her, but the girl's rigid, poised demeanor seemed to discourage friendliness. Sherry hesitated. No one else moved toward the car, either.

Sherry was startled to see Michal nudge Nechama and whisper loud enough for Sherry to overhear, "Who does she think she is, the queen of New York?"

Sherry couldn't believe it. *Michal isn't an unkind girl, so why is she being mean to a newcomer?*

Nechama snickered. "Doesn't she think she's grand?"

"Yeah," Michal said, her tone flat. "She probably thinks she's better than all of us. We're just plain British, while she's a high-and-mighty American."

Sherry scrutinized Rayla, failing to detect much of a difference between the girl in her Samphire uniform and the rest of the form. The only difference between Rayla and the other girls was that she had arrived in a somewhat ostentatious fashion. Her chauffeur had retrieved her bags from the trunk and was leading the way toward the school steps. Rayla glanced at the group of girls and hesitated, then followed him.

"Let's give her a chance," Sherry said. "We have no right to judge her like this."

Becky shuffled her feet. "I agree. It's *lashon hara.*"

Mindy Gross, who had also been a newcomer the previous year, nodded.

"Well, I, for one, am going inside," Nechama announced. "I have no intention of greeting some stuck-up American." She turned on her heel and flounced toward the school building, walking fast enough to be well ahead of Rayla and her chauffeur. Several girls followed her, including Leah and Keren. Sherry watched them go in consternation.

"Rayla doesn't need us," Michal said to Sherry, looking sidelong at the pretty, primped girl. "She seems so confident and sure of herself." She slipped an arm through Sherry's. "Come, let's help set the tables for supper."

Becky and Mindy looked uncertainly at Rayla, who was walking with her head held high and an intense expression on her face, then at Sherry.

"I think I'll say hello later," Mindy said. "Give her a chance to settle in first."

"Good idea," Becky added. The two girls followed the rest of the group.

But Sherry saw what the other girls didn't—Rayla's slightly faltering steps, the book she held close to her chest as though it could shield her from whatever lay in store for her, and her anxious, pasted-on smile. She was not as confident as everyone seemed to believe.

"I'm staying here," Sherry said. "I think we ought to show her around a little."

"I told you," Michal said. "She doesn't need us."

Sherry was puzzled. "Don't you remember what it's like to be new?"

Michal gave Sherry a long look and said nothing, but the wounded expression was back.

"Michal—"

"It's fine," Michal interrupted, turning to go.

Sherry sighed. "We'll catch up later, okay?"

"Sure." Michal walked toward the school, hastening to catch up to the other girls and avoid Rayla.

Sherry watched her sister, her heart heavy. Michal had done a marvelous job of dealing with her misery over the loss of her mother, and Sherry hoped it wouldn't take long for her to get lost in the joviality of school and settle down again this year. Her sister's hesitant steps seemed to beg Sherry to join her, but Sherry flipped her hair behind her shoulder and walked resolutely toward the new girl.

3 All the School's a Stage

Rayla walked into the building with her chin up. She let out a slow, controlled breath in an attempt to loosen the tension in her muscles. The act was on. She'd leave all her worries aside, and perform the part of the eager student to perfection.

She pasted on a wide smile and cocked her head to the side. "Did you say your name is Cherie or Sherry?" she asked the girl with the big brown eyes and confident stride who had walked into the school with her.

"Sherry."

"I think I'm going to go straight to Mrs. Pepper. Do you want to come with me?"

Sherry's gaze darted around the entrance hall. "Uh, okay, if you want."

"Whoa, you gotta be kidding me. Are you that scared of her?"

Sherry shook her head. "It's not that. It's just that, um ... I was hoping I could give you a tour of this place. You know, dining room, hall, grounds, and all. Samphire is simply splendid, there's so much to see. You're lucky to come here, you know. At least, that's how I feel about being here."

Rayla's mouth opened in surprise. "Wow, really? So are you all perfect students, then?"

Sherry chuckled. "I wish." Her expression turned serious. "It's a wiring problem."

Rayla couldn't make heads or tails of what the girl was saying.

"Our brains don't always relay the information fast enough," Sherry said, still poker-faced. She pointed to her heart, then to her head. "What I know and how I act are two different things." She scratched her ear and scrunched up her forehead. "But not all the time, I hope!"

The tension eased out of Rayla's hunched shoulders. *I like this girl. Maybe I will somehow fit into this British school Mom so wanted me to attend.* Thinking of her mother made her fingers tremble. She clenched them into a tight fist. *Remember that you're still on stage, girl. The curtains are wide open.*

Squaring her shoulders, she observed the scene. There were so many girls milling around the place. Aside from Sherry, no one had been welcoming. The reception she'd received was as cold as the milk the British added to their tea. And that petite girl with the neat auburn ponytail had seemed absolutely horrified by her arrival.

She tilted her chin up. *It doesn't matter what they think. The fewer people who want to be friends with me, the fewer people I'll have to play-act with. One nice girl might be enough.*

The girl—Sherry—interrupted her musings. "Mrs. Pepper's office is the last one there." She pointed to a paneled oak door with a plaque that read *Headmistress*. "She'll probably keep you a while."

Rayla shook her head. "I've changed my mind. Show me around."

Sherry clapped. "Yes! Then, let's go. The dining room is right over here ..."

Sherry made an awesome tour guide. Rayla soaked up the girl's enthusiasm as Sherry described the decor. The building was every bit as splendid as the girl had said. Why, even the hallways were beautiful, with lacquered wooden panels and fantastic murals featuring inspirational *pesukim*, with pictures illustrating them.

But of all the rooms, it was the music room that drew her in. She headed straight for the large guitar and strummed the strings as she looked out the window at the incredible clifftop views. There was something magical about the way the imposing whiteness met the endless canopy of blue.

If only I could be there right now, scaling the cliffs—together with Mom.

She blinked back some tears and settled on a white armchair, admiring the deep-blue cushions, their color matching the sea.

Mom would love these. She gulped, struggling to swallow despite her tightening throat. She smoothed the tassels, which were the color of seafoam on the crest of a wave. *Mom? Where are you now? What are you doing?*

It pained her to think about her mother stuck indoors for much of the time. *She probably won't even get to visit the ocean.* The unhappy thought reminded her why she had to come to Samphire this year instead of going to her old school in New York, and the energy Sherry had imbued her with during the tour faded.

Sherry was telling her how the grand piano had been a gift from Lord Jakobovits, when Rayla stood up abruptly.

"I'd better go to Mrs. Pepper now."

Sherry blinked in surprise.

"I'll come with you," she offered.

Rayla opened her mouth to respond, but said nothing. She had been glad to have company, but keeping up a cheerful demeanor all afternoon was exhausting. She wanted nothing more than to get her obligatory visit to the headmistress over with so she could go take a nap.

Receiving no response, Sherry shifted her weight uncomfortably and looked around the room. Then she turned toward Rayla.

"I'm just thinking back to my first meeting with Mrs. Pepper when I was a newcomer last year. She made such an impression on me—I was sure I would never get into trouble again." She grinned. "Well, guess what? I had more than my fair share last year!"

Rayla chuckled, despite herself. "You? You seem so smart. I mean, how do you know all this stuff?"

"Last year, my friends Baila and Rivi told me all about Samphire, just like I'm telling you. I bet you'd like them a lot." A cloud passed over her face. "I hope they like you too. I'll introduce you later."

Rayla sighed. She supposed she'd have to meet all her new classmates eventually. *Chin up, girl. This is only the beginning.*

She pasted a smile back on her face.

"Sure, you can come see Mrs. Pepper with me. Thanks for offering."

Sherry beamed. "My pleasure."

When they reached the office, Mrs. Pepper was standing there with the door open. She smiled warmly at Rayla.

"I'm so glad you've come, dear," she said.

Sherry gasped. Rayla couldn't help wondering if Mrs. Pepper's warmth was unusual for her. *It's nice to be so welcomed.*

The headmistress turned to Sherry. "Thank you, Sherry, for welcoming Rayla." She leaned forward. "Sherry, aim for the top. I know you can do it. I'm expecting great things from you this year."

Sherry's head bobbed and she swallowed. "I'll try, Mrs. Pepper."

Rayla held back a smile as the poor girl's face turned the color of beets. Mrs. Pepper patted Sherry on the shoulder, which Sherry took as a cue to leave.

When the door closed behind her, Rayla was struck by Mrs. Pepper's kind eyes—they looked like two blue wells of wisdom. Although she knew they shared a family connection, she'd never actually met the woman before.

"Please, sit." Mrs. Pepper indicated a chair in front of her impressive mahogany desk. Rayla sat on the wooden seat, and Mrs. Pepper leaned against the desktop, clasping her hands in front of her tartan pleated skirt.

"Every student wants to be successful," Mrs. Pepper began. "To some, that means doing well in exams. For others, it's making friends—and these are good things. But remember, Rayla, it doesn't matter how others view you as much as how you view yourself. Looking successful is about popularity and accomplishments. But it is *being* successful that matters most."

As the headmistress spoke, her inspirational words sent a tingle down Rayla's spine. They excited and unnerved her all at once. Rayla listened like she'd never listened to anyone before.

"To be truly successful, you must teach yourself to act with integrity and courage, compassion and honor, at all times and in each situation."

Rayla realized that she was nodding along. *Oh, how I want to be a true success!*

Mrs. Pepper said no more, but arched her eyebrows questioningly at Rayla.

"Oh! Yes, Mrs. Pepper. I'll do my best."

Mrs. Pepper smiled. "Excellent. I am sure you will. That will be all."

Rayla stood and hurried to the door to leave. She opened it, but before she could go, the headmistress patted her on the shoulder.

"If you ever want to call your mother, you can always knock on my door. My office is open to you."

Rayla swallowed the sudden lump in her throat. Mrs. Pepper was the only one at Samphire who knew why she was here. She hoped it would stay that way.

"Thank you," she said, tears prickling her eyes.

As she slipped out the door and closed it behind her, she spotted the ponytailed girl she had seen earlier staring at her from down the corridor.

Rayla frowned. *What's up with her? Did she overhear Mrs. Pepper giving me free access to use the phone? Maybe she's jealous.*

She dug her hands deep into her pockets, stuffing down the emotions Mrs. Pepper had just raised in her.

If only she knew I'm the last person she should be envying. But let her think what she wants. I don't care. As long as she doesn't find out the truth.

She flashed the girl a broad smile.

The play was on.

4 The First Day

Excited about her first day of lessons, Sherry rushed to the classroom with Michal, both girls eager to secure their seats early. The room was set up in rows of attached desks, and about half of them were already claimed. When she saw that both desks at the end of the center row were available, she let out a whoop of delight.

"Let's sit there."

She pointed at the seats, and she and Michal hurried to claim them, placing their books on the desktop and standing beside them to wait for their teacher. Sherry looked for Rayla, but the American girl wasn't there yet.

A few moments later Rayla slipped through the door, her beret at a saucy slant over her golden curls. The only empty seat was near the front of the room, by the window. Without looking around, she put down her own things and stood beside her desk facing the blackboard.

As soon as Rayla's back was turned, several of the other girls started smirking at her. Sherry watched her classmates with dismay. Even Michal crinkled her nose.

"Michal!"

Michal frowned. "What?" She scratched her nose as if it itched.

Sherry didn't buy the act, but let the matter drop.

Nechama turned around to whisper over her shoulder, "Have you guys heard anything about Mrs. Cohen?"

Leah, who sat next to Nechama, spoke up. "She taught my older sister, Suri, two years ago. She said she's pretty nice and pretty fair, but watch out if you misbehave! Suri said that when Mrs. Cohen is angry, she doesn't yell, but her eyes bore into you like they can see into your very soul." She made a creepy wiggling motion with her fingers.

Baila nudged Bassy. "I guess you'd better be careful, then."

"Hey, I'm not the only prankster in the group," Bassy said, folding her arms. "Remember Nechama and Sherry last year?"

Sherry swallowed. She had no intention of following up last year's performance with any more pranks. Well, she didn't want to do anything that would get her in trouble, anyway.

The girls turned to Nechama.

"Don't look at me," Nechama said. "I learned my lesson last year."

"Oh yeah, sure," Leah said in a disbelieving tone.

"I can hear footsteps—watch out! 'Tis Mrs. Cohen coming, no doubt," Bassy stage-whispered in her usual dramatic way.

Mrs. Cohen, a slim lady only slightly taller than most of her students, entered the classroom. Her *sheitel* had soft, bouncy curls that hung loose to her shoulders, accentuating her vibrant eyes. She scanned her students as though she were able to discern each one's flaws and strengths in only a few seconds. Sherry could see what Suri had meant about Mrs. Cohen looking into her soul. She squirmed uncomfortably.

"Good morning, class. Please be seated so we can take attendance."

Mrs. Cohen pulled out an attendance book and a pen, quickly working her way around the room. Of course, Bassy, instead of simply saying "present" when her name was called, had to say a little rhyme. Mrs. Cohen simply checked off the box next to her name and went on to the next girl.

When she had finished, she stood at the front of the room and clasped her curled fingers in front of her as though she intended to deliver a performance of some kind.

"Welcome, girls, to the new year. All of you, step up a gear. Work hard, be respectful and sincere." She looked at Bassy, who was blushing. "No messing up—is that crystal clear?"

The girls smiled, some of them covering their mouths and looking at Bassy, who slid down in her seat. Though a smile tugged at the corner of Mrs. Cohen's lips, she arched a brow at their giggles—a brow that would clearly brook no nonsense from her students. They took out their pens and notebooks without being instructed, ready to begin taking notes.

Rayla opened her pencil case and withdrew an expensive-looking fountain pen, elegantly putting it to paper as though she were signing an important form. Michal and Nechama exchanged looks. Some of the other girls nudged each other and gawked, taken aback by the flamboyant display.

Rayla peeked over her shoulder and noticed the stunned reactions. Her cheeks reddened. The girls seemed oblivious to her embarrassment, but Sherry caught her eye and gave her a kind smile. Rayla gave a small nod, clearly grateful for the show of friendship, but her eyes were dull. She glanced around at their classmates, who had pointedly lowered their eyes, before returning her attention to her own work.

Sherry squinted at Michal, who was ignoring Rayla as assiduously as everyone else. She frowned. Why was Michal acting so unkindly?

Rayla is kind of aloof, but I don't think she means it. She's not like that, not deep down.

She remembered how Rayla had seemed to be enjoying the tour she gave her the day before—and the faraway look in Rayla's eyes as she looked out the windows in the music room. She didn't think Rayla was aloof at all. There was more to this girl than it seemed.

Nechama flicked her gaze to the back of Rayla's head and mouthed something to Leah. Leah giggled quietly.

I might be aloof, too, if everyone treated me this way. If only Michal would give her a chance!

Mrs. Cohen began a discussion about the importance of starting the year on the right foot. Rayla tried to speak several times, but each time she opened her mouth, one of the other girls would jump in with a comment. Finally, Rayla put her fancy pen on the notebook in front of her and stared straight ahead at the blackboard, saying nothing. Her blue eyes shone with moisture.

Sherry looked around at her classmates, ashamed at their behavior. She made a silent resolution to give this year her best shot—starting with letting Rayla know that not everyone here was against her.

Ten minutes before the lesson ended, Mrs. Cohen stopped teaching to make a few announcements. After mentioning a new fire-escape route and several other routine matters, she stopped and looked around with a weighty gaze.

"I'm sure you've been anxiously waiting to find out the identity of this year's form captain."

All the girls sat up straight in their seats, eager to hear who would have the honor. A smile tugged at the corner of Mrs. Cohen's mouth.

Sherry glanced at Michal. Despite the way her friend had been acting toward Rayla, she could think of no one better for the job.

"It had better be you," Michal mouthed.

"We are delighted to have Mindy Gross as our form captain this year," Mrs. Cohen announced, smiling at Mindy.

The girls applauded and cheered. Sherry joined in. She had hoped Michal would be chosen, but she understood why the position had gone to Mindy. Like Sherry, Mindy had only joined the class the year before, but had easily gained the girls' admiration through her friendly, sincere manner.

Mindy looked around the room and returned a shy smile, her face growing red.

"Thanks, everyone. I'll try to do a good job."

Mrs. Cohen smiled, and her face transformed. "I'm sure you'll do just fine, Mindy. Now, girls, there are only a few more minutes left to the lesson. I suggest you use them to begin the assignment."

Sherry caught Mindy's eye and gave her a thumbs-up before returning to her work. Mindy smiled, obviously pleased. Sherry grinned back and picked up her pen.

The more she thought about it, the more she realized that Mindy was the best choice. Last year, Mindy had organized the second form end-of-year party and done a smashing job, even when all the cream had spoiled the night before the party. Everyone liked her. And, come to think of it, she was one of the only girls who wasn't being rude to Rayla.

As if to illustrate this point, Rayla's pen clattered to the ground. Mindy scooped it up and handed it back to Rayla with a smile. Rayla muttered her thanks and returned to work.

Michal watched the exchange and mock-pouted. "Good decision," she said, pointing to Mindy. "But really, it should've been you."

Sherry fiddled with her pen. "You're too generous, Michal. Have you forgotten the mischief I got up to last year?"

Michal smiled. "Well, the teachers don't know you as well as I do."

Sherry smiled. "And I *really* thought it would be you. Oh, well, there's always next year."

"What are you two busy with?" Mrs. Cohen asked, coming over to their desks.

"Sorry, Mrs. Cohen," Sherry said hurriedly. She snapped forward, worried about what Mrs. Cohen's penetrating eyes might do to her for speaking during class. Never was she gladder when the bell rang to signal the end of the lesson. Mrs. Cohen said nothing more as she went to gather her things from the desk.

Whew! All Sherry needed to start off her year on the *wrong* foot would be a tongue-lashing during her very first lesson of the term.

She wasted no time preparing for their next class, which was English with Mrs. Bergman, who was already waiting outside when Mrs. Cohen dismissed them. She marched in, her posture straight as could be. At once, Sherry sensed she was not a teacher to mess with.

"Good morning, girls," she said, her greeting firm, yet delivered with the tiniest hint of a smile. "We have a lot to cover this year and we will begin immediately. To help me assess the level of each student, I have an assignment that must be completed for next week. The guidelines are clearly explained on the cover sheet. You will each write a short story that demonstrates a good understanding of plot and character building. The story must be at least one thousand words."

Sherry couldn't believe it. *Homework? Already? We've only just arrived.* At the same time, the idea of writing a story intrigued her. She loved writing—last year, she had written an entire journal of stories that her Papa used to tell as a gift for Ma and Chava. She'd enjoyed working on it immensely.

Now, her annoyance faded as visions of bright scenery and vibrant characters flowed through her mind. She nearly grabbed her pen to begin writing, but her thoughts were interrupted by the teacher's clear voice cutting through the stunned silence.

"I expect each of you to do your very best, which is its own reward."

At that, the girls sat a little straighter, though Nechama rolled her eyes over her shoulder at Sherry.

Mrs. Bergman's midnight blue eyes sparkled at her students' reactions.

"However, to add a little excitement to the project, the best assignment from this class will be entered into a countrywide contest. There are seventy-five schools participating from around the UK, and competition is tough. The winner of the competition will receive a medal, and her school will be awarded a monetary prize. It would be wonderful to see one of you as the winner." She pierced her students with her forthright gaze.

A thrill rushed through Sherry. A writing competition? Could she be good enough to win? The idea of entering her writing in a competition intimidated her—but not enough to stop her from trying.

A flurry of questions from her classmates followed the announcement.

"Are all the classes entering the contest?"

"Can we submit more than one story?"

"Is it possible to extend the deadline?"

Mrs. Bergman answered patiently, then raised her hand to show the discussion was over. Once the girls had settled down, she began teaching a complicated grammar lesson about clauses and sub-clauses. It wasn't the most exciting topic and, judging from the girls' expressions, many of them found the lesson tedious. Still, Mrs. Bergman kept them on their toes, pouncing randomly on her pupils to make sure they understood the concepts.

Sherry answered a question about subordinate clauses and breathed a sigh of relief when Mrs. Bergman moved on. She'd gotten it right, but barely. This class would be a lot harder than last year. Still, that also meant she'd be learning more.

The idea excited her. She wanted to become as fine a writer as possible. Papa had always encouraged her writings. Her eyes misted over as she thought about the poem she had penned for him when she was just seven years old. Papa had hung it near his bed, and had never taken it down. She recalled it now:

I wake up in the morning and I see the sun,
I wake up in the morning and I want to run
Right to you, Papa, because—
Papa, you're the best of everyone

Of course, there were some spelling errors here and there, but Papa had loved it enough to keep it hanging in his room all those years. It wasn't there anymore. Ma had removed it when she remarried, and Sherry wondered now if she had kept it at all, or if it had been discarded. It had her signature at the bottom: Sherry Spencer.

Spencer. She stared at her name in the right-hand corner of her paper. *Sherry Lempel.*

Actually, she had started writing "Spencer" before she'd remembered, so it read *Sherry ~~Sp~~Lempel.* She twisted her pen in her fingers. She didn't know why the change bothered her so much, but she fought the sudden urge to cry. *Ridiculous. I'm no less Papa's daughter now than ever.*

Still, she turned the page over and started writing on the empty side, ignoring the relief that she could no longer see her new name.

Bassy raised her hand, an inexplicable grin on her face. "Mrs. Bergman, it's hot in here. Could you turn on the ceiling fan?"

"Certainly."

Mrs. Bergman turned on the switch. When the fan started to move, paper confetti in a rainbow of colors sprayed all over the room, landing on the heads of the girls and decorating the floor like technicolor rain. Mrs. Bergman turned off the switch immediately, but it was too late.

The girls broke out in laughter, but none so loud as Bassy.

"Bassy Joseph," Mrs. Bergman said, no hint of amusement in her voice, "are you responsible for this?"

Bassy stopped laughing and sat upright in her seat. She nodded, looking surprised that Mrs. Bergman had figured out the culprit so quickly.

Mrs. Bergman gave Bassy a baleful glare, but the corner of her mouth tugged upwards as she surveyed the rest of the students. "You all look like a party supply store exploded all over you."

Rayla brushed bits of paper out of her curls, wrinkling her nose, and Mindy collected the paper scattered on her desk to take to the garbage bin.

"That's enough, Mindy," Mrs. Bergman said. "Bassy can stay after class and clean up the rest."

Bassy's grin disappeared from her face. "But we have netball practice then."

Mrs. Bergman arched an eyebrow. "Remember, Bassy, there is a time and a place for jokes and pranks, but that is not in the middle of our class time, which would be better spent learning. Since you chose to use learning time for fun, you can use fun time to learn."

"Yes, Mrs. Bergman," Bassy said, and sighed.

Sherry looked sympathetically at her. She knew how much Bassy wanted to be in the annual match, and today Glenda Chiswick, the games captain, would be there. Judging from the amount of confetti scattered all over the room, Bassy would barely have time to eat. There definitely would not be any time left for a game.

Mrs. Bergman folded her arms as she inspected the room. "Since there are only a few minutes left to class, and it will be difficult to do any work under these conditions, you may be dismissed."

The girls got up in a flurry of giggles and excited whispers, brushing bits of colored paper off of themselves and their things before leaving the room. Bassy stayed behind.

Sherry was caught up with the rest of the girls in the excitement of the contest. They exchanged ideas and discussed plots and counterplots. But what could Sherry write about? Papa had been a master storyteller, and the stories he told still shaped the way she behaved today. It had been a special skill of his, and she dared to hope that she had inherited at least some of his genius.

Sherry couldn't stop thinking about the competition all day. She used every spare second she had the rest of the day to try to think of ideas, but came up with almost nothing she liked. By the time the final period—science—came around, she was exhausted.

The girls left their form classroom and trooped downstairs to the science lab. Miss Posen greeted them, then told them to put on lab coats and pair up to do their first experiment. She had an unfortunately narrow face and eyes like a young doe.

Nechama covered her mouth and whispered to Michal, "Hey, ne-e-e-ighbour." She pulled her chin down and adjusted some imaginary spectacles so there was no doubt about who she was impersonating.

Leah snorted, and Michal giggled.

Sherry wanted to laugh too. Miss Posen *did* remind her a bit of a horse. But she remembered her vow to start off the year on the right foot and pinched her arm to stop any hint of mirth from escaping. She wished she wouldn't have found it amusing in the first place. *There's nothing funny about making fun of people.* Papa had always marveled at the *chein all* Yidden possessed. Why couldn't she?

So, chiding herself, she looked around the room. Rayla was having trouble putting on her coat, so she went over to lend her a hand.

"Wanna be my partner?" Rayla asked as she slipped her arms into the coat Sherry held up behind her.

Sherry hesitated, unsure how to respond. Michal, she knew, would expect to be her partner. But Michal had other friends here too. Sherry could see her giggling with Leah and Nechama by the lab coat hooks. Rayla didn't have anyone. *I'm sure Michal will understand that I can't refuse Rayla. The girl is in such need of a friend.*

She nodded. "Sure. I'd love to."

Michal walked up to them. "Come on, Sherry, let's get started." Michal saw that the two girls were already partners and her expression fell.

Sherry swallowed. "I'm sorry. I thought maybe you and—"

"Oh, who needs plain Michal when you can be friends with rich Rayla?" Michal blurted. She stomped toward Becky Robinson, who still had an empty space beside her.

Sherry was aghast. Had Michal intentionally said that so Rayla would overhear? It couldn't be.

Rayla bore a stricken expression, but she quickly covered it with a tremulous smile.

"Maybe you'd better go with your friend."

"No. Michal will be fine. Let's start the experiment."

Rayla's smile became much more genuine—almost relieved.

Sherry decided she was glad she'd chosen to be her partner.

During the lesson Sherry surreptitiously observed Michal, who barely glanced her way. Michal's behavior left her dumbfounded. It was so lonely to be a newcomer. They'd all been through it at some point. She had a hard time fathoming how Michal could be so blind to the need to be kind to Rayla. More than that, why was Michal lashing out at *her* for doing so?

At one point during the lesson, she went over to Michal to explain herself, but Michal simply turned away.

Sherry tossed her hair behind her shoulder and returned to Rayla, ignoring the pinprick of hurt Michal's rejection had given her. *Michal is still settling in. I'm sure this will blow over quickly.*

5 An Adventure for Michal

When the day's lessons were over, the girls gathered in the common room to do their homework and relax. Michal came in late and noticed an empty spot on the couch next to Sherry—but Rayla was sitting on her other side, talking. Michal balked. *Sherry is spending all her time with Rayla now. She never has time for me.*

Sherry hadn't even noticed her standing in the doorway.

Forget her. I don't need her.

But that wasn't true. Tears pricked her eyes, and she threw her books into her cupboard, grabbed her coat, and fled out the door.

Ever since Tatty had married Mrs. Spencer, waves of loneliness and uncertainty would hit her when she least expected them to, threatening to wash away her brave facade. Seeing the girl who she thought would be not only her best friend, but the closest sister she could ask for, talking to that snobby American girl, made those feelings gain momentum. And now she felt as if she was being dragged down into the depths of the brackish sea.

She didn't know why she was acting this way. It wasn't like her. She didn't like this new version of herself, but she couldn't seem to stop her behavior.

She needed to get away—far from the school, her class, and Sherry. Tears trickled down her cheeks and her bottom lip quivered as she ran through the school grounds. Before she realized where she was going, she was standing on the cliffs above the sea near Samphire. There, she sat on the grass and hugged her legs tightly, her body wracked by bitter sobs.

The waves seemed to respond to her sorrow, throwing themselves against the cliffs. She looked on, mesmerized by the pounding rhythm.

Her mother had loved to watch the sea when it was like this.

"Look at how the crystal-pure water can turn into something so powerfully fierce," she would say.

Michal missed her so much. She and her mother would have sat here together and watched the ocean. Without saying a word, they would know exactly what the other was thinking. Her mother had shown her how to see every view as a *mashal* and every one of Hashem's vistas as a work of art.

"Will everyone I care about disappear one way or another?" she whimpered, giving the ocean a pained stare.

The water's only response was another round of pounding surf on the rocks. Still, it had a calming effect on her, and she soon felt at peace. She could almost sense her mother's presence as she stared at the foamy grey waves. Closing her eyes, she basked in the moment.

Thank You, Hashem.

An urgency to portray that scene and capture the emotions she was experiencing struck her. She wanted—no, *needed*—to pour this magnificent landscape onto canvas. She scrambled to her feet—she would have to fetch her supplies. That meant trekking back to Samphire.

For the first time, it occurred to her that she had broken the school's rules—they were not allowed to walk to the faraway cliffs, those that flanked the sea at its dangerous depth, without a staff member. But the urge to paint this scene was so powerful, she would not be deterred.

No one ever notices me anyway. What's a few hours of painting on the cliffs?

She tugged her blazer closed and rushed back to school. When she neared the common room, she took a deep breath and crept past the window. Using the camouflage provided by the shrubs to remain undetected, she headed for the art room to collect her painting supplies.

Before she left the room, she stopped to review her strategy. *I'd better leave through the back gate if I don't want to meet anyone.*

Her escape plan unfolded perfectly—down the back stairs, out the door near the kitchen, tiptoe behind the bushes. After a quick glance over her shoulder to make sure the coast was clear, she was through the painted white iron gate and walking down the lane that ran behind the school. But her carefully laid plans met a hitch when an elderly lady stopped her on the path. The corners of the woman's mouth were turned down in what seemed to be a perpetual frown.

"Where are you heading, young lady? You should be in school now."

The woman's tone was a bit sharp, and Michal pictured herself being dragged back into school by her earlobes. She thought quickly.

"I'm doing ... I'm doing an ... an art project," she stuttered.

The woman's demeanor changed, and when she smiled, it reached her eyes, behind her round spectacles.

"Oh! You're painting? I love painting." She shuffled closer, groaning in pain, but her eyes glittered. "You know, when I was your age, I considered myself quite the artist."

She chuckled, her eyes lost somewhere in a distant memory.

"Turns out, while quite arrogant, I was right about that. In fact, some of my paintings are hanging in the local art museum."

She looked at Michal's supplies and nodded approvingly, then adjusted the scarf around her neck before turning to leave.

"Good luck, then, my dear."

"Thank you," Michal said, relieved. Instead of the woman calling Mrs. Pepper to report her for being off school grounds, she had offered her wholehearted support.

Still, maybe she should reconsider her plan. Perhaps she shouldn't be out here. What if someone did notice she was missing and report her? Would Mrs. Pepper call Tatty about something like this? She couldn't bear to disappoint him.

No. Even if Mrs. Pepper did call him, he would understand her need to paint. He'd even made special trips to take her to places like the cliffs so she could paint. It was worth the risk.

A pink hair ribbon flashed on the pavement ahead of her. She picked it up and turned it around. It was almost spotlessly clean, aside for a few specks of dust that she brushed off with her fingers. *Whose hair ribbon could it be? Someone must have dropped it a few moments ago.*

She peered up and down the road. It was completely deserted. Save for the old lady she had bumped into, she hadn't met anyone at all. Of course the pink ribbon couldn't belong to that sweet woman. She chuckled as she imagined the woman's white hair tied back with such a girly ribbon. She studied the ribbed grosgrain. *It's only a simple ribbon, but you can never know what it might mean to a little girl. I wonder if there's a lost and found place around this area.* Putting it in her pocket, she determined to find out.

Her paint supplies were getting heavy. *Right, down to business.* She rushed along the path to the cliff and found a perfect spot, where she set up her supplies. With the canvas propped up before her, she divided it into sections and marked the center. Looking toward the horizon, she decided to make the formidable waves her main focal point.

Once she'd sketched an outline, she began an almost frenzied application of masses of paint, forming dark, abstract shapes to depict the sky, sea, cliffs, and trees. Sometime later, she stepped back and surveyed it. At last, the foundation was complete. Now the drama could begin.

Sharpening her focus, she closed her eyes and listened to the pulse of the sea as it thumped against the crags to a thrilling, dynamic tempo. Then, attempting to capture the immense energy with her brush, she poured this magical sea song onto the canvas in a chorus of intense blues and greens and greys.

She existed in a bubble outside of time, focusing on each stroke of the brush or on blending the paints on her palette to create just the right shade. This was all that mattered right now.

Michal loved telling stories through images. Everything in nature had a story to tell if you listened, Mummy would always say. When Michal painted people, those images told stories—when she could get the eyes right. It could be tricky, capturing a person's soul through the eyes. That's why she liked painting nature scenes like this. Then the only eyes that mattered were the ones looking at it.

A bee hovered above her wrist, the vibrations of its wings thrumming through the air. When she waved it away, she caught a glimpse of the hands on her watch.

Nine o'clock? She gasped. The last sliver of sun had disappeared over the horizon, fading her surroundings to shades of grey.

Oh, no! She'd missed supper, and it would soon be time to head to bed. In fact, her classmates would likely be wondering where she was. She hoped no one had become worried enough to report her absence to Mrs. Pepper.

Time to go. She snatched up her art supplies, placed the canvas in a special folder so the paint wouldn't smudge, and ran back to school. When the large gates came into view in the distance, it was nearly dark, and her knees began to tremble.

Is it late enough to be locked out of Samphire?

Icy fear coursed through her veins, sending a chill right down to the soles of her feet. Half-frozen from terror, she forced her legs to move faster and faster until they ached. Sweat poured down her face, and she licked salty beads from her lips. With darkness descending, her fear mounted, but she forced herself to run. *The back way is still best.*

As she approached the back gate, a figure peered at her through one of the school windows. It looked like Mrs. Pepper. A shudder ran through her at the thought of being called to task by the headmistress herself.

She slipped through the gate. There was a shed near the back entrance, and she stashed her supplies behind some gardening supplies. As she emerged, she prayed that her absence would remain unnoticed by the staff until she was safely inside. The figure in the window hadn't come tromping out to chasten her. Maybe it wasn't a teacher after all, or maybe whoever was looking out hadn't noticed the lone figure in the garden.

Her confidence returned, and she straightened to her full height. The side door opened with ease, and she peered cautiously inside.

The hall was empty. She slipped through and headed straight upstairs to her dormitory.

Sherry pounced on her the moment she entered. Michal looked past her. The curtains around everyone's bed were drawn closed. The dormitory seemed peaceful, with light snoring accompanied by the occasional rustling of books.

Sherry coughed. "Where were you?" she whispered. "I was getting ready to fetch help to find you. Were you outside?"

A wave of anger washed over Michal. *It's your fault I had to get away, Sherry, and you probably don't even know ... or care.*

She shook her head to shake off the unwelcome thoughts, knowing she was being unfair, but a bout of misery drowned out any sense of reason.

"I was painting."

"Where? I looked everywhere for you."

"Do I have to tell you everything?"

Michal folded her arms defiantly. A small part of her was gratified that Sherry had looked for her, but that didn't change the fact that Sherry was shutting her out, causing her to leave in the first place.

Sherry studied her face, then backed down.

"You're lucky it's the first week and supper was buffet style," she muttered. "Otherwise, I'm sure the teachers would have realized you weren't here."

"I couldn't care less what the teachers think," Michal said, moving toward her washstand and closet. "I'm glad I didn't get into trouble, but running back has tired me out. I'm turning in for the night."

"Good night, then," Sherry said softly. She didn't move, obviously waiting for a response.

Michal turned away, unable to offer one.

And it hurt.

6 Another Day

Sherry woke early the next day with a niggling feeling of unease. Her discomfort propelled her out of bed while most of the girls still slept soundly. She quietly washed *negel vasser*, got dressed, and went downstairs to the dining room for her morning tea, trying to shake the sensation.

And then she remembered. Michal.

She shivered as she thought of the icy reception her sister had given her the night before, and how curt she'd been when she'd said goodnight. Tears clouded her eyes. She rubbed them away, but her eyes—and her heart—still hurt.

A gentle tap on the shoulder startled her. She looked up. Rayla's cornflower-blue eyes were wide with concern.

"What's up, Sherry?" she asked, sitting beside her on the bench. She set a tray of mint tea and sugar cubes on the table in front of her.

"Nothing important," Sherry replied, trying to force a smile.

Just then, Michal came down the stairs. When she saw the girls sitting side by side on the bench, her face darkened. She descended the last few steps and came to stand next to the table.

"I'm glad Rayla's made such a *loyal friend*," she said.

Rayla took one look at Michal's unfriendly face and, with an apologetic smile at Sherry, picked up her tray and went to sit next to Becky and Mindy at the other end of the table. Sherry glanced up at her sister in annoyance.

"What is with you lately?"

"You like Americans, don't you?" Michal asked, ignoring her question. "I think I'll sit with Nechama this morning. Plain ol' Brits are good enough for her."

Sherry watched her leave, bereft. She felt caught, but not in the way Michal thought. She was trapped in the middle, trying to befriend a newcomer, while at the same time not wanting to alienate her true best friend.

Michal's sudden jealousy was hard to understand. Last year, Leah had been jealous when Nechama befriended Sherry. But Nechama hadn't spent any time with Leah at all then. Sherry hadn't been avoiding Michal — she and Michal still ate every meal together, were usually partners when the girls were required to pair up, and sat together in every class.

Well, they hadn't sat together this morning.

Sherry sighed. She tried to fit the pieces together in her head, but she couldn't come up with an answer, though one seemed to hover just out of reach. Her shoulders sagged and she released a heavy sigh.

Heavy steps thudded down the stairs, and then Bassy's cheerful voice punched through Sherry's somber mood.

"Sherry's up, it beggars belief. Are you turning over a new leaf?"

Bassy jumped down the steps, grinning. It was no secret that Sherry liked the snooze button. She was usually the last one downstairs, barely making it to the davening hall in time for Shacharis.

Sherry willed her lips to form a smile. "Stranger things have happened." She got up from the bench and looked at her friends. "Well, now that we're all ready, why don't we head to the davening hall?"

"Sure, Miss Lempel, I'm ready to obey. I'm coming, I'm coming, I'm on my way."

Sherry was glad she'd had a few extra minutes to prepare herself before davening, as it made all the difference to her *tefillah.* She asked Hashem to help her improve her relationship with Michal, with whom she had so hoped she would have a good year. Michal was a lovely girl and a wonderful sister, but her behavior belied her true essence.

She took a moment to calm her thoughts, but images of Michal's angry face kept running through her head.

Hashem, please help me figure out what to do about her. What's going on?

As she closed her *siddur*, she hoped some kind of answer would zap into her heart. That would sometimes happen to Papa when he chanced upon a particularly thorny issue in the Gemara. He always said that without *tefillah*, it's impossible to plumb the depth of the Talmud, and if he got stuck, it just meant he hadn't davened enough.

Maybe she too hadn't davened enough; she had taken her relationship with Michal for granted. She paused, considering. She had hoped that once she davened, she would receive the clarity she wished for, but no such thing happened. Disappointed, she shuffled toward the breakfast hall for some toast and scrambled eggs, intensely aware of Michal shooting daggers with her eyes at her and Rayla.

The first lesson of the day was maths. When Miss Bentley walked in, she was all smiles. This was her third year with the class—but only Sherry's second year with her, of course—and they had developed a good rapport.

Sherry shifted in her seat in anticipation. She liked Miss Bentley's way of explaining things. Her reasoning was always easy to follow.

Miss Bentley requested that the first exercise of the lesson be completed in pairs. "Let's see which pair can finish the sums first."

Sherry looked at Michal, but her sister was facing away, already absorbed in her work.

Sherry shrugged and began doing the sums on her own. Miss Bentley paused as she passed her desk, and Sherry tucked in her chair, aware of how unusual it must seem that Michal wasn't working with her.

Mindy and Becky were the first pair to raise their hands. Miss Bentley checked their work.

"Excellent," she said. "All correct."

Sherry looked up and groaned to herself. She was only about halfway through. *Why do things have to be so complicated?*

When Mrs. Cohen came into the room for the next period, Sherry was still upset. She was aware of the tiny seeds of anger growing inside, but they were buried by a stronger, deep-rooted concern. *What is causing Michal to act so out of sorts?*

"Why the scowl?" Mrs. Cohen asked her.

Sherry tried to smile, but her scowl-turned-smile only made her classmates laugh. Even Michal joined in.

"Well, it was a nice try, anyway," Mrs. Cohen said kindly. "Please take your seat, Sherry."

"Yes, Mrs. Cohen." Sherry's cheeks burned.

Mrs. Cohen launched into a lesson about the importance of

taking gradual manageable steps in order to reach one's goal.

Sherry found herself more interested than she'd thought she'd be—or maybe the lesson simply offered a welcome distraction from her worries about her best friend. She soon relaxed into the safe rhythm of learning. Friendships could be difficult, but school was predictable and safe. If she learned well, she could excel and make Ma proud. She'd make Papa proud too.

Mrs. Cohen was telling the story of Rabbi Akiva, who saw a hole that had been carved in solid stone by the constant dripping of soft water upon it, and reckoned that if he were to apply himself to Torah—which is as hard as stone—it, too, would make an indelible impression on his heart.

Sherry sat transfixed, trying to imagine simple water drops creating a passage through solid rock.

Abruptly, Mrs. Cohen dropped her chalk on the table—the cue that a probing question would follow. Sherry leaned forward.

"Which drop was it that held this power?" Mrs. Cohen asked. "When was it that the rock was breached?"

Mrs. Cohen looked around the class. Sherry followed her gaze. Everyone's faces were scrunched in concentration—Mrs. Cohen's questions had that power. They all knew there was a lesson somewhere.

Sherry frowned. How could a single drop be responsible for breaking through the rock? Then she remembered that Mrs. Cohen had introduced the lesson by talking about taking manageable steps toward a goal. Steps, not a single step.

Ah, that must be it.

She raised her hand.

"Yes, Sherry?"

"It wasn't any one drop. It was the consistency—without let-up, drop after drop after drop. And that's what Rabbi Akiva noticed. Just like a steady trickle of something as soft as water could penetrate solid rock, if we do something consistently, even something very small, it can make a dent in our negative habits—in our bad *middos*—and penetrate our hearts, changing us for the better."

Mrs. Cohen nodded. "Exceptional, Sherry. You've expressed how the power of consistency can penetrate our hearts and—"

Nechama snickered. "What's the connection? Is the heart made of stone?"

The class gasped. Sherry gaped along with the others. Nechama had always been impertinent, but outright insolence to a teacher? That was new. And had Nechama intended the insult for her or Mrs. Cohen?

Sherry looked at Mrs. Cohen's calm face, wondering how she would react.

The teacher studied her desk for several seconds, and then she fixed her gaze on Nechama. Nechama kept her own gaze steady. Mrs. Cohen said nothing, but continued to look at Nechama with piercing eyes; she squinted as she did so, and it seemed to Sherry as if the girl's heart and mind were under a microscope.

Finally, even bold Nechama couldn't take it any longer. "Sorry," she said, a slight tremor in her voice.

Sherry wondered what Mrs. Cohen saw when she fixed her penetrating gaze on her students like that. For a fleeting moment, she entertained the idea of volunteering to be dissected by the teacher's powerful lens. Maybe Mrs. Cohen would provide a breakthrough to help her with her troubles with Michal.

But she nixed the idea before it could ferment. No use asking for more trouble.

When Mrs. Bergman arrived at the door for English class, Sherry's heart was still heavy. Her friends' animated chatter broke through her introspection.

"I've been working hard on my story for the competition," said Rivi, her dark eyes glittering behind dark glasses. "I'm so excited. It's about the building of the Bevis Marks Synagogue in London. It's the oldest synagogue in the UK, you know."

Other girls chimed in with their ideas, and Mrs. Bergman nodded, offering comments and suggestions when necessary.

Sherry's heart fell. She had been too worried about Michal to write anything. She sighed. *I better give it my all after lessons today if I want my submission to stand any chance.*

"On Thursday, I will allow you to bring in your drafts for peer review," Mrs. Bergman announced. "You'll be able to show your stories to your friends and have them comment. This will help you develop your writing further."

The girls let out whoops of delight.

Nechama leaned toward Leah. "I can't wait for you to read my story. You're so good at noticing small details."

Other girls were also chattering about how they hoped their friends would help them improve. Sherry glanced at Michal, who looked away with a frown. At the front of the room, Rayla was gazing out the window, ignoring the din behind her.

Sherry observed the rest of her classmates. Keren was already scribbling ideas in her notebook. Even Nechama had a determined expression in her eyes. Yes, they were all keen to win. This would be a tough competition.

As soon as lessons were over for the day, they all hurried to the common room and began working on their stories.

Sherry put down her notebook in front of her and made a dash on the first line, where her first idea would be listed. Before long, she was staring out the window, still drawing a blank.

What would Papa say? He would never have had this much trouble coming up with a story.

Papa never seemed to run out of ideas. Of course, many of his stories were taken directly from the Gemara or Midrash—but not all of them. She remembered a story Papa had once told her of the fifteenth-century Spanish Marranos, who had been forced to convert under the Inquisition. They had kept their faith alive by telling stories to each other to disguise their teachings.

She'd always been fascinated by this. What must it have been like to hide their true beliefs, to go through the motions of a religion they'd been forced to adopt? And how clever to use stories to hide their Yiddishkeit in plain sight!

That's it! I'll write about the Marranos. She carefully noted the words on the first line of her notebook and stared at them. She chewed the end of her pen. *Now all I need is a plot.*

When it came to her, she could barely hold in her excitement. The pen seemed to move by itself as she imagined the life of Leon the Marrano—how he was paralyzed with fear when he realized his colleague had discovered his disguise. She could almost feel the frightful flames of the pyre when Leon grasped the horrible end that awaited him. Her breath quickened when Leon discovered that his would-be denouncer was a practicing Marrano too, only finally slowing when they plotted a successful escape together.

Sherry reread her piece and rubbed her hands together. *Yes, this story has a real chance of winning.*

Her classmates were still at work, heads down, writing feverishly.

Bassy looked around the room and laughed. "I say, our form has gone berserk. Since when are we all so hard at work?"

Rayla lifted her head and smiled at the sight of everyone else writing so earnestly. She grinned at Sherry.

Instinctively, Sherry scanned the room for Michal. *Oh good, there she is, totally engrossed in her story.* When the bell rang at half-past seven to signal suppertime, Michal was still hard at work.

Sherry beckoned to her, but her sister didn't even notice.

"Michal, are you coming to eat?"

Michal glanced up. "What? Is it suppertime already?"

Sherry grinned and pointed at her papers. "That must be a good one. I can't wait to read it."

Michal glanced at the stack of paper before her. "I hope so."

With palpable reluctance, she tucked her pages into her bag and headed to the dining room with Sherry.

Sherry glanced sideways at her sister. All her previous anger seemed to be gone, dimmed in the glow of creative fervor.

I don't think I've ever seen her so fired up before. I didn't even know she cared so much about the national competition.

Sherry wanted to win the competition. But, she told herself, if writing helped Michal stop being so jealous and angry all the time, she wanted Michal to win even more.

She'd much rather have her friend than an award any day.

7 A Parcel

For the next few days, the competition was all the girls could talk about. Sherry felt strangely reticent about sharing her idea, even when Rayla pestered her about it after they made their way from breakfast to their form room for their first lesson on Thursday morning.

"C'mon, I told you what mine was about," Rayla said with a teasing grin.

"I know, and it sounds really good. But ... I'm not ready yet. I'll let you read it after I've revised it, okay?" She had made a similar promise to Michal, and didn't want her to be hurt if she let Rayla give her feedback first.

Rayla sighed dramatically. "Well, if that's the best you can do ..."

From behind them, someone called Rayla's name. They turned to see Mrs. Hayley, the school secretary, hurrying down the hallway toward them.

"There you are, Rayla. There's a parcel for you," she said when she reached them. "Please come and collect it from the office."

Rayla quickened her steps to keep up with Mrs. Hayley's hurried pace, with Sherry close behind. They arrived to see a massive box on the floor, wrapped in brown paper. Rayla squatted, stretched her arms as far as she could to grab the package from the bottom, and heaved. Her face flushed from the effort of trying to pick it up, but it slipped from her grasp.

"Oops, this is heavier than I thought."

She glanced behind her and signaled to Sherry.

"Hey, could you help me with this?"

Sherry helped her carry the parcel to the common room, her hands shaking from the weight. Her stomach fluttered as she took in the massive box. *This is no ordinary package. I bet there's something exciting inside. I just wonder what!*

Rayla caught her eye and chuckled. "We'll have to leave it unopened until recess. We'd better rush if we don't want to be late." They dashed to their classroom just in time for lessons.

Sherry took out her English books and stood respectfully at her desk to wait for Mrs. Bergman. A few desks in front of her, Bassy kept giggling to herself.

"Bassy, what are you up to?" Sherry whispered.

Bassy looked over her shoulder. "You'll see."

A moment later, a bright "Good morning, girls" greeted them, and Mrs. Bergman walked in with purposeful steps.

"I'm happy to see you've brought your writing assignments with you," she said, nodding at the folders on their desks. "This lesson, I will allow each of you to pass your work to a classmate." She stopped and picked up a piece of paper from her desk. "What's this?"

Mrs. Bergman frowned and read, "'Open the cupboard for a smart surprise.'"

Glancing at the students, Mrs. Bergman went to open the

cupboard where all their textbooks were kept. She took a look, then swung both doors wide.

Inside, the thick literature books they were to study in their next unit were piled up like a statue. About a third of the way from the top, two books were open—one on each side, their cover flaps stretched out like arms with gloves attached to their edges. The top books were covered by a wavy, soft brown *sheitel*, with a pair of wire-framed eyeglasses roughly where eyes might go and a scarf around the "neck."

"So *that's* where Miss Posen's eyeglasses are. She was looking all over the staff room for them this morning. And how did someone get one of Mrs. Cohen's *sheitels?*"

Mrs. Bergman folded her arms and turned to face the girls, holding up the note so they could see it. The note was composed of letters cut out of a magazine, so no one could be identified by their handwriting.

"Who did this?"

Sherry glanced at Bassy. She was smiling, but so was everyone else—even Rayla was giggling a little. Still, Sherry suspected that Bassy had orchestrated the entire prank. *Didn't she learn anything last time? Mrs. Bergman doesn't like pranks.*

"Fine," Mrs. Bergman said.

She retrieved the costume pieces from the stack of books and closed the cupboard. Walking to the front of the room, she laid them on her desk and turned around, her face composed as though nothing had happened.

"Pass your folders to the person to the right of you, or, if you are sitting on the right, pass to the person in front of you. Please critique each other's stories carefully and respectfully."

Sherry's thoughts were instantly pushed aside at the excitement of having someone read her story. She handed her folder to Becky and took Michal's, both nervous and excited to let someone see her work for the first time. *What if Becky doesn't like it?* Her only consolation was that Michal looked as nervous as she felt.

The rest of the students seemed to share her feelings. Comments of "Don't be too hard on me" and "Wait until you get to page five!" filled the air as the girls exchanged papers. But soon, the room quieted as everyone became engrossed in the stories. Not long after, all she could hear were soft murmurs of "Wow!", "Poor him!", and "Oh, no!"

It wasn't hard to get engrossed in Michal's story. From the first sentence, Sherry was transported to the double life of Pardo, a high-ranking Marrano doctor who served in the palace of Ferdinand and Isabella, monarchs of Spain—that is, until his cover was blown. The turn of events made her flesh crawl. Hugo, the lower-ranking official who intended to turn Pardo over to the Inquisition, made her squirm with revulsion. How could anyone be so horrible? She read on voraciously, desperate to know what happened next. Sherry had just gotten to the part where the Marrano was plotting his escape when she suddenly stopped.

This has a similar storyline to mine.

She stared at the page in dismay. Michal's writing was good, there was no denying it—but Sherry had had more practice, and she felt confident that her own story had a bit more splash than this one. What if her own story, so similar to Michal's, won? Would Michal think she had copied her idea?

What if Michal's story came in second only to her own, and Michal could have won the class competition if not for Sherry? She didn't know for sure that her own story would win, but she knew that it would be a tough decision for Mrs. Bergman. And what if their teacher decided that their stories were so similar that one or both of them must have copied from the other? Sherry couldn't bear the thought. Once was enough for her, thank you.

She considered the hours Michal had put into her writing, knowing her friend had risen extra early in the morning to polish her piece. Michal had pursued this assignment with a passion that Sherry had only seen her pour into her art. Michal's melancholy might be lifted if she won. Maybe this was what she needed to break the gloom that had held her fast since Ma and Tatty's wedding.

Sherry sat up as she realized just how much space Michal was occupying in her heart. There was nothing she wanted more than to see her friend's smile again. She pulled at her lips. Her decision was made. She would not enter this story into the contest. She'd simply have to try again—and this time, not write quite on par with her ability.

Leaning forward, she tapped Becky's shoulder. "I don't want you to read the rest of my story," she whispered. "Please give it back."

Becky wrinkled her forehead.

"Really? But I want to know what happens to—"

"Just give it back, please," Sherry interrupted before Becky could reveal too much.

Becky sighed, but handed the work to her. Sherry handed over Michal's paper, and Becky raised a questioning eyebrow.

"Uh... it's just that..." She looked around the class, hoping the words would come to her. What could she say?

Becky didn't wait. She took Michal's story and flipped back to the beginning. She was usually unflappable, but she wore an annoyed expression now. Sherry couldn't blame her, but she wasn't sorry.

Michal glanced over, her brow furrowed, and Sherry cast her a reassuring smile.

"I love your story. It's so good!"

Michal brightened. "You think so? Thanks!"

"I know so."

Michal smiled shyly and went back to reading Bassy's paper.

Sherry skimmed her own story, lamenting the work that had gone into writing it. *It really is good. Too bad I won't get to share it with anyone.* She couldn't have been gladder to hear the bell ring a few minutes later, but most of the class uttered sounds of dismay.

"But I was just getting to the good part!" Rivi wailed, turning to hand Becky's paper to her.

"There's no way we've had our fill. This story's making time stand still," Bassy grumbled. She glanced at Rayla, whose paper she was reading, with a begrudging look of respect.

Sherry, however, was about to put her paper in her desk and prepare for maths class when Mrs. Bergman hushed them.

"Miss Bentley has kindly agreed to let us continue for another lesson, in exchange for an extra maths lesson next week. You can keep reading the compositions."

Grateful sighs flittered around the room, and the reading continued. Only Sherry had nothing to occupy her.

"Is something the matter, Sherry?" Mrs. Bergman asked sharply.

Sherry hastily picked up her paper again. "No, nothing."

Mrs. Bergman nodded and resumed marking assignments.

The students spent the rest of the period engrossed in their classmates' narratives.

Sherry, however, spent the lesson rereading her own story and trying to come up with an idea for an alternative. And then it came to her. She slyly pulled out some fresh paper from her desk and set to work. With each movement of her pen, the plot thickened—but not too much. She couldn't make the story too engaging, after all. Dumbing down her story took some effort. *Who would've believed that* not *doing well could be so much work?* A grin escaped her lips and she glanced up. Mrs. Bergman's face was as serene as ever—she must not have guessed what Sherry was doing. Sitting in the back had its fair share of benefits.

~

As soon as the break-time bell rang, Rayla called to Sherry. "Quick, let's get going. I wanna find out what's inside that package."

She spoke a bit too loudly, however, as all the other girls perked up as well.

Chairs scraped the floor as almost everyone rushed after them, obviously curious about the contents of this special package.

In the common room, the girls gathered around Rayla and the box with expectant expressions. Rayla glanced around, nervous about being the center of attention, then opened the box. She pulled a smaller, gift-wrapped box out of the larger parcel. Then, she eased out one bag after another, each one filled with delicious snacks. While she'd expected the parcel, she hadn't known when it would arrive. She hoped that sharing the goodies would help improve her standing in the class.

A small gift card and bow fell off the box and she bent to retrieve it, but Nechama was quicker. The shorter girl cleared her throat.

"Our dearest Rayla," she read dramatically. "Best birthday wishes. Love and kisses from Mom and Dad."

She snickered, and Rayla stiffened as her face burned. *That girl is truly awful.* But she squared her shoulders, lifted her chin, and forced the brightest smile.

"Yep, I'm fourteen today."

"Mazel tov!" Sherry shouted, patting Rayla's shoulder. "I've got the best idea. Let's have a midnight feast!"

Rayla looked around at the girls, who had brightened at the

words. *Should I? The other girls all seem pumped by the idea.* She bit her lip and glanced at Mindy, who gave her an encouraging nod.

"Why don't you open that?" Michal asked, pointing to a large white box inside the parcel.

Rayla blinked several times and rubbed her hands together. "I'm gonna leave that for twelve tonight."

Michal's eyebrows arched. "You're going to risk a midnight party?"

Rayla looked at Sherry. *Should I dare? If we get caught, how bad could it be? Mrs. Pepper wouldn't really send me away ... would she?*

"Yes, midnight!" Sherry said. "Tonight, we're going to have a super-secret birthday party. Now, quick, let's stash everything in the cupboard and go back to class before Miss Winter arrives."

Rayla beamed, delighted to see the excited expressions aimed her way for once. "Let's do it."

The girls cheered. At midnight, there would be a grand party.

Mine! How exhilarating.

But her excitement was short-lived. Nechama was glaring at her, whispering loudly to Michal, "Doesn't she think she's posh? Only *she* gets such fancy goodies."

Rayla fought to control her anguish. She pressed her thumb into her index finger to distract herself and soldiered on. Michal turned to her, and Rayla offered her a hopeful smile. *At least she didn't agree with Nechama.*

Michal smiled back. "That was some birthday gift," she said, and turned away to follow Nechama to class.

Rayla's smile faded. While the compliment had seemed genuine, Rayla couldn't decide if Michal had been envious or happy for her. Either way, it must have taken some effort for Michal to say it.

But it's a start.

8 Midnight Fun

That night, Rayla got ready for bed as quickly as she could. She snuggled beneath her covers, set her alarm clock for midnight, and placed it beneath her pillow. Around her, the other third form girls discussed the upcoming midnight adventure in conspiratorial whispers.

They're having a party for me. She could hardly believe it.

After the decision had been made, the third formers had been restless and fidgety all day, eager for the midnight party.

"What is going on with this class today?" Miss Abraham, their Chumash teacher, had asked, clapping once in frustration. "Strange ransom notes for Miss Posen's glasses, and now it's like you're all sitting on anthills. Stay on task, please."

At the mention of the note and the glasses, the girls started to giggle again, but they tried to settle down when they saw the stern look on Miss Abraham's face. Still, the day seemed to drag on. When it had finally been time for bed, Rayla's insides were coiled as tightly as a spring.

Clang, clang.

Midnight.

She jumped out of bed, almost knocking over her *negel vasser* cup. She caught it just in time. Going from bed to bed, she woke everyone and, in no time, the girls of Form Three had their robes on and were ready to tiptoe down to the common room.

"Shh, make no noise," Sherry reminded them. "The last thing we need is for one of the teachers to wake up."

They edged down the stairs, hugging the banister so the steps wouldn't creak, then snuck down the corridor and into their common room—the only one set apart from the main building.

The girls flowed into the room and started to prepare for the party. Sherry eased the door closed behind them, and Rayla caught her eye.

"Thanks for arranging this."

"Of course," Sherry said, smiling brightly. "Isn't our class terrific?"

Rayla looked darkly at the other girls. Next to the sink, Michal, Nechama, and Leah were laughing about something Nechama had said as they prepared some snacks.

"That hasn't been my experience so far."

Sherry glanced at the other girls. "It just took them a while to warm up to you. They're coming around."

Rayla pressed her lips together. She wasn't so sure about that. Then she gave her head a little shake and pasted on her best smile. *Time to be the birthday girl.*

Everyone did their part, setting up tables and chairs, placing food in bowls and pouring drinks into pitchers. Rayla's mouth watered at the sight of so much good food.

"This is a feast for queens, alright. Everyone knows food tastes best at night," Bassy said as she jumped off a chair, causing it to rock wildly.

Baila caught the chair before it landed on the floor with a crash. "Bassy! You're going to bring the night monitor down on us."

Bassy looked momentarily chastened before going to the cupboard to pull out a board game. "Who wants to play Cluedo?"

Several other girls joined her at the table. Rayla had no idea Cluedo could be such a loud game.

"Hey, look at this," Nechama said. She was juggling caramel toffees in the air, to the great merriment of the other girls.

Nechama always needs to be the center of attention, doesn't she? Is that why she's so jealous of me? Because I'm new, so more people were coming over to me when I first arrived?

She watched Nechama juggle and shook her head. That didn't make sense. She wasn't new anymore, and hardly anyone talked to her, which was fine. Still, Nechama had stolen the spotlight on her special night, and that stung.

It might not have been intentional, but so far, Sherry was the only girl who had shown her any kindness at all.

Never mind that. I've got a part to play and I cannot be hurt by them. Mom expects more of me.

Nechama caught another toffee, and Rayla laughed and clapped her hands. Baila took out her trusty 110 camera from her bag and snapped several shots.

Rayla curled her lips.

Nechama wants to get all the attention? Why don't I help her?

"I bet you can't do four at a time."

To illustrate, she threw four toffees in the air and caught them—or tried to, at least. Two dropped to the floor, one bounced onto the table, and the last one she caught and popped into her mouth.

Nechama grinned, eyebrows raised. "I'll take the dare."

She scooped four toffees from the candy bowl and, wonder of wonders, she actually managed to juggle them.

The girls stared at her, agape.

Rayla didn't want to be impressed, but she couldn't help it. "Hey, you're pretty good."

An expression of surprise flitted across Nechama's face, changing quickly to annoyance. "Thanks." She almost sounded like she meant it.

Rayla's smile slipped.

Sherry caught Rayla's eye and flashed her a cheerful grin. "Hey, why don't we sing?"

She sat down on the couch and patted the seat beside her, indicating that Rayla should sit there. Hesitantly, Rayla perched next to her. On her other side, Mindy gave her an encouraging smile.

Sherry began to sing, a jubilant song about *simchah*. The girls joined in, and Rayla found herself quite enjoying the impromptu choir. The other girls must have been enjoying it too, because their voices kept growing louder and more enthusiastic. Bassy even stood up and started gesturing with her arms, as though giving an exaggerated stage performance. The girls giggled and hooted. Rayla laughed too, relaxing.

Mindy leaned toward Rayla.

"Thanks for agreeing to this," she said. "I can't remember the last time I had this much fun."

Rayla nodded, and a warm feeling slowly spread from her chest and through her body. "Me too," she said, realizing it was true.

Sherry nudged her, pointing at the grand piano. "Should I play some music?"

Rayla considered, then shook her head. "It's pretty noisy as it is, don't you think?"

Sherry nodded.

They both resumed singing, but then Bassy started a new song, even louder than before. Rayla wasn't sure what to do. The singing had reached a risky level. Mindy rushed to hush them. Rayla looked at the form captain gratefully. Though their common room was far from the staff rooms, it couldn't hurt to be extra cautious. It wouldn't do to have her first happy night here ruined by getting in trouble.

Some of the girls quieted, but Nechama and Leah kept talking loudly near the food table, even after Mindy went over and asked them to quiet down. Rayla frowned. She wasn't the only one whom Nechama was rude to, apparently. How could she get their attention without shouting?

I know!

She went over to her package, took out the white box, and placed it on the table.

The action had the desired effect. The girls quieted down and crowded around, agog with curiosity as she lifted the lid. Even Leah and Nechama came and stood with the others.

In the box was the most luscious-looking chocolate mousse cake, decorated with dainty pink and purple sugar roses. Rayla recognized the signature cake from her favorite bakery. Her parents bought her birthday cake there every year—an expensive indulgence, even for them. *The company must have a branch in Manchester.*

Her heart pinched. How she wished Mom were here—but she wasn't. She should be thankful that her mother could even send a cake.

"Cake, anyone?" she asked brightly, tamping down her melancholy.

"Yes!" came the resounding response.

The girls *oohed* and *aahed* as she pulled it out, then kept their attention on the moist cake as she cut a piece for everyone. Runny chocolate gushed out like molten fudge from between the layers. The girls ate slowly, savoring every delicious bite. Michal even gave her a real smile when she accepted her piece.

Rayla put the last three pieces onto plates and looked around to see who had been missed. Standing apart from the others, Nechama watched them with her arms folded.

Rayla put a fork on a plate and carried it over to her. She pasted on a friendly smile. If she had won over the others, she could win over Nechama too.

"Here you go. I saved you the best piece."

Nechama looked down her nose at the cake as though deciding whether or not to take it. She must have really wanted a taste, though, because she took the plate with a begrudging "Thank you."

"You're welcome," Rayla chirped, hiding her annoyance at Nechama's rudeness. "I'm sure you'll love it. My mother bought it at Gelb's Patisserie."

Nechama glared at her like she couldn't believe Rayla would say that. "Of course she did."

"What? Did I say something wrong?"

Nechama just snorted and shook her head, then dug in to the gooey cake. Rayla stood bereft for a few seconds, then quickly walked away to eat her own piece. Somehow, it didn't taste quite as good as usual.

When Sherry began clearing up, Rayla realized how late it was. Michal and Becky rushed to help and were joined by almost every girl, collecting garbage and scrubbing the tables clean. Nechama looked on stubbornly until Leah handed her a cloth. With a glare at Rayla, even she started tidying up. In no time, everything was put away in its rightful place and the floor sparkled.

The girls lined up by the door to trek to the dorm. Sherry opened the door, but immediately closed it again. She backed up against it with wide eyes.

"I saw a shadow move on the wall at the end of the corridor," she said in a frantic whisper. "Someone must have heard us." She flailed her arms. "Everyone, hide!"

Terrified, the girls scrambled for hiding places. A few hid in cupboards, someone dodged behind the grand piano, and Rayla ducked behind the makeshift stage. Sherry flicked off the lights and looked around desperately, then joined the few remaining girls as they dived beneath the tables—just in the nick of time.

The hallway amplified the clicking of heels until they stopped outside the common room. The door creaked open and the lights switched on.

Rayla held her breath, afraid that even a simple exhalation could give her away. She curled up to make herself even smaller, praying to be left undiscovered as the footsteps tapped around the room. Next to her, Michal looked just as terrified, but when Rayla caught her eye, they were both simultaneously struck by the ridiculousness of the situation. Rayla looked away and covered her mouth, afraid she'd let out a giggle.

The heels clicked closer to Rayla's hiding place, and she and Michal tucked their heads down and held their breath. The footsteps stopped.

What was happening? Rayla couldn't stand not knowing. But her heart nearly climbed out of her throat when a voice whispered right above her, "Happy birthday, Rayla. Make sure everyone gets to bed soon, okay?"

Rayla and Michal both jerked. Rayla glanced up to see Mrs. Cohen's sharp eyes gleaming at her. She was about to apologize when the teacher placed a finger over her smiling lips. With a wink, she turned and walked away.

Rayla and Michal stared at each other in surprise and alarm until the door opened and the lights turned off once again. Mrs. Cohen hadn't gotten them in trouble.

Whew! That was a close call.

Rubbing her eyes, Rayla motioned for Michal to climb out. They shared secret smiles—their teacher obviously hadn't wanted everyone to know she was letting this slide.

"Whoa, the coast is clear," Rayla whispered as the clicking heels retreated down the corridor. She smiled as she looked around the room. "Party's over, I guess."

Michal glanced up at her. "That was a close one."

"Yeah. Lucky us."

Michal stood, looking as though she wanted to let out her giggle at last. Then, remembering that she was talking to Rayla, the mirth left her face. Begrudgingly, she said, "I'm glad you had a party, Rayla. This was kind of fun."

Before Rayla could respond, Michal spun on her heel and crept out the door toward the dorms, keeping a wary eye out for Mrs. Cohen.

The rest of the girls went on their way, content and full after such a grand party. They thanked Rayla heartily with smiles and kind wishes before sneaking out the door and up the stairs in groups of two and three.

Rayla glowed, basking in her classmates' praise and admiration. Sherry gave her a warm *brachah*, then went to peek out the door to make sure the coast was still clear.

Rayla was in her element—but then it was Nechama's turn.

"Thank you, Rayla," she whispered with a sneer. "But just remember, money doesn't buy friends."

She slipped out the door, leaving Rayla standing alone in the dark, speechless. All the goodwill she'd felt that night had been sucked out of her with a single, cruel comment, like a pin deflating a balloon.

She lay awake in her bed for hours, drawing the darkness around her like a stage curtain.

She'd resume her act tomorrow. For tonight, she let the tears fall.

9 Competition Winner

The weeks passed quickly, and soon more than a month had gone by since the writing assignments had been handed in. Every girl seemed pleased with her submission, and all of them waited expectantly to receive their stories back. All except one—Sherry was dreading the occasion, knowing her work was not up to par.

When Mrs. Bergman entered the classroom one day with a giant stack of papers, Michal let out a muffled shriek. Sherry glanced at her friend's nervous, excited face.

"You'll do great," she whispered.

Michal flashed her a hopeful grin.

Sherry returned the smile, feeling a bit better. She had absolutely no regrets that she hadn't submitted her first story, even if she would have liked Mrs. Bergman to recognize her true abilities.

"These papers are exceptional," Mrs. Bergman began, looking around the room. "They were a joy to read."

She returned the stories and the girls eagerly took their work.

They looked at their grades and read Mrs. Bergman's comments with relish. When Sherry received hers, she glanced at her mark, not really wanting to know how she'd been graded on her first English assignment of the year. A round red C mocked her. Not a fine start. But that had, after all, been her goal. Wasn't it a bit harsh, though? Or was she just upset that even her not-so-great work was, well ... not so great?

Hurriedly, before anyone else could see her mark, she stashed her work in her desk. There would be time enough to read the critique later. Out of the corner of her eye, she noticed Mrs. Bergman watching her. *Does she know I'm capable of far better?*

Michal was the only student who had not yet had her work returned. She sat with her mouth open a little, her face flushed with excitement.

Mrs. Bergman beamed. "Michal, this is your paper. A-plus plus. You have won the class contest."

Most of the girls congratulated her — except Nechama, who was smirking.

"I can't believe it's all that brilliant," Nechama whispered to no one in particular, fidgeting with her own paper.

Sherry stared at her, shocked. She hoped Michal hadn't heard her.

But Michal was aglow at everyone else's comments. If she had heard, she gave no indication of it.

Sherry slapped her new sister on the back. "Amazing, Michal."

"Thanks, everyone," Michal said, her face nearly as red as her pen.

For a moment, hearing all the praise Michal was getting and thinking of that big red C, Sherry regretted her decision. What would Ma think when she found out she'd done so poorly? Maybe she hadn't needed to do quite so badly to let Michal win.

But Michal's radiant smile wiped the thought away.

When the lesson was over, more girls came over to congratulate Michal. She was pleased by all her friends' accolades, but it was Sherry's praise that meant more to her than anyone else's.

For weeks, Michal had been trying to find a way to open up to Sherry about how she was feeling, but Sherry was always so busy with Rayla that there never seemed to be a good time. Watching the two of them, Michal often felt like a stranger outside the window observing two happy friends by a cozy fire, with no way to break inside and be part of the company. But today, for once, she wasn't just part of it—she was the center of attention. And Sherry was the most effusive of all.

When Rayla came over and expressed her warm wishes, Michal found it within herself to smile graciously. But she was glad when the posh American girl walked away without saying anything more. No one else had the power to make Michal feel so out of place just by being there. Rayla was so pretty and stylish—no wonder Sherry preferred to spend time with her.

Sherry asked if she should save her a seat at lunch, and Michal smiled. Maybe things would go back to normal now. After all her worries about Sherry, knowing that her sister was truly happy for her calmed her misgivings.

Later, in the headmistress's office, Mrs. Pepper commended her on writing such a fine story. Michal smiled with delight, savoring the warm, fuzzy feeling inside.

She was walking back to her locker to read her story one last time before going to lunch when a blue folder jutting out of the locker next to hers caught her attention.

That's Sherry's. I wonder how she did?

She looked around to see if anyone was watching, but the rest of the school was either in the dining room or had already gone outside for some fresh air. Seeing the empty hall, she tugged the folder free. Inside, visible through the semi-transparent cover, was a short story.

That's odd. I'm pretty sure the piece Sherry submitted wasn't this one. She noted the different layout and lack of a grade on the paper. Sherry had spent hours on her story—far more than anyone else. And she was a wonderful writer. She must have done well. Why was there no mark on this?

Unable to control her curiosity, she took it out and started to read. With the first few words, the story held her in its grip. The characters were so lifelike and the story so compelling that she couldn't have put the pages down if she'd tried. She laughed, she gaped in shock and horror, she even cried a few tears. When she reached the climax, the paper almost dropped from her hands, and it took effort to steady her trembling fingers. It was only when she read the conclusion that she let out a loud gasp of relief, her body still shaking with fright.

She shook her head in wonderment. *But why didn't Sherry submit this masterpiece?*

Approaching footsteps made her jump, and she slipped the papers back into the folder and shoved it into the locker. Then she fumbled in her own locker as Sherry arrived.

"So, where were you at lunch?" Sherry asked as she opened her locker.

"Lunch?" Michal frowned. Then she remembered. Sherry was going to save her a seat, but she'd been too engrossed in Sherry's story to remember to go eat. "I, uh, I had to, um ..." She hated lying. And she was terrible at it, anyway. She gave up and decided on the truth. "I'm sorry, Sherry. I forgot. And I wasn't that hungry. After I left Mrs. Pepper's office, I decided to read my story one more time."

That was the truth, even if she hadn't ended up doing it. She reached deep into her locker for a pencil to hide her flaming face. But Sherry moved the locker door aside and pinned her with a hard stare.

"Michal, what is the matter? You don't think your story shouldn't have won, do you?"

"Well ..." Michal began, not sure how to respond. She was no longer certain she did.

"Michal, I think your work is magnificent. You really deserved to win."

"What grade did you receive?" Michal asked, the question popping out before she could contain it.

"Oh, a C," Sherry answered. She shrugged and turned back to her locker, grabbing her things and slamming the door.

"What?" Michal was astonished that Sherry didn't seem bothered. *Something's not adding up.* "But your writing is far better than that. It doesn't make sense. You're easily top of the class."

Sherry looked down and twisted her watch. "I don't know," she said at last. Then she shrugged. "I don't know."

She's hiding something.

Michal pondered this, remembering how truly happy her new sister had been for her and how amazed she'd been by Michal's story when she'd first read it. Sherry had asked for her own story back from Becky and given her Michal's instead. Then she'd started writing a different story. At the time, Michal thought Sherry had come up with a better idea. But what if that wasn't what had really happened?

Wait, her story was about the Marranos too. Did she think I'd be upset if she used that idea? Or did she think I'd be upset if she used that idea—and won?

Then it hit her and she understood: Sherry had written a new story and done badly on purpose. She'd given up any chance of winning so Michal could have a chance to win. Her heart dropped at the thought of Sherry putting herself last—and more, that she felt she had to do so in order for Michal to win. A bubble of anger swelled in her. *She thought I'd only win if she didn't submit her story? How dare she?*

"Well, you'll do better next time." Michal gave her sister a half-smile.

Sherry nodded, looking relieved. "You bet."

Michal took out a geography textbook from her locker and walked away quickly. As soon as she turned the corner, she stopped and peeked behind her to see Sherry close her locker and walk toward the common room. After waiting a few moments, she returned to Sherry's locker and removed the blue folder. Glancing around to make sure she hadn't been seen, she clasped it to her chest and walked in the opposite direction that Sherry had gone.

When she arrived at the staffroom, she asked for the English teacher.

"Mrs. Bergman," she said when the teacher came to the door, "could I talk to you?"

Mrs. Bergman raised her eyebrows and led her to a vacant office. Michal thrust the blue folder into her hand.

"Read this," she said. "Please."

The teacher lifted the folder toward the light and began to read. Soon she was just as engrossed in the story as Michal had been. She read a page or two, then looked up at Michal in amazement.

"This is unbelievable," she said at last. "Is this Sherry's?"

Michal nodded, then explained what she presumed had occurred. She told how she had given Sherry her story to read, but then noticed Sherry asking Becky to return her own work. Michal suspected that Sherry had acted selflessly so Michal's chances of winning wouldn't be ruined. She tried to keep the bitterness out of her voice, but wasn't sure how successful she was—especially when Mrs. Bergman gave her a sharp look.

Mrs. Bergman held up the folder. "Michal, if you will allow me, I would like to submit this composition to the countrywide contest. This was the story Sherry originally wrote, and while she may have made her own decision, I've made an altogether different one. I think it has a very good chance of winning. I'm assuming, also, that's why you're here. You want the most deserving person to win, is that right?"

Michal's heart lifted. She might be upset about what Sherry had done, but if she deserved to win, Michal still wanted her to have that chance.

"Absolutely."

"With your permission, Michal, I'm going to ask Sherry if I can submit her story to the competition. You write lovely stories, and I hope you don't let this bring you down."

Michal shrugged. "I prefer to tell my stories through art, anyway. And I think you're right. That's why I brought this to you. But if you ask Sherry, I think she might say no."

Mrs. Bergman's eyes widened. "Why would she do that?"

Michal shifted her weight. Sherry had probably just been trying to be nice. But on the other hand, she must not think much of Michal's abilities. To purposely submit a lousy story when she could have easily won? Maybe Michal was wrong about Sherry's intentions, but she didn't think so. It was a very *Sherry* thing to do. Michal's stomach churned.

Well, she wouldn't let her get away with it. She didn't want a prize she didn't deserve. And she didn't want Sherry to think she had to let her win, either.

"I think ... I think she wouldn't want to take this away from me. That's why she did it in the first place. But I don't want to take this away from her, either. Is there any way you could submit the story without telling her?"

Mrs. Bergman regarded her thoughtfully. Finally, she nodded. "Yes, I can see your point, and I believe you're right. This time, I will do as you ask. Such a humble act of selflessness should be rewarded. This will be our secret, okay?"

Michal lifted her chin. She didn't feel like she was being particularly selfless at the moment. "Okay. And you don't need to send mine in at all. We both know Sherry's is better."

Mrs. Bergman inclined her chin. "If that's what you want."

Michal looked at the floor. "Sure. That's what I want."

But as she walked away from the room, she realized that wasn't what she wanted at all. She wanted Sherry to stop treating her like she was a disposable commodity that could be pushed aside when something better came along, or an object of pity that had to be given charity prizes because she couldn't earn it herself. She wanted Sherry to treat her with respect.

What she wanted was her friend back.

10 Michal in Trouble

Over the next few weeks, Michal avoided Sherry as much as possible. She went so far as to ask Rayla to trade seats with her, so Michal would be at the front of the room and Sherry could have her silly American friend sit beside her. When Sherry asked why she did this, Michal just said, "I thought you would prefer that she sit next to you," and then walked away.

She was too angry to talk to Sherry, and too sad to pretend everything was okay. The pressure of her emotions kept building inside her until she felt she might explode. She hated feeling this way, but nothing she normally did made her feel any better. She felt dull when she sang in the choir and draggy on the netball court. Then she remembered her painting stashed away in the garden shed.

That's what I'll do. I'll finish the painting.

She crept to the shed, making sure no one could see her. The way to the back gate was clear—there was a fifth form netball match going on, and the rest of the student body had gathered to watch it. As she was about to open the shed door, a large shadow darted off to the side and grass rustled. She edged away, too frightened to make a sound.

A long moment later, a head peeked around the corner. Rayla.

Whew!

When she saw Michal standing there, she emerged from the shadows.

"Hey, Michal," she said, catching her breath. "I was sure you must have been a staff member. What are you doing here?"

"I ... I, uh ..." Michal stammered. Rayla was just about the last person she wanted to talk to right now. Except, maybe, for Sherry.

"What are *you* doing here?" she asked to deflect the question.

Rayla looked at her, shifting her feet. Finally, she went into the shed and reached behind the potting bench, beneath the window. For the space of a heartbeat, Michal thought her secret had been discovered—but instead of hauling out her art folder, Rayla lifted a small guitar into view. What were the chances that another girl would stash her treasure in exactly the same place as Michal's folder? She surreptitiously eased herself between Rayla and the folder, trying to block her artwork from view, but this only served to draw Rayla's attention to it.

"Is that yours?" Her eyebrows arched in surprise.

Michal's shoulders drooped.

"It is," she admitted. She pulled the folder out of its hiding spot.

Rayla craned her neck. "Are you off to paint some beautiful landscape?"

The cover slipped from the painting, and Rayla shifted to the side to look at it.

"Wow! I know exactly where this was painted. It's so realistic!"

Michal was too flattered to be bothered by Rayla's intrusiveness.

"Just please, don't tell anyone," she begged. She didn't relish the thought of explaining to Mrs. Pepper how she'd made such a realistic painting of a place she wasn't supposed to visit without permission.

"Sure. No problem," Rayla said with a nod, which reassured her.

"Great. Thank you."

"Don't tell anyone I keep a guitar here, either, okay? I don't want them to get ideas about making me play in public. That's, like, my worst nightmare."

Rayla is afraid of something? She's so put-together. I wouldn't think she'd be afraid of anything.

Michal blinked and nodded. "Your secret is safe."

"Thanks."

For a moment, the two were silent. Michal couldn't bring herself to look at the girl, but did feel a small pang of regret for thinking poorly of her. At the same time, she was still upset that Sherry had put her on the backburner in favor of the American.

"Um ... I'm off to work on my painting," she said eventually, still not meeting Rayla's eyes.

"Oh, cool! Well, have a great time out there. It's totally stunning. I'll be here, practicing by myself."

Rayla held up her guitar. Michal nodded and turned away, tucking her painting under her arm and adjusting her bag of supplies over her shoulder.

She jogged toward the cliffs and found the spot where she'd previously worked on the canvas. Today, she would tackle the cliffs and hopefully finish the painting.

She sat on the grass, cross-legged. Then she propped the canvas against a large stone, arranged her brushes and paints, and got to work.

She studied the view, awed by the way the cliffs ran into one another, changing angles and forms as they followed the curvature of the coastline until they disappeared from view. She mixed her colors, then added shadows with a variety of dark blues, browns, and reds.

She glanced at the cliffs again, homing in on tiny details like fractures and spots and the sleek edges where the water had worn the rock smooth. Some cliffs faced away from the sun, making patterns of light and dark that thrilled her artistic soul. She focused on each spot individually, capturing the angle of the light with her brush.

When highlighting the sunlit areas, she made sure they didn't become overly pallid and chalky. When painting the cliffs in the distance, she softened the edges and diminished the details. In the foreground areas, she kept the edges of the features crisp. Her painting took on a life of its own as she developed a scene so astonishingly detailed, it looked real.

She wondered what Rayla would say about the painting now. Before, there had only been some waves and a few indistinct details. Now, the painting had an almost photographic quality. Pride burned in her chest.

Let's see Sherry throw me a bone for this one. There's no way she could paint like this.

"What have we here?" came a crackling, shaky voice from behind her.

Startled, Michal spun around. It was the same old lady who had greeted her some time ago near the back gate.

"Oh, it's you again, is it?" the old lady said. "I haven't seen you about for a while and thought you must have given up, but I must say, your work is absolutely beautiful."

"Oh, hello," Michal said. "I'm Michal."

"Mostyn. Mrs. Mostyn."

The woman seemed frozen in thought for a moment before

taking a seat on the grass beside Michal. Michal noticed that the lady's emerald eyes, though somewhat milky with age, sparkled with strength and wisdom, as though they'd seen enough pain and joy to know something about the seasons of life.

"This painting is good enough to sell!" Mrs. Mostyn declared. "Now then, would you like me to give you some tips to polish it even more?"

Michal remembered how the lady had said she'd been an artist, and she eagerly agreed.

Mrs. Mostyn repositioned her glasses, which had slipped down her nose, then focused on the painting.

"See this spot? If you apply some of this bright hue, you can add a wonderful glow that will make it even more luminous." She raised a small glass container. "Here, let me show you."

Although Mrs. Mostyn's body trembled, her fingers were steady as she showed Michal the skilled techniques she had developed over many years of practice. Her hands moved with remarkable grace, and as she spoke she demonstrated. Her comments were short and sometimes breathless, accompanied by occasional, tinkling laughter. Mrs. Mostyn gave Michal the best art lesson of her life and, together, they completed the painting.

After a few minutes of mutual admiration as they took in the beauty of the work, Mrs. Mostyn heaved a sigh.

"I'll be on my way now, dearie. The sky looks overcast and I wouldn't want to be caught in the rain. Help an old lady up, would you? I'm not as spry as I used to be."

Michal jumped to her feet and helped Mrs. Mostyn up from the grass. The pink ribbon fell from her pocket, and Michal remembered that she had meant to advertise that she had found it. She silently chided herself, when Mrs. Mostyn cut in.

"Where did you get that?"

Michal looked curiously at her. *It's just a simple ribbon.*

"Uh, I found it on the ground, just after I met you last time. I was hoping to advertise that I'd found it."

"Do you mind if I have a look?"

Michal handed her the ribbon, finding her interest very strange.

"I think this may be mine."

"Huh?"

Mrs. Mostyn smiled. "My granddaughter's, I mean."

"Oh." Michal was glad to have found its owner.

The lady chuckled. "My son purchased a ribbon in a hideous green color." She leaned forward. "He's color blind, if that explains it. When I saw this pretty one in the shop, I couldn't leave it. Now, I'm so glad I can give it to her—she'll be so pleased."

"It *is* pretty. Your granddaughter is lucky to have such a devoted granny."

Mrs. Mostyn smiled again. "That's a lovely thing to say." She surveyed the horizon, then dusted off her hands and gave a kind smile. "Thank you for your time. It's been lovely."

"An absolute pleasure," Michal replied. "And I can't thank you enough." She gestured at her painting. "Your kind and generous advice really gave this painting that extra touch."

With a stiff flick of her fingers, Mrs. Mostyn waved goodbye and walked off at a slow but steady pace.

Michal sat back down to linger over the painting a little longer. It was better than she ever would have imagined. If there were a national art competition, she'd win, hands down. Nobody would dare give her a pity prize then.

Eventually, she put the painting in her folder and gathered her supplies. The evening was wearing on—surely Rayla would be done practicing and would have gone to the common room to study. But Michal didn't feel like going back to the school yet to be ignored by Rayla and Sherry. She especially didn't want to see Sherry and be reminded of what her sister had done.

The path leading toward the sea beckoned, and she decided to follow it for a while. She found an old hut down the path and stashed her folder and materials in a corner, then continued on her way.

She picked her way along the path, melancholy thoughts about Sherry and Rayla threatening to overturn her good mood, much as the grey clouds in the sky above her hinted at rain.

No. She wouldn't let them steal this from her. With fierce determination, she studied the gleaming wall of white flanking the blue expanse. The sinking sun flashed golden rays that turned the sea into glittering gems. A frosty wind blew sand against her cheeks and moistened her lips with splashes of brackish water from the waves below.

Before long, she was once again lost in the beauty of nature. She sat down on the path to admire its splendor, but her mind soon wandered back to her biggest concern.

What was she going to do about Sherry? She didn't want the situation to continue as it was, but she didn't know how to fix it. If only fixing a friendship was as easy as painting a canvas.

A drop of rain landed on her cheek, and she glanced skyward. Above her, the roiling clouds had changed from grey to an ominous charcoal. *I should get back.*

She stood and began to ascend the way she'd come. Light droplets of rain peppered her face—in a calming pitter-patter at first, but they soon turned into brutal bullet-like hailstones. Icy-cold gusts whipped through her hair and clothing. She pulled her flimsy jacket tighter around herself. Then lightning flashed, thunder crackled, and the thunderstorm was upon her.

I'm in for it now.

Torrents of water cascaded in every direction. Thoroughly drenched, she tried to move faster, but the hammering rain made it difficult to see where she was going. One moment, she was making her way forward, step by step, and the next, her feet slipped out from beneath her. She stumbled and skidded.

She caught onto a wet ridge with her right hand, but the rugged edges cut into her skin, weakening her hold. The wind tugged at her jacket and the rain pounded her like it was trying to wash her away. She tried desperately to hold on, but her fingers were getting tired. *Hashem! Help me!*

Then she lost her grip.

She slid down the slope, thrashing about to grasp hold of anything that would slow her fall. Her legs and knees scraped against the rocks, and her thigh slammed against a jutting slab. She screamed, twirling and jerking as she fell. She seemed to be picking up speed. Her throat constricted and she could hardly catch her breath.

She was falling ...

Falling ...

Falling ...

She had a vague sense of the massive expanse of water below as she fell, flailing her arms, desperate to grab hold of a rock—to grab hold of anything. She couldn't allow herself to be swept into the sea.

Then she landed on a ridge projecting from the cliff, the impact jarring her to her bones. Too terrified to look, she squeezed her eyes shut and curled into a ball. Her eyelids fluttered open, then shut as she became engulfed in a chilling blackness.

Is this all a nightmare?

The sound of the gushing rain seemed distant. She wasn't sure if she was even conscious. Or alive.

Do dreams visit the dead too?

Back at the school, the entire student body was in the dining room, watching a film on the *halachos* of *brachos*. The lights were dimmed and Rayla ate silently, watching the scenarios playing out before her. Every now and then, she scanned the door, watching for Michal to make her appearance and slip in.

A crash of thunder jolted everyone, and they stood up to recite the appropriate *brachos*.

Rayla stared out the window. *Oh no! Where is Michal? I hope she's not stuck somewhere on the cliffs in this awful weather. But what if she is?*

With the lights off, it was easy for her to slip out of the room. She took a quick look in the coat closet—Michal's jacket and boots were still missing. Rayla chewed her lip, looking at the rain pelting the windows at the end of the hall. She closed the closet door.

Should I tell anyone about Michal? I can't. Michal didn't want anyone to know. And it's not raining so hard now. I'll look for her myself. I'll be fine on my own.

She yanked open the closet again and put on her jacket. At the last minute, she grabbed the warm cardigan she kept in her locker for particularly chilly days and tucked it inside her jacket, just in case. If Michal was still out in the storm, she would be soaked to the skin. Then Rayla walked as quietly as she could through the large entrance hall and slipped out the door.

She was grateful the storm had started to abate, making the way less difficult and treacherous. She ran to where she knew Michal had been painting. When she arrived at the spot, she noticed the little hut and thought maybe Michal had taken cover there.

Michal wasn't there, but her art supplies were. At the sight of them, Rayla drew a sharp breath. *Where can she be?*

She followed the path past the hut, but couldn't see Michal anywhere. She thought about heading back, but a tremendous sense of foreboding propelled her forward.

Then, far below, she spotted a flash of yellow, the color of the Samphire School uniform.

Michal!

She leaned over carefully to get a better look. It was definitely Michal, lying on a ridge partway down the cliff. She chewed her lip again. *How am I going to get her out of there?*

She thought about running back to the school for help, but knew Michal's precarious situation might not afford her much time.

Who knows how long she's managed to hang on there? She must be drenched, and she could be hurt.

She examined the cliff before her until she found a path that led down toward the ridge. With steady, careful steps, she began her descent.

"Michal! Michal!" she called. "Don't worry, I'm coming."

Something far away nudged Michal out of her darkness. It took her a while to rouse herself, but when she did, a sound startled her.

Someone was calling her name.

She unfurled enough to look in the direction of the voice, and her heart soared.

Rayla!

But she was too spent to open her mouth, unable to utter the words her mind was screaming. She couldn't see any possibility of Rayla reaching her.

Rayla dragged and shoved a flat boulder, working to angle it in the direction of the ridge. The slab was clearly heavy, and Rayla wasn't muscular. Michal watched breathlessly. It was a precarious attempt if ever there was one.

"Ouch!" Rayla lost her balance. She started to slip, her shoes gliding over glossy rocks. Michal's fears rebounded. She squeezed her eyes shut. But then the large stone clunked into place, one edge caught on the lip of Michal's sheltering ledge. Rayla caught her balance and stood strong and upright.

Safe.

Michal blinked rapidly. A moment ago, she had thought there was no hope, and now a stable path lay before her. She maneuvered to her hands and knees and inched her way toward the temporary bridge.

Rayla held on tight to the boulder to make sure it wouldn't give way as Michal crawled over it. Her progress felt painstakingly slow. Rayla was in obvious pain from bearing Michal's weight, and Michal hoped her muscles wouldn't yield.

Finally, she was over it and standing beside Rayla—dazed, shocked, and soaked, but safe and uninjured, apart from a few scrapes on her legs. And that was all that mattered.

They made their way up the slope, with Michal's progress slowed by a pain in her thigh and the uncontrollable shivering that had overtaken her body. When they got to the hut to collect her art supplies, Rayla took out a woolen sweater from beneath her jacket. Michal put it on and clenched Rayla's hand in gratitude, her fingers trembling. Then they walked toward the school as fast as Michal was able.

Fortunately, the rest of the students were still watching the film in the dining room when they arrived, and Rayla was able to help her to the empty dorm unnoticed. Once Michal was dry and in fresh clothes, she accepted a cup of tea, which Rayla forced her to drink. It was strong and sweet and, bit by bit, Michal came back to herself.

"Rayla," she whispered, "I have no words to thank you. You saved my life."

Rayla smiled at her and waved a hand dismissively. "Nah, I didn't do much. You would have done the same, wouldn't you? Do you think you should see the nurse?"

"Oh, no. I can wiggle my fingers and toes. The only thing that really hurts is my thigh, but it's not bleeding, only bashed up a bit. I'm fine, just a bit tuckered out. You go back to the common room. I think I'll stay here and rest."

Rayla chewed her lip, as she often did. "Do you want me to stay with you?"

Michal blinked. She wasn't sure if she was more surprised at the offer, or by the fact that she wanted to take Rayla up on it.

"Um, sure. Yes, I do. Thank you."

Rayla smiled shyly and sat next to her.

The two spoke with each other for a long time, bonding as only those who have been through a terrifying ordeal together can. Michal told Rayla about her mother's passing and her father's remarriage, though Rayla already knew all that from Sherry.

"You and Sherry have got pretty close, huh?" Michal tried to keep the bitterness out of her voice.

Rayla nodded. "*Baruch Hashem*, for her. Her and Mindy and Becky. Without those three, I wouldn't have had any friends here this year."

Michal's heart pinched. She knew she had been part of the reason for that. All her unkind words and actions toward Rayla during the past term came to mind, and her cheeks started to burn.

"Well, you've got another one now."

Rayla smiled. "That's good to know. Thank you." She squeezed Michal's hand. "How's the tea?"

Michal examined the dregs of her cup. "Fine, thanks." She set it down on the nightstand.

Rayla was quiet for a moment, then brightened. "Say, do you want to see my photo album?"

Michal was exhausted, but her heart was still hammering too hard to allow her to sleep. Besides, she felt she owed Rayla her time—and not just because the girl had saved her life. Shame wormed through her heart.

"I'd love to."

"I'll be right back!"

Rayla dashed to her closet on the other end of the dormitory, and Michal stretched out on her bed, aching inside and out.

How could I have been so blind for so long?

11 Rayla's Secret

Sherry rested her head on her hands, glued to the screen, amazed by the intricacies of the *halachos*. Without warning, there was a loud *pop*. The screen went blank and the lights went out.

She looked around in the darkness, wondering what had happened. Bassy, two seats away and cheery as ever, called out to answer the unasked question.

"No worries, there's nothing frightening—just a power cut caused by lightning."

And she was right. The entire ground floor had been plunged into darkness.

"It's so dark in here," a first former whined.

"I can't see anything!" another girl shrieked.

"I'm scared!" her friend yelped.

Sherry squinted in the darkness as her eyes adjusted. She barely made out Bassy creeping to the first form table, feeling her way with her hands. When she got there, she leaned close to the girls and stage-whispered conspiratorially.

"There's nothing here that we can't handle. Wait a moment, I'll fetch a candle." She took a step away, then turned around and leaned close again. "While I'm gone, why don't you play blind man's bluff-I spy, okay?"

"How do we do that?" one of the younger girls said, her voice quivering.

Sherry smiled at her friend's trademark impromptu rhyme. Trust Bassy to turn a power outage into a game. She got up to help. "Why, you take turns feeling things in the dark, and then ask others to guess what it is, of course."

Bassy peered at Sherry in the dim light coming through the windows from the occasional flash of lightning and gave her a thumbs-up. Henya Sherwood, the head girl this year, got in the spirit and stood on her seat in the back of the room.

"That sounds like a wonderful idea. Perhaps we should divide up into teams by form. Form captains, help your groups find each other by calling out so they can come to you. Careful, now, we don't want anyone to get stepped on ..."

As Henya organized the game Bassy had just invented, Sherry came over to the table and took Bassy's place next to the younger girls.

"I'll take it from here," she said quietly.

Grinning, Bassy scrambled out of the dining room to perform her self-appointed task.

Sherry bent to talk to the first form girls, who peppered her with questions about the new game. *Where's Michal? She would do much better with these girls than I would.*

A dreadful realization came over her—she hadn't seen Michal for hours. It wasn't like her to disappear for so long. She bolted upright, straining to see in the dark room.

"Michal!" she called over the din of laughing girls shouting "I spy" at the top of their lungs.

But there was no answer.

Becky came over. "Is something the matter?"

"I haven't seen Michal for a while. Have you?"

Becky shook her head. "No, I'm sorry, I haven't seen her since before supper."

Sherry's mouth went dry.

"Would you stay with these girls, please?"

Becky nodded, looking concerned in the dim light. "Sure. Let me know when you find her, okay?"

Sherry gave her a tight smile and made her way as quickly as she could through the crowd.

If Michal had somehow gotten hurt, Sherry would never be able to forgive herself.

~

In the dorm, Michal and Rayla sat together, engrossed in Rayla's photo album, when a noise made them jump. Bassy had entered the room. She made her way straight to the cupboard with the emergency supplies next to the door. When she noticed them, she stopped.

"What are you two doing, hiding up here?" She stepped closer. "You don't look well at all, Michal. I'll go down to the office and get you some medicine. I'm sure you'll feel better in no time. Just let me fetch some candles first. I remember seeing them in here."

She rummaged through the cupboard shelves as she searched.

"Candles?" Rayla asked. "What do you need those for?"

"Oh, there's just been a power cut downstairs. The first formers are scared out of their wits." She rolled her eyes, unable to hold back a wide grin.

"Ah, here they are." She held up a handful of white tapers. "I'll be back in a jiffy."

With that, she hurried out of the room.

Michal and Rayla looked at each other and then burst out laughing.

"She wasn't even rhyming, she was in such a hurry," Michal said.

"But she's got a good head, er, she doesn't lose it in a flurry." Rayla made a face. "Oh, that wasn't very good. I don't have Bassy's talent for it."

"Well, you haven't had her practice, either."

The girls giggled again. They were still giggling uproariously when Bassy re-entered the room, medicine in hand. She put the tablets down on the night table and perched on the corner of the bed.

"Mind if I see?" She gestured at the photo album.

Rayla shut the leather-bound album and clutched it. "I—I'm sorry, it's just—"

"No worries," Bassy said. "They're playing blind man's bluff-I spy downstairs, and I want a turn." She grinned and gave a quick wave, then jumped up and left the room.

The girls exchanged glances.

"Blind man's *what?*" Rayla arched her brows.

Michal shrugged. "Search me. It sounds very *Bassy*, though."

"You've gotta admit, that girl sure knows how to cheer someone up," Rayla said.

"She does, doesn't she? Despite all her mischief, it usually turns out right in the end."

Michal thought about this. Bassy naturally drew people to her. It was a talent Michal envied. She glanced at Rayla. Despite the perpetual smile the girl wore, she seemed to push people away. She wondered if Rayla was thinking similar thoughts, judging from her frown. Truthfully, Rayla wasn't so bad, once you got to know her—but getting to know her was the trick.

Rayla reopened the album and gave a low cough, as if inviting Michal to take another look. Michal gazed at the next photo. "Who's this?" She pointed at an older girl who looked very much like Rayla. She was looking through a pair of binoculars.

"Oh, that's my sister, Linda. She loves bird-watching when we're on one of our family vacations."

"Yeah? Sounds like fun."

Rayla's eyes sparkled. "Whoa, you have no idea." And she was off on another story about her family.

Michal had been surprised when Rayla dug out the album from where she kept it hidden in her drawer, but she understood. Maybe since Michal had looked so forlorn, Rayla felt safe sharing her own feelings. Or perhaps it was because Michal had finally stopped being so mean to her. She sighed. It was probably both reasons. The album was filled with pictures of Rayla's parents, along with her two brothers and one sister. Rayla, it turned out, was the youngest.

"Your mother is a perfect sport," Michal said, touching the photo of Rayla's mother jumping from stone to stone in a river. "And look here," she exclaimed, pointing at a different photograph. "What is she doing with that snake around her shoulders?"

Rayla laughed. "That was taken when we visited my sister in California, at a place called Venice Beach."

In another photo, Rayla's mother was holding a massive carp, which must have weighed at least thirty pounds.

"This was when we went to Town Lake in Austin, Texas," she explained. "Fishing for carp is really hard, but my mother found a way to lure them in. She threw a handful of corn into the water and waited until the carp came to feed. When she felt a tug, she raised the fishing rod skywards, and kept the tension on until she was able to reel the fish in. A few anglers nearby cheered and clapped. Not one of them had been as lucky as her. When she drew out the enormous fish and held it up, everybody laughed. It almost dwarfed her."

As she spoke, her eyes sparkled. Those memories were obviously precious to her. Then, eyes dimming, she leaned forward.

"Can I tell you a secret? One I haven't even told Sherry or Mindy?"

Michal sat up. "Of course. I think I'm pretty good at keeping secrets."

Rayla gave a small smile. "Somehow, I thought you might be."

She paused, fingering the pages of the album and staring at the picture of her mother. Just when Michal thought she might not say anything else, she spoke.

"My mother is really sick. She's actually been in the hospital more than at home these past two years." Her words were barely audible and her hands shook as she spoke. "The doctors are really worried." She took a deep breath and shuddered. "Her ... chances of survival are slim."

Michal's heart felt like a heavy stone had been placed on it. She knew exactly what Rayla was going through. Her own mother had been sick for a year before she passed away.

"I'm so sorry." She touched Rayla's hand. "Is that why you came here?"

"Yes," Rayla answered, so quietly Michal had to strain to hear. "Mom's receiving a special new treatment at a hospital in Manchester. It's our last hope." She sighed and shook her head. "Her last hope. Well, according to the doctors, that is."

She pointed to a photo of her mother, looking rather pale and thin, with one arm around Rayla. Both of them were covered by pigeons.

"This one was taken at Trafalgar Square, in London, just before school started. We stayed at Granny's vacation home, in the London suburbs. She loves exploring the UK during her vacations. Mom wanted us to have a few days of fun when we arrived here before I went to Samphire in the south and she began her treatment in the north." She heaved a sigh that almost broke Michal's heart. "Sometimes it feels like she's on the other side of the planet."

Michal nodded. "I know what that's like." She stared at the photo. "How on earth did you get the pigeons to land on you?"

Rayla chuckled.

"We walked around and she insisted that we feed the pigeons there. She actually put birdseed on our shoulders for that photo." Her cheeks dimpled with a half-smile. "My mother is an active, nature-loving person, and this illness has ravaged her. But more than that, I know how much she's always wanted to make us happy."

Michal wrapped her arm around Rayla's shoulders. She understood her now, in a way no one else could. They were silent for a few moments.

"She'll be okay," Rayla said, abruptly closing the album and standing up. "She'll get better. She has to. I don't stop davening for her."

"She will," Michal said, her voice low. "And I'll daven for her too."

She was shaken by her new friend's secret, knowing exactly what the girl must be going through. There was so much more to Rayla than met the eye.

Michal recalled her initial misjudgment, and guilt and shame filled her. She'd had no idea that when Rayla stepped out of that limousine, holding her head as high as she could, she hadn't been haughty—she'd been trying to hold it together.

Rayla wasn't a snob. She was kind and heroic. And, despite her immense worries and the way she'd been treated by most of her classmates all year, she'd managed to keep a cheerful demeanor.

I was wrong to judge her. I thought she had everything going for her, including having the benefit of speaking privately to her mother on the phone in Mrs. Pepper's office. She covered her eyes with her hands and shook her head. *How could I have been so callous? And the way I've treated Sherry is totally unacceptable too.*

There was a lot of mending to do, and she resolved to tackle it as soon as possible. She should go find Sherry now, before another second passed.

No sooner had she thought that than Sherry burst into the dorm, her eyes wild. When she saw Michal, she rushed over to her.

"There you are! You had me scared to death. I thought maybe you'd gone outside to paint and—oh, hello, Rayla."

Rayla smiled. "Hi, Sherry. Michal's been with me this whole time. She's fine."

Sherry glanced skeptically at Michal.

"Are you sure? I ran into Bassy on the stairs on the way up, and she said she brought you medicine because you looked horrible. You weren't outside on the cliffs again, were you?"

All of Michal's annoyance at Sherry's bossiness flared again. She knew she should apologize for how she'd behaved, but it was hard to do that when Sherry acted like Michal was utterly incapable of doing anything at all. She folded her arms.

"What business is it of yours?"

Sherry looked incredulous. "I'm—I'm your sister, Michal. *And* your friend. I think that makes it my business."

Rayla looked away uncomfortably. "Maybe I should go ..."

"No," both girls said at once, exchanging belligerent glances.

"Stay," Sherry said first. "I'll go. They'll need help cleaning up downstairs."

She looked at the two of them, finally taking in the photo album on the bed and the way they were sitting close together.

"I'm glad you two are spending time together. It's been horrible trying to be friends with only one of you at a time."

She turned and disappeared through the door.

Sherry's final words hit Michal like a slap. She didn't need Rayla's reproachful look to realize that she had made a terrible mistake.

She sighed and wrapped her arms around her knees. "Do you ever feel like you sometimes turn into someone else? That you're not yourself at all, but this mean, terrible person takes over and you have no say?"

Rayla looked at her with sympathy, but shook her head. "No, I don't. I've been working hard all year to seem like I haven't a care in the world. I don't want anyone to know what's really going on, but that's my choice."

Michal nodded and fidgeted with her blanket.

"I'm so sorry for how I treated you, Rayla. Thank you for coming out to look for me. I don't know what would have happened to me if you hadn't."

Rayla smiled. "Think nothing of it." She bit her lip. "You're not gonna tell anyone my secret, are you?"

Michal glanced up, startled. "Of course not!"

Rayla looked relieved. "Thanks."

"But, you know ..." Michal started, then stopped.

"What?"

"Well, if you were a little more open with people, I think you'd be surprised by how many friends you might make. I think people think you might be a bit of a ... a fake. Because you seem too happy all the time, but you don't talk about yourself at all."

Rayla chewed her lip. "Maybe so. But that's the only way I can keep it together most days."

Michal nodded. "I understand. More than you know."

She squeezed Rayla's hand, and the other girl gave her a tight-lipped smile. Then Rayla closed her photo album.

"Are you going to apologize to Sherry? You two shouldn't fight."

Michal sighed and nodded. "I know. And I will. Eventually."

Exhaustion hit her hard, and she could barely keep her eyes open.

"You look wiped out. You should rest," Rayla said. She stood up and held the album to her chest.

Michal burrowed under her covers, already half asleep.

"Mm-hmm," she mumbled. "Goodnight, Rayla."

Rayla smiled. "Goodnight, Michal."

Michal didn't even hear Rayla leave. She was glad she had finally seen past Rayla's aloof exterior, but now she had another apology to make. No matter how annoyed she was with Sherry, her sister didn't deserve to be treated the way Michal had treated her.

Her last conscious thought was, *I'll do it first thing in the morning. Maybe.*

12 A Purim Prank

When Michal woke up the next day, she recalled the pledge she had made the night before to apologize to Sherry as soon as she had the chance. That chance came at lunchtime.

Not without some trepidation, she waited at her locker until Sherry arrived to put her books away.

"Can I talk to you?"

Sherry smiled. "Sure. What's up?"

Michal looked up and down the hallway. Girls were milling about on their way to or from the dining room. "Alone?"

Rayla approached. "Hi, Michal. Feeling better today?"

Michal nodded. "Much, thanks to you."

"Awesome."

Rayla flashed her too-bright smile at her. Michal frowned. She knew why Rayla kept up her act, but that didn't mean she agreed with it.

Rayla put a hand on Sherry's shoulder.

"So, Share-bear, are you ready to go play netball? The other girls are already on the court." Rayla gestured in the direction of the field with her thumb.

"Yeah, but go ahead without me. I have to talk to Michal."

Rayla smiled knowingly at Michal. "Okay. See you out there."

"Sure, Ray-Ray."

Rayla smiled again at Michal, then turned and walked away.

Sherry faced Michal again. "Where do you want to go? The art room?"

Michal stared blankly at her. *Share-bear? Ray-Ray? Why don't we have nicknames for each other? We're the ones who are family!*

Unbidden, the jealousy she thought she'd overcome grasped her heart.

"Uh, never mind. It's just about the notes from English. I can ask you later."

"No problem." Sherry pointed to the lockers behind them. "In fact, I have them right here."

She pulled her English folder from her locker and started flipping through the pages, then took out a couple of sheets of loose-leaf paper covered in blue ink. She handed them to Michal, who took them sheepishly.

"Hey, any news about the writing competition yet?" Sherry asked.

Michal hadn't been expecting this. She definitely didn't want to talk to Sherry about the writing competition.

"You know as much as I do."

Sherry's brow furrowed. "Um, okay." She hesitated. "Do you want to come play netball with us?"

Michal shook her head, not trusting her voice. "I think I'd better study. We have that test coming up in history."

Sherry smiled uncertainly. "Okay. See you in class."

"Uh-huh."

Michal spun on her heel and walked away before Sherry could see the moisture in her eyes and the sadness in her heart.

~

Purim was approaching and the girls were getting into the spirit, bored of work and tired of tests. They sat in the common room, trying to decide what pranks to pull.

Rayla sat in a chair behind a large group of girls, watching from where she wouldn't be noticed. Her mind was preoccupied with the phone call she'd had with her parents the previous night. They had told her they were waiting for test results. Dad's voice had been strained, and Mom's tone had been unnaturally cheery. Rayla recognized that tone. It was the same one she'd been using all year every time someone asked how she was doing, and she chirped "Oh, I'm fine" in response.

Yet she was not fine. And Rayla couldn't help but wonder if her mother was hiding something.

"We could turn all our chairs backwards and pretend that nothing is different," Leah suggested. "Can you imagine Miss Bentley's face when she tries to teach maths and we're all looking at the back wall the whole time?"

Bassy sat on the piano bench, plunking keys at random with one hand. She wrinkled her nose. "Nah, it's been done."

"I know!" Nechama said. "What if every time the teacher calls on someone, she stands up and recites a limerick?" She stood to demonstrate:

Miss Bentley was hanging a pic,
When a student came out real quick
That blu tack you're usin',
Poor you for choosin'—

My chewed gum, though 'haps it will stick

The girls broke into giggles, and Nechama sat with a satisfied smile.

Even Bassy chuckled appreciatively at that one. She stood up and recited:

Nifty Nechama got that slick
With her eccentric limerick
A tad too sticky
Yet mad and shticky
A fantastic, bombastic trick

Nechama high-fived her. "You're some competition."

"Rhyming Bassy has found her match-y," Sherry said, as she and her friends looked on, amused.

"'Tis quite likely catchy," Nechama remarked.

"Not all of us are as quick with rhymes as you and Bassy, though," Becky pointed out.

Rayla tried to imagine herself composing impromptu poems, and almost laughed out loud. It wasn't one of her greatest talents, and she was more than glad when the other girls agreed with Becky.

"What do you suggest, Bassy?" Rivi asked.

The girls turned to face the master of pranks, but she just spread her hands wide and said in her typical singsong, "What makes you think there's any pranks I'd play, before we break up for Purim—aka Pranking Day?"

Baila, who sat on the bench next to her, chucked her friend on the shoulder. "Bassy, you're too much sometimes."

Bassy laughed, but said nothing more. Whatever pranks she had up her sleeve, she wasn't telling them about it.

"I have it!" Sherry said, wiggling her eyebrows. "We'll blow up balloons, hundreds of them, and fill the entire classroom until there's no space. Then we'll present the teacher with a needle and she'll have to pop the balloons so we can get in."

Rivi squealed. "Just imagine how bright the room will look with all the colorful balloons. Totally Purim'dik."

"But that will take an awful lot of blowing up," Nechama said.

Against her will, Rayla was inclined to agree with her. When Nechama saw her nodding, though, she turned away.

"Where will we store the balloons?" Mindy asked, worry shadowing her eyes.

"I know how we can make this even better!" Nechama cried. "We could fill some of the balloons with water. Oh, won't it be funny to watch the teacher as water bursts all over the place?"

"We can't do that!" Becky said. "That's worse than the confetti."

Thankfully, the rest of the class agreed.

Bassy stood and pushed the piano bench back into place. "Count me out, girls. I've already cleaned enough colored paper out of the grates this year. Besides, I want to keep fit for the matches. I'm to be goal attack, remember?"

Disappointed murmurs passed through the room, but Bassy held up her hands to forestall further grumbles, then went and grabbed her history textbook to begin studying for their next exam.

The rest of the girls huddled together and plotted and schemed until their plan fell into place. Rayla volunteered to go to the village and buy the balloons with Sherry. That earned her scowls from both Michal and Nechama.

I thought Michal and I were getting along now. What's with that girl? She decided to give Michal a wide berth from now on. She didn't need such disloyal friends, not when it had been so hard to share her secret with her. *I'm better off just keeping to myself.*

She gave Michal her best smile as though she wasn't upset at all.

As Purim came closer, the girls in Form Three got to work. Whenever they had spare time, they pumped balloons and placed them in one of the designated hiding areas, which were rapidly filling up. Unfortunately, they weren't always as good at concealing them as they could have been.

"Why is Form Three so busy with balloons?" Rayla overheard Miss Bentley ask one day in the hall.

"They really do seem obsessed," Mrs. Bergman said. "I've already stopped three girls carrying armfuls of them. So much color."

Bassy and Baila happened to be passing by, and Mrs. Bergman arched a brow at the shorter girl.

"I don't suppose you have any idea what's going on with all these balloons, Miss Joseph?"

Bassy stopped short, eyes wide and innocent. "Honest, I have nothing to do with any balloons, here or in the past. I learned my lesson about party favors."

"Hmph," Mrs. Bergman said, though she gestured to the girls to go.

"I think the teachers are on to us," Rayla whispered to Sherry when she got to class.

Sherry nodded. "We'll have to be more careful. We'll talk to everyone this afternoon to make sure they're more discrete."

Rayla shifted uncomfortably. At the front of the class, Michal looked back at the two of them, then faced forward.

"Maybe I'll leave the talking to you," Rayla said.

Sherry followed Rayla's gaze and sighed. "I don't know if certain people will take it any better from me, but I'll do the talking. No problem."

Later, in the common room, the girls agreed to be more cautious. But since Purim was only a few days away, they wouldn't have to hide their balloons for much longer. Now they just had to work out the final details.

"In which lesson should we carry out our plan?" Baila asked.

Mindy surprised everyone by speaking up. "I think first period would be most practical, don't you? This way we'd have enough time to prepare the room."

Nechama's eyes gleamed. "Practical and perfect."

"Our last day before Purim is Tuesday—we'll have Mrs. Cohen first," Leah said. "It couldn't be better."

The rest of the girls started chattering excitedly in agreement.

Rivi looked at Bassy, who was listening but not participating in the discussion. "Good idea. Definitely not in Mrs. Bergman's class. I think she's already had enough 'fun' this year."

Bassy grinned, but held up her hands as though to proclaim her innocence. "I don't have any idea what you're talking about."

"Mm-hmm," Rivi said.

"Mrs. Cohen it is, then," Sherry said. "I think we may need a few more balloons, though. Our supply is running low. Michal, would you like to come to the village with me this time?"

Michal narrowed her eyes, looking back and forth between Rayla and Sherry. "I'm busy at lunch tomorrow. You'd best take *Ray-Ray* again."

She got off the couch and left the room.

Sherry exchanged glances with Rayla and sighed. "Do you want to come with me again, Rayla?"

Rayla blinked. She had thought Michal might be a true friend.

Oh, why did I ever trust her? Why was I so naïve? So foolish?

She squashed her feelings of hurt and betrayal into a hidden closet deep inside and slammed the door shut. Then, turning to Sherry, she pasted on a broad smile. "Sure, I'd love to. I'll pay this time. Maybe we could get a few of those fancy foil balloons to hide in with the rest."

Nechama smirked at Rayla. "Because that's what matters most, isn't it? Showing off that you can afford more than anyone else can?"

"Nechama ..." Sherry said, a warning tone in her voice.

Nechama jumped to her feet. "I've got homework to do. You all do what you want."

She left the room, and the rest of the girls stared at each other awkwardly.

Rayla, feeling that the tension was somehow her fault, tried to brighten the mood.

"Well, we'll see if she feels differently on Tuesday when Mrs. Cohen pops a balloon and a bunch of Belgian chocolates fall out. Oh, I can't wait to see the look on her face!"

A few of the girls shook their heads and whispered to each other.

Sherry looked around, chewing her lip. "Let's go, Rayla. Maybe we can get to the shop before it closes. And I could use some air, couldn't you?"

Rayla heaved a sigh, glancing at the other students. How could she get these girls to like her? Why did she always say the wrong thing?

She ignored the tightness in her chest and grinned brightly. "After you."

~

Tuesday morning, even Sherry woke up early. In groups of three, the girls walked to their allocated hiding places. Amid incessant giggling, they went back and forth to the classroom, filling it with colored balloons. Every time she saw the room, Sherry felt ready to explode with laughter. If it wasn't for Baila, who covered her mouth with her hand, it was likely her raucous laughter would have woken the teachers.

Michal helped fill the room with the rest of the girls, only speaking to Sherry when she asked how she'd slept and if she was excited about the prank—and then only responding with a few sullen syllables. Sherry couldn't understand it. She'd thought Michal and Rayla had made up—so why was Michal still so upset? Michal still wore that guarded, tight expression every time she saw Sherry. On the rare occasion Sherry did get her sister to smile, it was like Michal quickly remembered herself and yanked it away.

It broke Sherry's heart. And, if she was being honest, it made her a little angry. What right did Michal have to be upset with Sherry? Hadn't she always done her best to make time for Michal? Michal didn't really expect Sherry not to have other friends, did she?

Sherry had wracked her brain, trying to figure out if she'd done anything to offend Michal, but hadn't been able to think of anything. Whenever she tried to talk to her sister about it, Michal turned and hurried the other way before Sherry could even say anything.

I wonder if we'll hear about the story winner any time soon. Michal should be excited about that. But then another thought came to her. *Why are you so sure that Michal's entry will actually win? It looks like you let yourself do badly for nothing! But that's small fry next to Michal's melancholy.*

The situation was looking a bit hopeless. Maybe she should call Ma and ask her what to do.

Sighing inwardly, she decided to have fun, sulky sister notwithstanding. She stuffed her last armful of balloons into the classroom, barely able to close the door without a few drifting out. Then she shut the door tightly.

"What should we do with these?" Leah asked, holding up a large box filled with balloons. Behind her, two other girls had similar burdens.

"Why don't we cover the door?" Rayla asked.

Nechama's gaze flitted to the American girl, and her mouth twisted. "That's actually a pretty good idea," she muttered, and put down her box of balloons.

Rayla blinked at Nechama in surprise. Sherry smiled to herself, then ran to borrow some tape from a nearby classroom.

Soon the whole door was covered in a rainbow of colors.

"Just for good measure," Bassy said, taping the final few balloons to the window in the door so it was impossible to see inside.

"I thought you weren't helping," Baila teased her friend. She whisked out her camera, and took several worthy shots.

Bassy chuckled. "I can't let you have all the fun."

"That's the Bassy we all know and love," Rivi said, gathering up their supplies. "Now, who wants to hand Mrs. Cohen the needle?" She held up a sewing needle.

The girls looked at each other. No one wanted to do that. What if Mrs. Cohen regarded their prank the same way Mrs. Bergman had? No one had wanted to mention it, but a stunt like this might get them all in trouble. Maybe Bassy had been the smart one for once.

Finally, they decided to tape the needle to a large note and hang it on the door handle. With the job finished, the girls trooped down to the davening hall.

"Be right there," Bassy said, turning around. "I forgot something."

Sherry watched her rush back the way she'd come, wondering what it could be. She turned to the rest of the girls just before they entered the davening hall.

"Perfect behavior," Sherry reminded them. She didn't want to give the teachers reason to suspect anything was up.

Bassy joined them before the last girl was seated. She was panting, and her forehead was glistening with sweat.

After breakfast, they lined up neatly outside the classroom and remained silent, waiting for Mrs. Cohen to arrive. From the end of the corridor, the teacher saw the perfect line of girls and cocked her head.

Sherry held her breath. *Does she know something's up?*

With firm, even steps, Mrs. Cohen walked toward the classroom. The girls solemnly wished her a good morning, keeping up their docile behavior.

She reached the balloon-covered door and saw the note attached to the handle.

"Girls." She looked sternly at them. "What is this?"

Sherry glanced at Michal, but Michal kept her eyes on the teacher. Still, Sherry was happy to see a small smile on her sister's face. At least she was enjoying the prank.

Mrs. Cohen took the needle, eased open the door and, with a broad smile, began bursting the balloons one by one. The girls chuckled at the sight, relieved, and pressed up to the open doorway to watch. Rivi and Leah squealed with delight as each balloon was popped, and Nechama gave a cheer.

Surprisingly, Bassy stood on the far side of the hall and watched, grinning.

Mrs. Beckerman came out from her empty classroom next door to see what the noise was all about, and smiled when she saw the balloon-filled classroom. She removed a pin from her *sheitel*, then stepped in and helped Mrs. Cohen pop the balloons. Every time she popped one, she recoiled with an exaggerated blink and said, "Oh!"

That finally broke through Michal's melancholy, and she began to laugh. Sherry watched her sister, afraid to say anything to ruin the moment. Michal was having some fun for the first time in weeks—maybe months.

"I've never seen anything so funny in my life," Michal said through her giggles, tears streaming down her cheeks. She whispered to Sherry, "This was a wonderful idea. You really do come up with the best ones."

Sherry smiled. "Not all the time. You wrote the better story for the competition, didn't you?"

Michal stopped giggling, and her smile became inexplicably strained. "Yeah. Right." She quickly turned away and went into the classroom to pick up colorful remnants.

Rayla came to stand next to Sherry. "Your sister is sure moody. Is she always like that?"

Sherry wanted to say no, of course not. But she'd only known Michal since last year, and her sister had been even more reserved and withdrawn then, reeling from the recent loss of her mother.

But now she had a new mother, so her sullen behavior couldn't be because of that.

And Sherry had a father.

At the thought of the man Sherry barely knew, she knew that her assessment wasn't fair. Just because their parents had gotten married didn't mean they were a cohesive family. It had been years since Papa was *niftar*, and she still missed him. How much harder must it be for Michal?

"She's usually ... more cheerful," was all she could think to say. "She's been through a lot the last few years."

Rayla nodded and frowned. "I know most of it, I think, but I don't think that's an excuse to be rude and standoffish, do you? We all go through things. Why should we make that someone else's problem?"

Sherry glanced at Rayla. As she silently agreed with her, she wondered how Rayla had come to learn that particular lesson. She suddenly realized how little she knew about the American girl.

Rayla's frown was replaced by a bright smile, and Sherry returned it.

"I don't think she means to be rude," Sherry said. "She's just not as resilient as you and me."

This time, it was Rayla's smile that slipped, but she quickly pasted it back in place. Sherry chewed her lip. There were times when she thought that Rayla might be hiding something. She let the matter drop, though. She wanted at least one friend she could still talk to, and didn't want to risk upsetting Rayla by pushing her to reveal a secret she may or may not have.

Ten minutes before the lesson was due to end, the task of popping all the balloons was finally complete. All that remained was a floor littered with deflated, colorful rubber. The girls filed into the classroom and took their seats, and Mrs. Beckerman returned to her own classroom, her eyes twinkling at the girls as she left.

Sherry sat straight in her seat and gave her full attention to Mrs. Cohen. Their teacher had been a real sport, she had to admit.

"Girls," Mrs. Cohen announced, brushing off her hands, "there's no point in starting the lesson with so few minutes left. Instead, let's talk about balloons."

She held up a red balloon—a stray one that hadn't been popped. It bobbed slightly as she pinched the knot between her fingers.

Sherry's eyebrows lifted. What lesson could she possibly draw from their prank?

The teacher held up the pin in her other hand.

"What will happen if I pop this balloon?"

"It will deflate," Nechama answered.

"It will fly around the room," Bassy said. "And make that funny noise."

Mrs. Cohen chuckled. "I believe that would happen if I released a balloon that hasn't been tied, Bassy."

"It will be torn apart," Rayla said quietly.

Mrs. Cohen turned to her, looking impressed. "Well said, Rayla."

With a flourish, she tapped the tip of the needle on the balloon. In an impressive percussive finale, it burst apart and the pieces went flying. One landed on Rivi's desk, and she picked it up and giggled.

"The balloon," Mrs. Cohen continued, holding up the red rubber knot she still held, "represents the people in our lives—our friends, our family, or someone you may have just met. And this," she brandished the needle, "is our words. When we say words that are sharp as needles, we can tear lives apart. Remember this, girls."

Just then, the bell rang. Nechama rushed out of her seat, making a beeline for the door. She almost crashed into Mrs. Cohen, who handed her the pin.

"As a souvenir," she whispered.

Nechama blinked at the pin through her spectacles. "But the prank wasn't my idea, Mrs. Cohen."

Mrs. Cohen arched a brow. "I never said it was." She looked around at the mess. "Now, girls, you should have just enough time to tidy up before the next class."

A few girls groaned in response, and she gave an impish smile before walking out of the classroom.

Nechama looked around the room. "I don't know why she gave this to *me*," she said, looking at the needle.

"I think the rest of us do," Rayla muttered to herself.

"No one asked you," Nechama snapped.

Rayla sucked in her lips, composed herself, and then flashed Nechama a bright smile. "You're right. Sorry. What was I thinking?"

Nechama's glare faltered. She glanced at Leah for support, but her friend wouldn't meet her eyes. Sherry looked at Michal, who was sitting in her seat at the front of the class and looking back at Sherry with an unreadable expression. Sherry didn't want to know what Michal was thinking now.

"Come, girls," Sherry said with forced cheerfulness, jumping to her feet. "Let's clean up before Mrs. Lee gets here."

The uncomfortable, awkward silence that blanketed the classroom while the girls worked couldn't have been a starker contrast to their earlier merriment.

Sherry walked around with a trash bin, collecting the bits the girls were picking up.

Some fun this is turning out to be.

The next period was with Mrs. Lee. She'd scheduled a test for that day and Sherry hadn't prepared for it as well as she should have, since she had been occupied with the approach of Purim. Mrs. Lee handed out the test papers and began reviewing the rules.

Just then, Baila jumped up from her seat and pointed beneath a desk. "I saw a rabbit!"

Indeed, there were rabbits scampering all over their classroom.

Mrs. Lee looked around in shock. "A rabbit? How on earth did that get in here?"

Seconds later, other girls were squealing in fright, jumping out of their seats and running about.

"I saw it too!" Becky shrieked, uncharacteristically distraught.

"Look, it's there!" Sherry cried.

"No, I saw it go that way!" Leah yelled.

Mrs. Lee was red-faced. "Girls, return to your seats now," she ordered.

But the girls were too jumpy to obey.

"Here, I'll help you catch them," Bassy said. She made a big show of catching a rabbit. "Hey, look, this rabbit has a label. It says 'Four.'"

"Bassy, put that out at once," Mrs. Lee said. And then she gave an enormous sneeze.

Bassy took it to the door, and Sherry thought she might be about to let the rabbit scamper down the corridor. To her relief, Bassy carried it outside.

Mrs. Lee sneezed again, this time louder than before.

"Mrs. Lee, what is the matter?" Mindy asked, hovering next to the teacher.

"I'm ah ... ah ... CHOO!" She took out a handkerchief and wiped her nose. "I'm allergic to rabbits," she finally managed to say.

Bassy and Baila exchanged nervous glances.

Oh, no! Sherry redoubled her search. They had to find the other three rabbits, and soon.

Mrs. Lee kept sneezing every few seconds as the search continued. Soon, Rabbit One and Rabbit Three had been caught and released as well. Only one rabbit remained.

The girls looked all over for it. Mrs. Lee seemed to be losing her temper.

"Have you checked the cupboard?" Bassy asked. "It might have jumped in there."

Sherry inched open the cupboard, scared the rabbit would spring out at her. She looked up and down, but it wasn't there. Michal climbed onto a chair to see if the rabbit had leaped up on the shelves.

Baila crawled along the floor, calling, "Bunny, bunny, come here."

She looked around surreptitiously, then took out her camera and snapped a few photos of the girls rushing around before Mrs. Lee was any the wiser.

If she hadn't been so anxious, Sherry would have laughed at how comical she looked.

"Girls, sit down now," Mrs. Lee tried again, as unsuccessfully as before. Her face was a little red and swollen, but her sneezing seemed to be subsiding.

The girls kept looking all over for the rabbit. "Might it be under your desk, Mrs. Lee?" Mindy asked worriedly.

Mrs. Lee frowned. "I think not. Please sit down, Mindy. We'll never find the poor thing if it's too scared to come out."

Mindy sat, but kept lifting her feet in case the rabbit ran at her. As much as the girls searched for it, the missing rabbit eluded them.

"I think we have to check the desks," Baila said. "Who knows, maybe it managed to hide in one?"

"Check your bags," Bassy cried delightedly.

"It might be in the dustbin," Leah squealed.

Shrieking girls and shifting desks and chairs raised the commotion in the room to near-deafening levels. Mrs. Lee stood at the front of the room, fuming and occasionally rubbing her red eyes with the palm of her hand.

"What is going on here?" a loud, strict voice called out above the din.

Sherry looked up and froze, petrified. Mrs. Pepper stood at the door.

"Someone please explain the meaning of this mayhem," she ordered. "I could hear you all the way in my office!" She took in Mrs. Lee's puffy face and her eyes widened in alarm. "Mrs. Lee, are you all right?"

Mrs. Lee nodded, sniffling a little. "Yes, I am doing better. I just have a little allergy to rabbits. No harm done, though."

Mrs. Pepper's eyes widened. "An allergy to rabbits? What triggered it?"

Mrs. Lee filled her in and told her that the girls had been searching for the missing rabbit for the last fifteen minutes. Then she smiled. "But I haven't sneezed once in the last ten."

Mrs. Pepper squinted and shook her head. "A rabbit that cannot be found does not exist," she said through pursed lips. "That could be why."

She stiffened, straight as a ramrod, and glared at the students one by one.

"Now, who has played this trick?"

The girls looked around at each other, but no one came forward.

"If the girl responsible does not own up in the next sixty seconds, the entire class will be punished."

Sherry was shocked to see Bassy raise a trembling hand.

"Follow me," Mrs. Pepper snapped. "And the rest of you will sit and listen to your lesson in silence. I sincerely hope that this is the last mischief I will hear of from Form Three today."

Bassy left the room, visibly shaking. Sherry couldn't believe it when Baila stood up.

"Please, Mrs. Lee, I have to go. I was part of the prank too."

At a nod from the teacher, she exited the room, her head down. Sherry watched them leave, biting her lip.

Has Bassy's mischief gotten the best of her at last?

13 Netball Match

"So what happened with Mrs. Pepper?" Nechama asked Bassy and Baila when they finally appeared in the common room.

Sherry was studying for the history test Mrs. Lee had postponed for lack of time, but she couldn't help perking up to listen. The other girls gathered around to hear what the two pranksters' consequences had been.

"Actually," Baila said, "it could have been worse."

Bassy crossed her arms. "Says you."

Baila rolled her eyes, then told the rest of the girls what had happened.

Apparently, believing from their terrified faces that they'd learned their lesson, Mrs. Pepper had let Bassy and Baila off more easily than they'd expected. Still, they had to write an apology note to Mrs. Lee, which they dreaded. They were also excluded from playing in the annual netball match planned for the next week. Bassy, the top goal shooter in the third form, was none too pleased about that.

Baila impersonated the headmistress, standing tall with her

hands clasped in front of her. "The way I see it," Baila said, tilting her head to look commanding and aloof while she quoted Mrs. Pepper, "you have already had your fun, and that has been more than enough."

Bassy harrumphed. "I don't think Mrs. Pepper would know fun if it came up and said hello."

"Bassy!" Becky chided.

Michal put a comforting hand on Bassy's shoulder. "Baila's right, it could have been much worse. Think of poor Mrs. Lee. You could have done some serious damage."

Bassy's shoulders slumped. "I suppose. I hadn't planned on her having an allergy." She rubbed the back of her neck sheepishly. "I have been rather a handful this year. Maybe it's time I tamed my mischievous spirit and put my energy into more constructive things. Like netball. When I'm allowed," she added dejectedly.

Michal patted her. "It is upsetting. I wish you could play, but I'm sure you'll be back in the match next year."

"Maybe without you there, I'll have a chance to score a goal," Sherry teased. "It's hard to shine when you're so brilliant all the time."

Inexplicably, Michal narrowed her eyes at Sherry. "At least she never *let* you win."

"Why would you say that?" Sherry asked, startled.

Michal stared at her for a minute, then shook her head. "Never mind. Forget I said anything."

But Sherry didn't think she could.

~

The weather the next week was perfect for netball. The blue team, while upset to lose Bassy, knew they had to make the best of it. Glenda, the games captain, shuffled positions, and Sherry ended up playing goal attack for the red team. Michal put on the blue goal defense bib. She'd be defending against Sherry. *Great.* Sherry didn't relish having Michal's mysterious grudge between them throughout the game.

Leah, a decent player herself, was selected to take over for Bassy.

"I'm sorry you can't play," Leah said to Bassy as she donned her blue goal shooter bib. "And I think the rest of the team is miserable about it too."

Bassy patted her on the back. "You'll do a good job. And I'll be rooting for you."

Nearby, Rayla put on the red goal defense bib, taking Leah's usual position.

"You know, if it hadn't been for Mrs. Lee's allergy, that would have been a great trick, Bassy," she said. "It was so funny how we were all looking for Rabbit Two, but it didn't exist because you'd intentionally labeled them incorrectly. You fooled us all, but definitely whipped up some fun. It's just too bad it ended so poorly for you."

"Who says I mislabeled them?" Bassy said, winking.

Rayla's eyes widened. "But Mrs. Lee! She stopped sneezing. You didn't really have another rabbit in there somewhere, did you?"

Bassy grinned. "You'll never know, will you?"

Rayla laughed uncertainly, then turned toward the court.

Sherry caught Bassy's eye, wondering the same thing as Rayla. The twinkle in her friend's eyes gave her no answers.

Becky was refereeing again. She blew the whistle to bring the players onto the court. The teachers sitting at the edge of the court ceased conversation and hushed the students, who were seated on benches along the perimeter. All chatter ceased. The sudden silence increased the intensity of the moment. Sherry was the last to rush to her position, moments before Becky blew the whistle again and the game began.

The girls from each team chased the ball, seizing it, passing it, and intercepting their opponent's catch. They jumped, scuttled, and leaped, not taking their focus off the ball for even a second. It was a tight game, and the spectators cheered, riveted.

Sherry ran for the ball. Michal cut in to catch it but Sherry was faster, grasping the ball and throwing it as the referee blew the whistle for half-time. Everyone seemed to hold their breath as it flew through the air ... and into the goal.

"No!" shouted Nechama, the blue goal attack, in dismay.

"She scored! She scored!" Bassy cried, dancing on the spot.

Michal gave Sherry a small, approving smile. It was less than Sherry would have liked, but better than the glare she'd been giving her for most of the last few months. Considering that Sherry had cut in front of Michal for the ball, she was mildly surprised at the reaction.

"Two goals for blue, two goals for red," Becky announced. "The game will resume in ten minutes."

The players left the court, their cheeks flushed and sweat pouring down their faces. Bassy gave out cups of water, and Sherry drank hers gratefully.

"Not bad, Miss Lempel," Bassy said.

Sherry glanced at Michal to see her reaction to Bassy's praise, but Michal was looking at *her*. With a start, she realized that Bassy was too.

"Oh! You mean me," she said, flustered. "Thank you."

Baila wiped water from her chin and began to stretch. "Michal's doing pretty well, too."

Bassy grinned. "Those who once were friends can now say 'sis.' Never does a Lempel miss."

Michal chuckled. "I bet you never knew becoming a Lempel

would mean you'd gain a court advantage," she said to Sherry.

Sherry nodded. Michal had been teasing, but Sherry's throat felt thick. *I wonder when I'll* feel *like a Lempel, though.*

"Right," she said with forced cheerfulness. "That's just one of the *many* reasons I'm glad to be a Lempel now."

She gave Michal what she had intended to be a friendly smile, but something in her voice made Michal look oddly at her. Perhaps she wasn't hiding her discomfort over her new name as well as she thought. *It would help if Michal hadn't been so standoffish all year.*

Becky blew her whistle and the players returned to their positions. Sherry smiled at her sister from near the center line. "Good luck." Michal nodded from her position on the other side.

"You too, sis."

She sounded like she meant it.

With the game tied, both sides would have to work extra hard to score the winning goal. The second half was played at a frenetic pace. Sherry gave it her all, and Michal hardly ever got the ball away from her. However, she seldom let Sherry make a complete pass, either. The other players were having no better luck. By the time only two minutes remained, no goal had been scored.

"Work harder," Glenda urged.

The blue team had the ball. It was heading for their goal shooter, Leah, when Rayla darted in at an angle and caught it, then swiveled on the spot and threw it to Mindy, the red center, who threw it up the court to Rivi, the red goal shooter. Keren, the goal keeper, bumped it with her hands and tossed it to Baila, the blue center, who tossed it to Nechama. The tension was palpable, and the spectators buzzed with excitement.

Rayla managed to catch the ball again, but with less than a minute to go, she had hardly enough time to get it near the blue team's goalpost. She caught Sherry's eye and threw it toward her, way above their opponents. Sherry leapt into the air. Several hands grabbed for the ball, including Michal's. Sherry jumped above them all and grabbed the ball.

"Ten, nine, eight ..." the fans chanted from the sidelines as they counted down the seconds.

Cold beads of sweat trickled down Sherry's back. She had just five seconds left to score the winning goal. Girls lunged at her and she swerved left, then right. Just as Michal reached up to block her perfect shot, she squinted, focused on the net, and flung the ball into the air. She froze as it made a neat rainbow arc and slumped through the net.

It was in. She looked left and right, not quite believing that she'd done it. *I've shot the winning goal. The red team has won!*

Michal was looking strangely at her. Did she think Sherry had been too aggressive, that she should have given Michal a chance to get the ball?

"You did your best," Sherry said. "You almost got that last shot from me."

Michal nodded. "Thank you for showing me the respect of returning the favor." She walked off the court to get a drink.

Sherry cocked her head. *What did Michal mean by that?*

It wasn't the first odd comment Michal had made. Sherry remembered what she'd said yesterday about Bassy never letting Sherry win, and now she'd made this comment about giving her best effort.

Wait. Did Michal think Sherry had been letting her win at Scrabble? She hadn't. Michal had just beat her soundly four times out of seven—something that irritated Sherry to no end.

Deafening cheers from the jubilant onlookers boomed around the field. She wiped her forehead and couldn't hold back a huge smile as her teammates crowded around her to rejoice. She'd worry about Michal later.

"Wow, Sherry, you played so well," Rayla said as they walked toward the benches.

"It wasn't half as hard without Bassy on the opposing team," Sherry responded, flicking a sidelong glance at Bassy.

"There's our Sherry, modest and humble. But who on earth am I to grumble?" Bassy replied.

After many of the girls, and some of the teachers, had congratulated Sherry, she noticed Mrs. Pepper coming toward her. *Calm down, Sherry. It was only a game. There's more to life than scoring goals.* Still, she couldn't help but feel tiny bubbles of pride inside her when the headmistress greeted her with a "Well done, Sherry!"

As she turned back to talk with her friends, she tripped over a tree root and toppled to the ground. She shot up, ignoring the pain in her hands. She smoothed her hair and brushed off her skirt, hoping no one had noticed.

But of course, someone had.

"Pride comes before a fall, my dear," Nechama said, smirking and tossing her hair over her shoulder.

Mrs. Pepper, talking to some teachers nearby, gave Nechama a sharp glance, but the girl didn't seem to notice. Sherry was glad Mrs. Pepper didn't say anything. The last thing she wanted was a big scene calling attention to her embarrassing moment.

Rayla gave Nechama a big smile. "Are you still wondering about that needle, Nechama?"

Nechama glared at her, then flounced away, Leah beside her.

Rayla let out a breath and turned to Sherry.

"Whoa, I can't believe I said that. My knees are knocking together!"

Sherry wondered at her too. She scratched her nose, thinking.

"I'm not sure you should have said that, but it sure took pluck. Brave, aren't you?"

Rayla blushed. "You're right. I shouldn't have said that loud enough for everyone to hear. I'll do better next time."

She grew quiet and bit her lower lip.

"I can't be called brave, can I? I'm not here to fix anyone's issues, except my own, I suppose. Now, my mom, she's *really* brave. I wish I could be more like her."

Sherry put a hand on her friend's arm. "You came to a new school in a new country and you've done very well, despite how most of the other students have treated you all year. I think you're more like her than you realize."

Rayla's eyes were round and wet.

"Thank you, Sherry. You have no idea how much that means to me. I'm so glad I met you."

Smiling, the two girls returned to the school.

Neither one had noticed Michal listening to their conversation nor seen her stricken face as she watched them go.

14 The Trouble with Polka Dots

Visiting day was approaching, and the entire student body was eagerly preparing for their parents' arrival. They displayed needlework and hung paintings, decorated common rooms and dorm rooms, and gave the whole building a thorough scrubbing.

Rayla threw herself into the work, her pasted-on smile never leaving her face. Whenever anyone asked if her parents would be coming to visit, she just said no, they couldn't. Of course, the only ones who asked her were Mindy, Sherry and Mrs. Pepper. Michal looked like she wanted to say something once, but changed her mind.

It didn't matter. Rayla was determined to make the best of the day and help the other girls enjoy the festivities.

Maybe then, she could forget about the test results her mother had said she and Dad were waiting for—the ones that would tell them if Mom was getting worse, or if the treatment was having some effect. *Hashem, please let it be good news.* But as Rayla took in the commotion around her, she wished she could share in the fun for real, not as an act.

One day after school, she was sitting in the common room and reading the latest letter from Mom when Bassy, face flushed with excitement, interrupted her dismal thoughts.

"I say, let's paint the garden shed and put up a stand of drinks and goodies for when our families come." She rubbed her hands together. "Just think of the fun we'll have."

"The shed could do with a bit of cheering up," Baila said, nodding in agreement. "And nothing is as refreshing as a new coat of paint."

"Mrs. Pepper will never agree," Nechama said.

Bassy frowned. "You wait and see."

Rayla watched as she headed off to the headmistress's office. *Some pluck, that girl has.* Then she remembered her guitar, which she still kept stashed behind a bag of potting soil in the shed. *I'm going to have to move that, and soon.* She'd barely played lately, and the callouses on her hand were starting to fade. Maybe she could find a more accessible place to hide the guitar. But where?

She wondered if Mrs. Pepper would let her keep it in her office and then decided she didn't have nearly as much nerve as Bassy to ask.

Minutes later, Bassy reappeared, beaming with excitement. "Guess what? Mrs. Pepper has given us permission."

Several girls perked up at this announcement and gathered around Bassy.

Rayla folded the letter and put it in her bag. *Time to stop feeling sorry for myself. If Mom can keep being brave, so can I.*

She straightened, took a deep breath and joined the group, her smile back. "What color should we paint it?"

"Pink," Nechama answered. "Bright pink." She laughed. "With yellow polka dots."

Leah nodded. "I love polka dots. So festive!"

"Sky blue," Mindy suggested.

Baila clapped. "Fluorescent yellow."

Sherry also clapped. "Stripes! Let's do stripes."

Bassy jumped at the idea. "Ooh, stripes! That's fantastic!"

Nechama narrowed her eyes. "I say we vote. By show of hands, who wants polka dots?"

Leah, Nechama, Michal, and two other girls raised their hands.

"And who wants stripes?"

Sherry, Baila, Becky, Mindy, and Bassy raised their hands. All eyes turned to Rayla, who hadn't voted for either option.

"It's down to you, Rayla," Nechama said, an edge to her voice. "Which one do you want?"

Rayla looked at her classmates' faces. Something like this shouldn't be a big deal, but she could tell by the expression on Nechama's face that it *was* a big deal to her. She almost voted for polka dots, just to avoid conflict. But why should she appease Nechama? The girl had been mean to her all year long. And even though she'd thought that she and Michal had become friends after Rayla saved her life, Michal had still been distant. Not mean and rude, like before, but not exactly friendly, either. The only girls who had been nice to her were on the *stripes* side. She couldn't care less how the shed was painted, but since the pressure was on, she knew which side she'd vote for.

"I dunno. Stripes, I guess."

The girls who wanted stripes cheered. Nechama shot Rayla a nasty look, which she shrugged off. She'd expected no less.

Now that they had decided on a design, the girls began discussing the colors in earnest. All the girls but Nechama, that is. She sat in the corner of the room with her arms folded, fuming.

Rayla ignored her and smiled despite herself. The girls' excitement was contagious. They soon settled on stripes of peach, coral, and blue. All they needed to do now was purchase the supplies and their project could get underway.

Mrs. Pepper gave them money for paint and brushes and decided that Bassy and Baila would go to the shops together. While they were gone, the other girls changed into their work clothes.

Rayla took the opportunity to slip into the shed and get her guitar. Upon opening the door, she saw that Michal had had the same idea.

They stared at each other in silence. Michal held her painting folder in one hand and Rayla's guitar in the other.

"I was going to move this for you," she said. "I didn't know if you'd thought of it."

Rayla held out her hand and Michal handed her the guitar.

"Thanks," Rayla said and turned to go.

"Wait," Michal said.

Rayla turned. Michal shifted on her feet, fidgeting with her painting and looking at the ground. At last, she met Rayla's eyes.

"Look, I'm really sorry for how I've been acting. I'm upset with Sherry, but it's not your fault. It's just hard to see my only real friend here spend more time with you than with me."

Rayla blinked in surprise. *That* was what Michal had against her?

"I thought we were going to be friends after what happened at the cliffs. We could all spend time together, you know."

Michal nodded miserably. "I know. And I'm not ... I'm not normally like this. It just feels like everything's changing. First, I lost Mummy. And now, my father remarried and I've got two sisters and a brother I barely know. I mean, I know Sherry, and she's great. Well, most of the time ..."

She trailed off, frowning at something Rayla couldn't see.

"You know," Rayla said gently, "Sherry has been just as upset by how you've pushed her away all year as you are by, er, by whatever made you do it." She leaned against the door. "She wanted to spend time with you, but every time she asked you to do something with us, you said no or were nowhere to be found."

Michal blinked, her eyes suddenly moist. "What? I haven't been pushing her away. I've been ..."

Her shoulders slumped slowly, like a tire deflating. She sat on top of a large overturned terracotta pot, a stunned look on her face. "I have been pushing her away, I guess. How did I not see it?"

Rayla came and put a hand on her shoulder. "Sherry means a lot to me. But I know she means a lot to you, too. I mean, you two are sisters! I wouldn't ever want to come between you. We can all be friends together, can't we?"

Michal looked up at her, blinking away tears. "Yes. Yes, of course we can. I'm sorry, Rayla. I'll start doing better. Right now."

She looked at the painting in her hands and the guitar in Rayla's. "Now, what are we going to do with these?"

Rayla smiled. "I have an idea about that too. You know that cupboard in the music room? Not the main one, but the one in the corner that holds all the broken instruments that need repair? I'm sure they would fit in there, and no one ever looks inside it."

Michal nodded and stood, putting out her hand. "Friends?"

Rayla shook her hand. "Friends."

The sound of laughing girls spilling out of the school reached them.

Rayla looked at Michal in alarm. "Oh, no!"

Michal smiled. "It's okay. We'll go out the back way. Follow me."

Once Rayla and Michal had stashed their secrets in the instrument cupboard, they joined the rest of their classmates, who were waiting for Bassy and Baila at the shed. The two girls soon appeared, walking as fast as their heavy supplies would allow them.

"Great to see everyone in their work clothes," Bassy said. "We couldn't risk our uniforms getting splashed."

"Yeah, well, most of us managed to find work clothes. Some of us are better than that, apparently," Nechama said, with a meaningful glare at Rayla's outfit.

Rayla glanced down at herself, embarrassed. She hadn't come to Samphire prepared for this kind of work, and the best outfit she'd been able to find for the job was a pink twill skirt and white cotton blouse she'd worn to the seaside last summer.

"Knock it off, Nechama," Michal said. "You look fine, Rayla. Just be careful not to get paint on your sleeves."

"Thanks," Rayla whispered to Michal.

"Don't mention it," Michal said.

Sherry gave them a curious glance, but said nothing.

The girls had already cleared the debris and spiders' webs from the walls, window panes and ceiling while they waited for Baila and Bassy. Now, they used sandpaper to rub away the loose and flaked paint, which seemed to have been there for decades. As Rayla worked, her mind kept returning to her mother's letter. Whenever it did, she only worked harder, trying to banish the thought from her mind.

Once in a while, she caught Nechama glaring at her. Whenever the other girl noticed Rayla looking, she bent her head over the spot she was sanding. She seemed to be sanding the same spot for a very long time.

At last, Bassy declared the shed ready for its first coat. She took a brush and applied white primer around the edges, then moved to the ceiling. A few girls grabbed the paint rollers and got to work on the walls. They rolled up and down, moving around until they were sure every inch had been covered.

Sherry worked beside Rayla.

"Looks like you and Michal have patched things up?"

Rayla smiled. "I think we really did this time. High time the two of you worked things out too, wouldn't you say?"

Sherry started. "You mean, she wasn't just mad about you and me being friends?"

Rayla glanced at Michal, who was working on the other side of the shed. "Not *just* that, I don't think."

Michal caught her eye, and Rayla flashed her a genuine smile. It felt so good when Michal smiled back.

When the primer coat was finished, the girls took a break to let it dry. They went to drink lemonade and play Pictionary in the common room.

"No playing ball," Bassy had warned. "You're going to need all your strength for this job."

Nechama didn't join in the game. "There isn't an even number," she grumbled, glaring at Rayla as though it were her fault. "It wouldn't be fair."

She spent the break doodling in a notebook by herself.

Rayla kept glancing at her, thinking of her own advice to Sherry that it was time to clear the air with Michal. Wasn't it time she did the same with Nechama? She looked around at the other girls, who were busy shouting guesses at Mindy and her sketch on the chalkboard. She didn't want to confront Nechama here, in front of everyone.

But I'll do it soon, she promised herself.

After two hours, the primer had dried and the top coat could be applied. Michal measured even stripes, and Sherry marked them with masking tape, leaving every third stripe clear. Meanwhile, the other girls opened and stirred the paint, poured some of each color into wide paint trays, and dipped in their brushes and rollers.

Rayla caught Nechama looking at her dripping roller with a wicked gleam in her eye.

What could she be up to?

Once all the walls were marked, Michal walked around the whole shed, checking everything with a practiced eye.

"Excellent," she said at last. "We're ready to begin."

"Hey, everyone, start your rollers," Bassy said pompously, holding her roller aloft. It was saturated with peach paint.

Rayla stood poised with her roller, from which sky-blue paint dripped. As soon as she heard the word "Begin," she painted from the ceiling downwards. She hadn't realized how much energy it would take to keep the roller flush while applying an even amount of paint to each stripe. But her efforts were well rewarded.

"What a pretty color," Rivi said, admiring her work. "Rayla, I'm so glad you voted for stripes."

Rayla stopped and surveyed their progress. "Me too."

No sooner had she said that than she felt a roller run right down her back. Horrified, she turned to see Nechama standing there with her coral-colored roller extended and a wild look in her eyes.

"Nechama, what have you done?" Rivi exclaimed. "Rayla's outfit will be ruined!"

Nechama glanced at Rayla's back as though she had never seen it before. "Oh, oops. Didn't see you there."

Something snapped in Rayla. "What is your problem with me, anyway? What have I ever done to you?"

Nechama looked taken aback. She had obviously never

expected to be confronted so openly about her behavior. Then her face darkened.

"What's the big deal? You can just buy another outfit, can't you? You, with your rich parents and your limousine and fancy chocolates? Why does it even matter if you got some paint on you?"

By now, all the other girls had stopped working and were staring at them in awkward silence. Rayla didn't care.

"You think because my parents have money that I don't have problems, or that I don't want to take care of my things?"

She reached around her shoulder to touch her back. Her fingers came back wet with paint, and the moisture made her shirt cling to her.

"My mother and I made this shirt together. I didn't want to wear it today, but it was the closest thing I had to something appropriate for this activity. And now you've ruined it."

Her eyes filled with tears, and she knew that her emotions would spill over soon. Her act would be ruined. It didn't matter that Nechama no longer looked smug. Rayla had almost reached the breaking point.

"Rayla," Sherry said, taking a step forward.

But Rayla didn't dare stay another moment. She threw her roller in the direction of the paint tray and fled toward the school.

When she ran past the headmistress's office on her way to the dorm, Mrs. Pepper stepped into the hallway.

"No running in the halls, young—Rayla! What on earth has happened to you?"

"Ask Nechama," Rayla said, barely pausing before she dashed up the stairs.

She rushed to her washstand and let the warm water wash her tears away.

I'm sorry, Mom. I let you down. I just couldn't keep it up anymore.

Sherry and Michal Plan a Surprise

Michal, Sherry, and the other girls stood and stared at the defiant Nechama.

"Are you satisfied?" Leah asked, folding her arms.

Nechama shifted her weight. "Not you too, Leah."

One by one, the girls resumed painting the shed. Michal stepped over to Nechama. She could see Mrs. Pepper standing on the school steps, watching them with her arms folded.

"Nechama, that wasn't right," Michal said in a low voice. "You must know that. Rayla has done nothing to you."

Nechama glared at her, then threw her own roller into the paint tray and stalked away. When she saw Mrs. Pepper, she turned around and marched toward the trees in the backyard instead of toward the school. After a few minutes, Mrs. Pepper disappeared through the school doors.

Michal resumed her work, her thoughts preoccupied with Rayla and Nechama. Jealousy was such an ugly emotion, and in Nechama's jealousy she saw a reflection of her own.

All year, she'd been jealous of the time Sherry spent with Rayla. Michal was pretty sure, based on what she knew of Nechama's background, that she was jealous of Rayla's money. But because of the way both she and Nechama had behaved, someone innocent had been hurt. All Rayla had done was try to put on her best face, despite the difficult situation she was secretly going through. Even though Michal was still upset that Sherry had let Michal win the writing competition, she knew her sister's heart had been in the right place. She'd probably only wanted to help Michal feel better and perhaps mend their friendship. It was the type of thing Sherry would do.

Shame filled her stomach like a hot fire. That's *exactly* something Sherry would do. And Michal had been using Sherry's attempt at kindness as an excuse to push her sister even further away.

She approached Sherry, who was touching up a blue stripe with a brush. When Sherry noticed Michal, she gave her a surprised smile.

"Alright, Michal? Poor Rayla. I hope she can get the paint out of her shirt."

Michal nodded. "So do I." She paused. "Is it okay if I work here?"

Sherry beamed. "Please do."

They painted next to each other in silence, finishing the last few stripes on the wall they were working on.

"We're done," Bassy said a few minutes later, clapping her hands.

"It looks splendid," Rivi said with a dreamy sigh. "I mean, it's no Dover Castle, but it's wonderful."

Michal and Sherry cleaned up their supplies. When everything was put away, Michal turned to Sherry. She almost lost her nerve, but knew that it was time to deal with her own green monster. There was no more avoiding the issue.

She swallowed and took a deep breath.

"Would you come with me, please, Sherry? I want to show you something."

Sherry nodded. "Okay."

She led Sherry to the music room and took her art folder out of the instrument cabinet. They sat down next to each other.

Sherry raised an eyebrow. "What's this about, Michal?"

"Here," Michal said as she opened her folder and withdrew her painting.

Sherry's eyes were like saucers.

"Wow. Wow!" She could hardly speak. "I ... I've never seen a seascape as realistic as this," she said at last. "It makes me feel like I'm right there."

"I went to the cliffs to paint it," Michal explained.

"You did not!" Sherry's mouth hung open. "You, breaking the rules?"

"I know, I can hardly believe it myself. I was just so ... I don't know. I was feeling lonely and sad. I had to get away. I was scared, Sherry. I thought you were choosing Rayla over me, and it terrified me." She tugged her ponytail. The ribbon came undone and her hair fell loose around her shoulders.

"What made you think—"

"I know, I know, I was acting irrationally. Looking back, I think everything that happened lately—my father marrying your mother—shook me up more than I realized. I kept dreaming about my mother and wishing she would come back. Somehow, the marriage meant my fantasy would never come true. That hurt. I had this hollow, horrible ache. It made me act in a way that didn't make sense. And I thought I was losing you, too."

She twisted the ribbon around her fingers, then retied her hair into a neat ponytail.

Sherry studied the painting in stunned silence. Then she held Michal's hand and leaned closer.

"Michal, we're sisters, remember?"

"Yes, and your mother is very special." Michal looked at the floor. "If my father had to remarry, there's no one I would have wanted more as a new mother. I can't stop thanking Hashem for all the good I have."

She met her friend's eyes.

"Of course, I'll never stop missing my own mother. It wouldn't be possible for anyone to take her place. And yet, Sherry, what can I say? I'm so grateful."

Sherry looked thoughtful for a moment. Then her eyes twinkled and a smile crept over her face—a reaction that gave Michal much joy.

"This means so much to me," Sherry said. "It makes me so happy to know you're happy. And ... oh, how can I explain this?"

Michal nodded and blinked, compelling her to continue.

"I always wondered what you felt towards Ma, because she's my mother, and all. But even more than that, I felt we could only be a real family if you would realize how much she adores you in a way only a mother can."

A wave of relief and joy spread through Michal. "I don't remember the last time I felt this glad."

She looked at Sherry, her eyelids fluttering. "Sherry?"

"What is it, Michal?"

Sherry's face was full of sympathy. It reminded her of the time they had sat together during visiting day last year, and she had finally summed up the courage to tell Sherry about Mummy.

She took a deep breath. "Uh, can you forgive me? I'm sorrier than you can imagine. I've repaid your kindness in the most awful way. I feel so bad." She knew she was blushing a furious crimson but didn't care. Sherry deserved more than that. "Ouch. It's so painful to face one's mistakes."

"And yet so calming and purifying once we do," Sherry whispered. She rubbed Michal's shoulder. "We're all good," she said. A faint blush crept up her cheek. "Michal, I know what it feels like to make mistakes. But you know what Mrs. Pepper says, right? The main thing is to learn from them and not repeat them."

Michal nodded slowly.

They were quiet for several moments. Sherry stared at the painting.

"I have a confession to make too, Michal," she said at last.

Michal blinked. Was Sherry going to come clean about the writing competition? "Yes?"

"You know, Michal," Sherry said, and stopped. It seemed to Michal that Sherry changed her mind about something mid-sentence. "It's Ma's birthday next week, the day after visiting day," Sherry said. "I was wondering if you would like to choose a present for her together. She would be so touched."

"Oh, really?" Michal sat up and then looked down at her hands. "But what can we give her?" Her eyes fell on the seascape that her own mother would have loved so much, and it came to her. "What if we give her my painting?"

Sherry looked again at the artwork. "Are you sure?" she asked. "It's yours. You put so much work and heart into it."

"And there's nothing more I want to do than give it to Ma."

"Wow! That is something. You know how much she loves paintings. She'll absolutely adore this. Especially when she realizes you painted it."

"I've got an idea. Let's make this gift-giving even more exciting.

You know that art store on the corner of Lake Avenue? Let's have it framed there and wrapped up. That way, she won't know I painted it—at first."

Sherry chuckled. "And when she finds out, she'll be so stunned. It will be as if she's received the present all over again."

Michal put her painting back in the folder and, together, the girls planned their excursion. During their lunch break the next day, they would sneak out to have the picture framed and then present it to Ma when she came the following week. With that decision made, Michal stashed her painting in the cupboard, and they went to clean up for supper.

"I noticed that you and Rayla seem to be getting along much better," Sherry said lightly as they left the room.

Michal's face flushed. Sherry raised an eyebrow.

"I know," Michal said. "I acted nastily towards Rayla as well, but I think we've made up now. Asking Rayla *mechilah* was possibly the hardest thing I've ever had to do. And it was then that I realized how I've behaved similarly towards you. Why don't we go check on her and see what happened with her blouse?"

Just then, Nechama walked by holding a shirt with coral stripes. Rayla's shirt. She refused to meet Michal's or Sherry's eye. Down the corridor, Mrs. Pepper looked on with a satisfied gaze, then retreated into her office.

Sherry and Michal exchanged glances.

"Well, let's hope that's the end of that," said Sherry. "She must be going to clean it for Rayla. I've had quite enough stormy winds for one year, haven't you?"

Michal jumped. Did Sherry know about her accident at the cliffs? Had Rayla told her?

But Sherry's bright smile showed no indication that another

meaning lay behind her words. At that moment, Michal realized she was no longer angry with Sherry about the writing competition. In the end, it didn't seem to matter that much.

Michal squeezed her friend's shoulders. "I'm glad we're friends again."

Sherry smiled back. "Me too. I've really missed you."

Michal smiled too, glowing. "Now let's go see if Rayla is feeling well enough to come down to supper."

16 Nechama Is Taught a Lesson

Rayla was unusually quiet throughout the following week, even for her. Sherry watched her worriedly. Was she very upset about what Nechama had done? She thought not. Nechama had been mean all year, and Rayla had borne it with bravery and kindness. No, there was something more going on. She was determined to find out what it was.

But whenever she asked Rayla what was bothering her, her friend only turned her smile up a notch and said, "Nothing, why do you ask?"

During lunch break on Tuesday, Michal, Sherry, and Rayla were passing by the office on their way to the dining room when Mrs. Hayley caught Michal's attention.

"I have a parcel for you. For both of you, actually," she said, indicating Sherry.

She handed Michal a medium-sized box. Sherry peeked at the address.

To the Lempel girls.

Sherry's heart skipped. That *did* include her, but it still felt so strange.

"It's from Ma and Tatty," Michal said. "What do you think it is?"

"I don't know. Let's go open it and find out."

They took the box into a nearby classroom and set it on a desk to open it. Sherry waited patiently as Michal slit the tape that bound it and withdrew items one at a time. There was a tag attached to each item.

Michal squinted at one. "This is for you from Ma."

She handed over a hardcover book with the title *The Exiles of Crocodile Island.*

Sherry clapped. She'd wanted this book for ages, but it had gone out of print long ago. Ma had promised to look for it the next time she was in London.

"Ma found it," she said, tracing the gold foil-stamped letters on the cover.

Michal had already pulled out the next item—a how-to book for painting detailed watercolor flowers. "Oh, how thoughtful. Ma always knows just what to get."

She flipped through the book. Rayla admired the paintings in the book over Michal's shoulder.

The next box contained freshly baked flapjacks. Sherry cracked open the lid and held out the box.

"Only one for now. We don't want to ruin our lunch. We'll share them with the class later."

"Good idea," Michal agreed.

Rayla peeked in the box, her flapjack in one hand. "There are two more things."

Sherry looked inside and pulled out a new set of paintbrushes. She handed these to Michal without even reading the tag. Michal accepted them and peeked at the label.

"Tatty bought these at Holdsworth's, he says. How nice of him to think of me." She placed the paintbrushes on top of her new book. "What did he get you?"

Sherry read the tag on the last item, a set of ordinary school-grade colored pencils. A simple *For Sherry, from Tatty* was all it said. She turned the package over in her hand. What was she meant to do with this? Did he think she might have run out of pencils?

"Here, Michal," she said, thrusting them toward her sister. "These are addressed to me, but I think you would make better use of them. You sketch way more than I do, so you use your pencils up more quickly."

Michal took them, looking troubled. "Are you sure? Tatty must have wanted you to have them for a reason."

Sherry shrugged. "I just don't know what. I have plenty of colored pencils left. Oh, well. It's the thought that counts, I suppose."

But as they took their new treasures to their lockers and went to join their class in the dining room, she couldn't help thinking that not much thought had gone into the gift at all. It had seemed like an afterthought, something her new father had grabbed while he was in the art section so she wouldn't feel left out, not something that would have real meaning to her.

She exhaled slowly. Tatty would be driving down Ma and Chava for visiting day. She'd make sure to thank him for the pencils then. At least he'd tried.

Later that day, still feeling despondent, Sherry pulled out the journal of the stories that Papa had told her and she had written down. She'd given the good copy to her mother as a gift the previous summer, but she'd kept the rough drafts for herself. Wanting to be alone, she went to sit in the music room rather than take it to the common room where her classmates might want to talk to her.

She had so many good memories of Papa. Rabbi Spencer had been an engaging lecturer, but an even kinder, gentler father.

She was flipping through a story Papa had told of "Glad Gadi," who survived all his trials with a *siddur* in his hand and a smile on his lips, when the door of the room swung open. She looked up to see Rayla standing there, surprise and a bit of dismay on her face.

"I'm sorry," she said. "I didn't know anyone was in here, Sherry. Do you want me to leave you alone?"

Sherry smiled. "No, come in. What are you doing here?"

Rayla's face grew red, but she made her way to the cupboard—the same one where the framed, wrapped painting for Ma was stashed behind a broken xylophone—and pulled out a guitar.

"Don't tell anyone," she said. "I came to practice."

Sherry grinned. "I *thought* that guitar looked a little too new to be in that cupboard. I mean, uh ..."

"It's okay. I know all about Michal's painting and your surprise for your mother."

"You do? Oh."

Sherry looked at the journal in her hands. Rayla always seemed to know much more about her and Michal than either of them knew about her. Maybe that was because she was more observant—she listened more than she spoke. And she spoke so seldom.

"Would you mind if I stayed to read while you practice? I won't be a bother, and I could use a little cheering up right now."

Rayla hesitated, then smiled. "I suppose. I don't like playing in front of people, but if my music would make you feel better, then I'd love to help."

She sat and began to strum through a poignant chord

progression in a gentle, rhythmic beat. Sherry tried to go back to reading, but soon found herself caught up in the music. Rayla was humming a melody beneath her breath, and Sherry caught just enough to know it was unfamiliar.

"What song is that? I've never heard it before."

Rayla stopped playing and rested her hands on her instrument. "Oh, it's nothing special. It's a song I wrote. Just a ditty, really."

Sherry straightened, impressed. "Not at all! That's one of the loveliest songs I've ever heard. I can't believe you wrote it."

Rayla's face turned the color of beets. "Thank you," she mumbled.

"Would you sing it for me?"

Rayla looked like she was about to refuse.

"Please?"

"Okay," Rayla said reluctantly, putting her fingers back on the strings.

Sherry closed her eyes and listened, carried away by the music. The lyrics spoke of Hashem's endless kindness, how He never leaves us. Like a shepherd caring for his sheep, each of them is always in His tender care, no matter what dark valley he may be walking through. Rayla had obviously taken the inspiration from Tehillim, but she had composed the song completely on her own.

When the notes faded, Sherry opened her eyes.

"That was incredible," she said.

Rayla ducked her head in embarrassment and got up to return the guitar to the cupboard. Then she turned around, suddenly decisive.

"It's for my mother."

Sherry smiled. "I know she'll love it."

Rayla nodded. "If she gets to hear it."

"Can't you play it for her at the end of the year when you go back to New York?"

Rayla shook her head and took a breath. "She's not in New York. She's in Manchester. She's been there with my father all year so she can undergo treatment."

Rayla sat beside Sherry. Sherry swallowed. *Treatment.* She knew what that meant, even before Rayla continued.

"My mother's sick, Sherry. And ... oh, I can't bear this alone anymore. When I spoke to her last night, she had just gotten some test results back. The treatment doesn't seem to be working." She swallowed, her eyes moist. "They think she's only got about three months to live."

Sherry's throat thickened. *This* was why Rayla had come to Samphire this year? This burden was what lay behind all her bright smiles? No wonder Rayla had been so subdued lately.

"I've been as blind as Nechama," she said to herself.

"What? No, you haven't," Rayla said, frowning.

"But why didn't you tell anyone earlier?"

Rayla looked at the floor. "I did. I told Michal, after I saved her on the cliffs."

"What?" Sherry's heart thumped.

Rayla's gaze flew up to Sherry's. "Oh! I thought she must have told you... Never mind. I wasn't supposed to tell you about that. Please don't tell her I said anything."

"It was while she was painting?" What had Sherry missed while she was overlooking Michal's moodiness all year? Guilt stabbed her. She'd promised herself that she'd make Michal feel welcome in her family, but Michal had felt alone—so alone that she'd kept breaking the rules to paint on the cliffs. And she'd nearly had a bad accident, apparently.

Rayla nodded. "But it ended well, *baruch Hashem.* As far as how the others have been behaving, it didn't bother me that much. I mean, someone who is going to judge someone she just met is not someone I want for a friend, anyway. It was enough for me to have a few friends—you, Mindy, Becky, and eventually Michal. Besides, I had bigger things to worry about than a few mean comments."

"Did you ever." Sherry was pensive. "No wonder you were so upset when Nechama painted the blouse you made with your mom. Was she able to clean it?"

Rayla sighed. "Not really." She looked up at Sherry. "You know, even though you and Michal haven't been on the best terms this year, seeing the two of you and hearing your story gives me hope. I mean, I'm really sad about Mom. But of course, we're not giving up. I just have to keep trusting Hashem that He's going to make something beautiful come out of all this pain. Just like the song I played for you. He's been walking with me the whole time." She looked down and shook her head. "*Im yirtzeh Hashem*, Mom will get better. And one day, we'll look back and see that the journey was all good."

Sherry stared at the American girl, once again amazed at her. Her *bitachon* was real. Even when her world was falling apart, her faith didn't waver.

"You're really something, you know that, Rayla? I'm glad you came to Samphire this year."

Rayla smiled shyly. "Me too." She stood up. "I'll leave you to your reading. Have fun."

"You too."

As Sherry looked down at her journal, a warm feeling filled her heart. She *was* pretty blessed. It might take some time for their family to blend, but that's all it would take—time. Time was something that Rayla's mother apparently didn't have—according to the doctors. *Hashem, please help Rayla's mother pull through.* She thought of Papa's story about "Glad Gadi" and how he had taught her to count life's endless joys and blessings. She'd been focusing on the small things that were going wrong instead of on the gifts she had been given. She still didn't know what Tatty had meant by giving her the pencils, but she had to recognize that it was a present of sorts.

And she was grateful beyond belief.

"I'm Sherry Lempel," she whispered.

And smiled.

No sooner had Rayla closed the door behind her than the curtains rustled and Nechama fell out of them with a tremendous crash.

Sherry stared in horror. "Have you been there all this time?"

What would Nechama do with all the secrets that had just been shared?

Nechama didn't look aggressive, though. She was holding her calf and wincing in pain. "Yes. Popular place to go to be alone, apparently." Her face scrunched in pain. "Wow, I thought she'd never leave. I got the worst cramp in my leg and didn't think I'd make it."

She bent her head to massage her leg for a minute, and Sherry got the impression she was hiding her face. When she looked at Sherry again, her expression was stricken.

"I've been a total heel this year, haven't I?"

Sherry chewed her lip, but nodded. "It certainly hasn't been your finest performance."

"I know." Nechama squeezed her eyes shut as though that would change everything that had happened before, then opened them. "I haven't had a moment's peace since I ruined the shirt. And now this. Rayla's mother. It really puts things in perspective, doesn't it?" She shook her head. "The poor thing."

Sherry almost gagged at her words. "I don't think she'd be very happy if she knew you know. She's kept it a secret all year for a reason."

Nechama nodded. "I wonder what I can do to show her how sorry I am and help her feel better without letting on that I know her secret."

Sherry blinked. "You're going to keep her secret?" That seemed so unlike Nechama.

Nechama smiled sheepishly. "I owe her that and more, don't you think?"

"Oh, much more."

Nechama wrapped her arms around her knees, still sitting on the wooden floor. She frowned, obviously deep in thought. Then she brightened.

"Do you remember when Mrs. Pepper gave us that strange lesson earlier this year? The one with the flowers?"

Sherry thought back to the lesson. They'd each been given two potted plants and some very odd instructions.

"You mean the one where we each froze one of our plants for several nights and took care of the other one properly?"

Nechama nodded, as though Sherry had just said something brilliant. "That one. Rayla was so upset that she had to put one of her plants in the freezer. She knew it would die. She practically cried when it turned black and wilted."

Sherry frowned. "Where are you going with this, Nechama?"

Nechama got to her feet. "Don't you see? The point of the lesson. I can't believe it took this long for me to grasp it."

The lesson had been given months ago, in the depths of the winter when tensions between the students had been running high—in particular, tensions between Nechama and Rayla. And the situation had only escalated since then.

"It's easy to understand how Plant A flourished so well," Mrs.

Pepper had said. "You watered it so it had the nutrients it needed to grow. You provided it with sunlight so it had the energy to thrive. But what happened to Plant B?" She looked around the room. "Why does Plant B look so forlorn?"

"The cold damaged it," Rayla had answered.

"Cold can cause damage," Mrs. Pepper had agreed. "Now, while I hope you enjoyed this little horticultural exercise, there was something more I wanted to teach you. Can anyone think what it was?"

After several guesses that were not quite right, she elaborated.

"You are each blessed with an abundant supply of water and sunlight, so you can enable your buds to flourish. What is this water and sunlight?"

"Kindness," Sherry answered, catching on.

"A good word," Becky said.

"Tolerance," Leah suggested.

"Gentleness," Mindy offered.

Mrs. Pepper went around the class, allowing each girl to give an answer.

Nechama's answer had taken the longest to come.

"Uh ... um ... uh ... compassion!"

Mrs. Pepper seemed satisfied. "Good." Her gaze traveled across the classroom. "So, you see, 'water' and 'sunlight' hold power. Now, I want you to remember this lesson. Each one of you can make a difference in the lives of the people around you."

She held up Bassy's Plant B for everyone to see. "What causes the buds to droop?"

"Mean comments," Bassy answered.

"Icy stares," Rivi said.

"Acting coldly," Michal suggested.

"Cold and darkness damage both plants and people," Mrs. Pepper said. "Badly. And this is one power we never, ever want to use."

But Mrs. Pepper wasn't finished. "And now I want to show you something." A half-smile lifted the corner of her mouth, and she had a glint in her eye. "Each of you take your pot with Plant A and gently unscrew the top part of it."

The memory faded and Sherry blinked at Nechama, who now stood over her in the music room.

"You finally get it," Sherry said.

Nechama nodded solemnly, heading toward the door. "I finally get it. And I know just what to do for Rayla."

Sherry watched her go, remembering the final part of the lesson Mrs. Pepper had imparted.

Each girl had done as Mrs. Pepper had instructed and loosened the top part of the pot containing the thriving green sprout, by twisting it. Sherry had stared, shocked by what she'd found. Beneath that pot was a second pot that contained a vivid, slender flower.

"A fuchsia," Mrs. Pepper had explained, pointing to the flower. "It requires just a bit of sunlight, but it, too, needs watering. Each time you watered the plant, some of the water seeped into the pot beneath it. And what happened? A beautiful flower started to grow.

"Girls, remember this—each time you perform an act of kindness or pay a genuine compliment to someone else, you are watering your own plant too. Nothing helps you grow more than helping another person to flourish."

She smiled as she gathered her things. "That's it, girls. And happy watering to you all."

Sherry came back to the present, looking at the journal in her hand. At last, she stood and left the music room, turning off the light and closing the door behind her.

She had some watering of her own to do.

17 Back in Manchester

It was the day before visiting day. Rayla's thoughts and heart were in Manchester. There was a hollow pit in her stomach that kept growing bigger. The school was abuzz with excitement, but the day held no merriment for her. She breathed in deeply. The act was still on, but she was fed up with playing her part. She was sad, sad, sad, and all she wanted was to hide in her bed and cry. Around her, clusters of girls were chatting amicably. Her gaze passed over them, almost unseeingly. Nechama noticed her and gave her a strange look. Rayla couldn't figure out what it meant, but she didn't care. Her mother was ill in Manchester. And that knowledge was all-consuming.

She shook herself and gritted her teeth. *What's with you, Rayla? Stop drowning in your own misery. Think about Mom. She's the one who is unwell, and is she falling to pieces? No. So pull yourself together and act your part—just as Mom would want you to.*

She pasted a smile on her face and took a step toward Nechama and her group. *Hey, here we go—Smiley Rayla, on stage once more.*

In Manchester, Rayla's parents, Danny and Leora Russell, were sitting on plush living-room couches, both on tenterhooks. Leora had gone for a new experimental treatment, despite the doctor's misgivings—they put all their trust and faith in the Ultimate Doctor. Now, the latest test results had come in and they were waiting for Dr. Wilson's call.

The phone rang and Leora jumped. "Hello?"

"I am calling from Blue Bananas. Would you be interested in a sample of our latest beauty product ...?"

Leora gritted her teeth. *These telemarketing calls should be banned. How dare she call me now?*

"What is it?" Danny mouthed.

"A telemarketer."

He grabbed the receiver and banged it down.

Almost instantly, it rang again.

Leora lunged forward. "Hello?"

"Hi, Leora, what's up?"

Please! Not now.

"Er ... great, Nava," she said to her new neighbor.

"Want to join me for a stroll?"

"Er ... maybe. Er ..."

"What's going on? Why are you acting so weird?"

"Er, nothing. Nothing at all. Listen, Nava, I'm ... I'm in the middle of something now. I'll call you in a bit, okay?" Her shoulders slumped and she sank into her seat. "I can't do this!" She closed her eyes. *This is all too much.* In her weakened state, she barely heard the phone when it rang again.

"Danny, you take it," she mumbled. She shut her eyes tighter.

A few moments later, his shout made her eyes fly open.

"Are you sure?" he cried. Then he danced a jig, right there on the Oriental rug. Placid, unflappable Danny. Leora sat up. Danny came toward her, his eyes bright enough to drive away the darkest of nights.

"*Baruch Hashem*," she whispered. Right then, she felt more alive than she had ever felt before. "I'm calling our kids. There's nothing I want more than to take them someplace beautiful and feel the wind on our faces as we run, carefree."

He shook his head, the smile not leaving his eyes. "You mustn't tire yourself out just yet. Doctor's orders."

"You know what?" Her breath quickened. "Let's go to a hotel in Samphire. I could do with some fresh sea air." Now he was smiling, too. "But let's keep this a secret and surprise Rayla once we arrive."

In a jiffy, he arranged the trip—tickets, hotel, and all. Then Leora picked up the receiver to call Mrs. Pepper.

The phone rang for a long time, but there was no answer. Danny raised a questioning eyebrow.

"Mrs. Pepper's not picking up," Leora mouthed.

"Then we'll have to surprise her too," Danny said, laughing. "We better get cracking—there's no time to waste."

18 The Finale

Visiting day arrived, and the girls got out of bed bright and early. They had arranged to daven at *netz*, so they would have ample time to prepare for their families' arrival. As soon as Shacharis was over, many of them headed to the garden to wait for their parents to appear. Sherry and Michal stayed indoors, choosing a strategic window that afforded them a good view of the driveway. They had deposited the gift-wrapped painting next to the wall, in a secluded area of the parking lot, ready to present to Ma at the right moment. It was visible from their lookout spot, so they could still keep a watchful eye.

Sherry could hardly wait for Ma to see it. She patted her pocket where a treasure of her own waited to be presented—poems of appreciation she'd written to each member of her family. Finding time to write them when Michal was otherwise occupied had been tricky.

Michal tugged on her ponytail. "Oh, I hope she likes it. Do you think she'll like it?"

Sherry laughed and batted at her hand. "Stop doing that, you'll ruin your ribbon. And of course she'll like it. There's no need to be nervous."

Michal nodded, but the worried gleam didn't leave her eyes.

Soon, Tatty's car pulled up in the driveway.

"Say," Sherry said as they rushed out the building, almost tripping at the entrance steps, "has Mrs. Pepper said anything about the writing competition? I'm certain you're going to win, and I can hardly stand the wait to find out."

Michal gave her an unreadable look. "Not yet. I'm sure you'll know as soon as I do."

Sherry smiled. "Okay. Just checking."

Ma and Chava came toward them, and Sherry and Michal threw their arms around their mother and sister, who both exclaimed at how much the girls had grown.

"We're so glad you could come," Sherry gushed. "I can't wait to show you the challah cover I made. The embroidery is gorgeous."

Ma's brown eyes twinkled. "I'm sure it's lovely, Sherry—it will look beautiful on our Shabbos table."

Tatty locked the car, turned to them and grinned.

"Good to see you both," he said, fixing a long gaze on Michal.

Michal cleared her throat, and Sherry remembered the cue. She gave a few loud coughs to distract her family. Meanwhile, Michal stepped over to the wall and picked up the gold paper-wrapped painting. Then she handed it to an astonished Ma.

"This is from me and Sherry. It's for your birthday."

Ma's face lit up with delight, and Chava beamed at her sisters.

"You remembered!" Ma exclaimed.

She ran her fingers beneath the tape and pulled off the paper, which Chava took so she could look at what was inside. Her face was agog as she examined the painting.

"Oh, my. I've never seen such a beautiful painting. It must have cost a pretty penny."

Michal's face flushed. She made several attempts to speak, but no words came out. Sherry nudged her and smiled, delighted that she was so happy.

"Look at this, Yehudah," Ma said, showing him the painting. "Look at the exquisite detail on the cliffs, and the play of light. The artist is exceptional. Do you think Bubby would like one too?"

Tatty nodded, his glasses slipping, as he bent close to admire the intricate rock texture. "I'm certain she would. Where did you girls get it?"

Sherry thought she might burst from excitement. She waited for Michal to speak up and reveal the best part, but her sister seemed to have lost her voice.

"Oh, Ma," Sherry said, "the painting comes from a special place. It's called ML."

"I don't think I've ever heard of that store before."

"Of course you have, Ma," Sherry teased. "In fact, you spent much of your summer in the company of the artist."

Ma looked sharply at her. "What are you talking about, Sherry? Are you playing a joke on me?"

"But, Ma, it's true! In fact, ML is standing right in front of you."

Sherry linked her arm with Michal's. Standing behind Ma, Chava grinned and shook her head as she caught on. Ma squinted at the artist's signature in the bottom corner, and her eyebrows rose in comprehension and surprise.

Michal smiled as though her heart might burst.

"Don't tell me," Ma blurted out. "Michal painted this? But the artwork is magnificent. Michal, you must have spent hours on it. And ... you did it all for me?"

She handed the painting to Chava and gathered her newest daughter into a crushing hug. "Thank you, sweetheart. This means so much to me."

Michal only nodded. "You deserve it."

Sherry waited for them to separate, wondering if she should present her own gift now. But no. She would wait until Ma had had a chance to properly absorb Michal's gift. There was no need to steal her sunshine.

Chava helped Ma put the painting back into the paper to protect it, and Tatty took it with him to the car so they wouldn't have to carry it around. There was so much to catch up on as they made their way toward the hall where the Form Three artwork was displayed. Chava told them about her experiences in the classroom and Ma talked about her garden and Mrs. Meisels, the elderly lady who had just moved in next door.

Then Chava asked about new developments at Samphire, gazing about with a nostalgic air. "I can't believe it's been almost a year since I was here. Everything looks exactly the same, but it feels like ages have passed! Tell me everything."

"But lots *has* changed. Bassy is our star netball player now."

"She was always pretty good," Chava commented.

"And so is Sherry," Michal said. "She scored the winning goal in the matches."

"Did you?" Ma raised her eyebrows at Sherry, and a feeling of warmth radiated in Sherry's chest. "Well done, Sherry."

Sherry couldn't help but notice the happy smile on Michal's face too.

"We also made a new friend," Michal added. "An American girl named Rayla."

"Yes!" Sherry said. "I can't wait for you to meet her."

She stopped short and looked at Michal. "Say, I haven't seen her this morning. Where *is* Rayla?"

Michal shrugged. "I don't know. Probably in the snack shack by now. She had her name down in almost every slot, remember?"

Sherry nodded and resumed being the enthusiastic hostess. "Great. You'll get to meet her when we go for lemonade later—and you'll get to see a special surprise too, but I'm not saying anything else for now. Let's go to the common room next ..."

While the other girls woke up early and hurried to prepare for visiting day, Rayla had remained in the dorm, huddled beneath her blanket. The sky was brushed in colorful strokes of faith and promise, but for Rayla it was all black. She shielded her eyes as if to block out the false hope that the sunrise heralded.

I must be the only one dreading today.

How she wished things could be different—that her parents could come visit, and that the visit would be unmarred by the anguish of her mother's illness. But then she thought of the rest of her classmates: Sherry and Michal, Becky and Mindy, and Bassy with her on-the-mark rhymes. In a flash, she threw off her covers and stood up, telling herself that she wouldn't let the day bring her down. The show was still on.

I'll make fresh lemonade and let the other girls have the full day to spend with their families.

Once she was ready, she headed straight to the shed, where the girls had allocated themselves time slots to manage the stall. She had volunteered to serve in the stand for most of the day to keep her mind off the fact that she had no family coming to see her. That, and the dreadful test results.

Her heart thumped as she thought about her mother lying

miserably on a hospital bed instead of spending a glorious day outdoors.

She shook her head. *Don't go there! What does Mom always say? "It's one's attitude alone that has the authority to determine whether a day will be good or bad."*

"Well," she said to herself, "I choose *good*."

Mrs. Pepper saw her at the shed while she was making her rounds. She excused herself from the family she was speaking with and came over to get a cup of lemonade.

"It's kind of you to volunteer," she said as she accepted it, then leaned closer. "You're a strong girl, Rayla."

Rayla gave a doubtful smile. *It's all an act. I wish I really were strong.* "Thank you," was all she said.

Rayla was hard at work, mixing freshly squeezed lemons with sugar and cold water in a jug. Then she looked up and saw Nechama standing at the window, only her head and shoulders visible.

Her stomach twisted in dread. While she could usually handle Nechama's poison, she didn't think she was up to it today.

"May I have a cup of lemonade and a Chelsea bun, please?" Nechama's voice showed no hint of disrespect or malice. In fact, it was pleasant, even. And then she did something completely unexpected—she gave Rayla a sweet, genuine smile.

Rayla poured liquid into a cup and placed the bun on a paper napkin, watching Nechama surreptitiously out of the corner of her eye. She had to be up to something. Something that was likely to ruin Rayla's day for good.

But when she brought over the lemonade and the snack, Nechama blushed a little and held up her hands so Rayla could see a potted hydrangea with plush, lilac blooms.

"Here," Nechama said. "This is for you. I want you to have it because ... because I'm really sorry for how I've acted all year. I know a plant can't make up for how terrible I've been, but I know how much you love flowers, so I hope it brings you a little joy."

Rayla blinked in shock as she accepted the pot from Nechama's hand. "Er, thanks, Nechama."

Nechama smiled. "No thanks necessary. I owe you at least that much." She picked up her lemonade and took a sip. "This is delicious. Thank you."

She lifted her cup in a mock-toast, then turned and walked away, leaving Rayla standing in dumbfounded shock, the plant still in her hands.

Bassy's head appeared in the window. "When every tour is said and done, there's nothing like snacks for everyone. Three lemonades, please."

A short distance behind her, Rayla noticed Bassy's mother and a little girl who must have been her sister, judging from the matching unruly hair and freckles.

"Er ..." Rayla looked around and spotted a place to put the plant near the back of the shed, on a bench that had been scrubbed and painted blue. She prepared the lemonade and set the cups in a small cardboard box on the window ledge. "Just bring back the box when you're finished, please."

"Sure thing," Bassy said. She handed Rayla a potted tulip with yellow buds nearly ready to open. "Payment in kind."

"What?" Rayla said, finding herself holding another pot of flowers in her hands.

But Bassy had already taken the makeshift tray and walked away, and Baila's head popped into view. She placed a potted iris on the shelf.

"Two lemonades, please."

Rayla stared at the third plant in amazement. With the tulip still in her hands, she stepped out the door to see every girl in the third form standing in a line snaking around the shed—and every single one of them had a potted flower in her hands.

Rayla gaped. "What is going on?"

Sherry heard and turned toward her, her eyes twinkling. "It was Nechama's idea. She asked her mother to bring all these flowers from a shop in town."

"She did?"

Rayla searched for Nechama in the yard. When she found her, she saw Nechama watching her with her arms folded—but instead of the familiar sneer on her face, she was beaming with joy.

"Uh-huh." Sherry came close. "She told me she noticed how much you love flowers. She wanted to make up for her behavior all year."

"I—I don't know what to say." Rayla looked in shock at the tulip she still held. Never in a million years would she have guessed that Nechama was capable of such kindness. She blinked back tears. *If only Mom had been able to come and see it.*

"Thank you, everyone. I don't know what to say," she repeated.

She took the pot into the shed and blinked at another surprise. While she and Sherry had been speaking, the rest of the girls had filed into the shed and placed the pots along the shelves at the back and sides, leaving just enough room for the snacks and lemonade. It looked like a charming English cottage bursting with cheer.

Rayla found a little space next to a Gerber daisy and wedged the tulip in. When she turned around, her classmates were all smiling at her just outside the door, with Nechama at the front.

"No, thank *you*, Rayla," Nechama said. "You have shown me what kindness and bravery really mean."

Something in her face made Rayla look twice. Did Nechama

know something she shouldn't? But Nechama just smiled and returned to her family, and the other girls did the same—except for a few who lined up because they truly did want some lemonade.

At a quiet moment, Nechama came up to her again, a brown envelope in her hand. "Rayla," she said, "my mother lent me some money. I… I'm going to do some odd jobs for neighbors during the holidays to pay for the shirt I ruined." She twisted her watch. "I'm so sorry, Rayla. I've acted so unkindly to you. I guess it was hard seeing you with so much money… when things are…" She ran her fingers through her short black hair. "Uh, when things are different for me back home."

Rayla stared at her. Suddenly, she saw Nechama in a way she hadn't seen her before. Not that she could ever justify Nechama's nasty behavior, but maybe she could try to understand her anyway.

"It's okay," she said, offering her widest smile. "All is forgiven."

Nechama let out a deep breath. "I really can never thank you enough."

A group of girls rushed toward the shed, and Nechama waved and left.

Just then, a first former came dashing up to her. "Rayla, Mrs. Pepper is calling for you. She's in her office."

Rayla looked helplessly at the line of girls.

"Go," Mindy said, stepping inside the shed. "I'll cover for you."

"Thanks!" Rayla hurried toward the school.

What could Mrs. Pepper want from me?

When she stepped inside the office, the dazzling smile on the headmistress's face startled her. The woman was positively beaming. Rayla glanced about the room, not sure how to respond.

"Rayla, I have something wonderful to tell you." Mrs. Pepper's voice was soft and tender. She patted Rayla on the back. "It's good news. Wonderful news. Your mother ..."

"What about her?" Rayla's voice came out in a squeak. What could have happened since they spoke only two days ago?

Mrs. Pepper pressed her lips together. "Perhaps I best let her tell you herself."

Rayla glanced at the phone, which was on the receiver. Mrs. Pepper followed her gaze.

"No, she's in the third form common room, with your father."

"What?!" Rayla couldn't talk. Mom and Dad were *here*? How was that possible?

"What are you waiting for?" Mrs. Pepper made a shooing motion. "Run along."

Rayla rushed out of the room, running until she burst through the door of the common room, out of breath.

Sure enough, there were her parents, sitting on the couch next to the fireplace. She dashed toward them and stopped, suddenly uncertain.

"Mom! Dad! You've come! Mrs. Pepper said you have wonderful news. Please tell me. I can barely stand the suspense."

Her parents were beaming.

Mom's smile was arresting, spreading warm rays all over her face. "The test results—the latest ones are glorious. The treatment *is* working."

Rayla stared at her mother in shock, barely daring to believe her ears.

"Mom is getting better," Dad said, grinning.

Rayla whooped and threw herself into her mother's arms, weeping tears of boundless joy. Her father patted her on the head, then stood and watched the happy scene until Rayla pulled away.

She looked at them both again, bowled over by everything that had happened in the last half hour. She had woken up this morning feeling bleak, and now not only had Nechama and the rest of her classmates made her feel like a princess, but her mother was also getting better. She wanted to pinch herself to make sure she was awake.

Dad coughed. "Okay if I go out for a bit? I may just catch a *minyan* for Minchah if I'm quick."

Mom waved her hand. "Of course. Go ahead."

Rayla watched Dad as he went out, his gait lighter than it had been for a long time.

Her mother gazed out the window. "I passed those at sunrise," she said, pointing to the faraway cliffs, as she gently combed her delicate fingers through Rayla's hair. "What a pretty world Hashem has made for us—a world of beauty and promise."

Rayla gulped. "I saw it too," she whispered. "The beauty and promise—only I didn't know what I was seeing."

She closed her eyes, letting the sunshine seep through her. Never had she felt so protected and cared for. She thought about the song she had composed, a deep feeling of gratitude to Hashem almost overwhelming her.

"Rayla?" came Sherry's voice from behind her.

Rayla turned and saw Sherry standing near the door of the common room with an older girl who looked startingly similar, and a woman who could be none other than their mother. Michal was there too.

Sherry held out Rayla's guitar. "I thought you might want this." She turned to Rayla's mother. "I'm Sherry, Rayla's friend. I'm so glad you were able to make it."

Mom stretched out her arms. "What should I say?" She smiled. "Hashem's wonders never cease to amaze."

She and Mrs. Lempel exchanged pleasantries while Rayla took hold of the neck of the guitar, her throat tight. "I—I'm not sure I can even sing right now."

Sherry smiled encouragingly. "Try."

Rayla turned to face her mother. Mom's eyebrows were raised questioningly.

"Rayla? Have you started performing in public?"

Rayla sucked on her lower lip. She glanced at the Lempels, then back at her mother.

"On an occasion like this, I'm ready to try."

She settled herself on a chair. As she sang the words inspired by Tehillim, telling of Hashem's kindness and His protection, tears of pride glistened in her mother's eyes. Rayla glanced at Sherry, who was listening in rapt attention along with her family, and was startled to see Mrs. Pepper and several other teachers, as well as more than a few third form girls standing just inside the door, too. As soon as the final note faded, they all burst into applause.

"Thank you," Rayla mouthed to Sherry.

Her friend beamed and gave her two thumbs up. No one said a word, almost as if they were afraid to break the spell that the music had created. Quietly, the audience slipped away.

Rayla turned to her mother and leaned her guitar against the wall. "Mom, do you feel up for a walk? There's something I want to show you in the garden."

"I'd be delighted," Mom said.

Rayla helped her stand and held her arm as they made their way out to the shed.

"What a lovely garden shed. So cheerful!" Mom commented, admiring the colorful stripes.

"That's not even the best part," Rayla said, smiling.

She saw Nechama sitting on a bench with her family near the pond, and Rayla beamed at her. She had a reason to be doubly grateful to the girl now—Nechama's gift to her would be the perfect gift for her mother.

They reached the shed. At Rayla's encouragement, Mom stepped inside. Her face lit up when she saw the chaotic color sitting in splendor on the bench and shelves.

"Oh, Rayla." She put her hand over her heart. "It's beautiful. What is it for?"

Rayla glanced at Nechama. "You, Mom. It's for you."

"But you didn't know I was coming, did you?"

Rayla giggled. "No. But Hashem did."

Her mother linked arms with her. Together, they admired the beauty that had grown from the murky soil. Rayla nestled next to her mother and rested her head on her shoulder, waves of happiness frothing inside her.

An actress receiving a standing ovation could never have felt this grateful.

~

Standing in the parking lot, next to Tatty's car, Sherry watched Rayla and her mother walk between the parked vehicles.

"Oh, that was wonderful," Ma said. "What a talented group of girls you are. Takes me back to my own school days."

Sherry glanced around, grateful that the rest of the crowd had dissipated somewhat.

"Ma? Uh ... Tatty? I have something for everyone too." She reached into her pocket and pulled out the envelopes, somewhat crumpled now, and handed one to her parents and sisters. She gave another envelope with Moshe's name on it to Ma. "Can you make sure he gets this, please?"

Ma raised an eyebrow. "What's all this?"

Tatty smiled, obviously intrigued by the mystery, and pulled out his letter from the envelope. "T is for Thank you," he read. "A is for Appreciated. T is for Thoughtful." He looked up at Sherry. "It's an acrostic."

"C is for Creative," Chava said, reading her own poem. "H is for Humble." She looked up. "Did you make acrostics for all of us?"

Sherry nodded, blushing. "Yes. Except, since 'Ma' is so short, I added 'Lempel' onto hers."

Ma chuckled, examining her letter.

"I know it seems like a silly gift," Sherry continued, "but I just wanted you to know how much I am grateful for you. *All* of you," she said, looking at Tatty.

"And I see you used my gift to write them," he said, admiring the multi-colored letters she'd used to add artistic flair to each line.

Sherry nearly choked. She exchanged glances with Michal.

"Uh, I really appreciated the colored pencils, Tatty. But I thought Michal needed them more than I did, so—"

Tatty frowned. "Didn't you see my note?"

"What note?" Sherry looked at Michal to see if she knew what Tatty meant, but she seemed as clueless as Sherry.

"The one inside the box."

"One minute," Michal said, and hurried away to her locker. She returned a few moments later with the box of colored pencils and handed them to Sherry. "I haven't even opened them yet."

Sherry hadn't noticed before, but the seal was already broken. She opened the box and, sure enough, there was a folded slip of paper tucked in next to the rainbow of colors.

"Dear Sherry," she read aloud. "Each pencil in this box is different. One might even say they come from different families. But when they are put together, they make a beautiful, harmonious whole. Just like our new family. I am so very proud to call you my daughter. Tatty."

She exchanged glances with Michal, moisture streaking her cheeks. She didn't even wipe the tears away.

"Oh, Tatty," she said. "You have no idea how much this means to me. And you're right. We do work pretty well together." She put an arm around her new sister's shoulders. "Don't we, sis?"

Michal smiled, returning the hug. The cold distance of the past few months had completely melted.

19 Silver Linings

The last term of the school year always seems to hurry by faster than the others. And once visiting day had passed, there wasn't much time left to the year at all. Sherry was looking forward to the summer, but at the same time she wanted to hold on to the year and savor it for a bit longer.

She was putting her books in her locker after the last class of the year when the sound of pounding footsteps caught her attention. Michal came up beside her and placed her own books in her locker.

"Isn't it a perfectly glorious day? Let's go for a walk outside."

Sherry grinned. She was still getting used to this new, happier Michal—but she quite enjoyed the change.

"I'm game," she said.

They made their way to the exit, but as Sherry put her hand on the door handle, she stopped.

"Let's call Rayla to join us."

Michal's eyes widened. "Why? What's wrong with ... uh—" She

stopped short. "Yes, you're right, I'm calling her right now. She's in the common room. Wait here for me."

Sherry watched her hurry down the corridor. *That was so strange. It's almost as if she had to fight with herself to include Rayla. But why? I thought they were friends too.*

"Come on, Sherry," Michal said, pulling her out of her thoughts. Rayla stood beside her in a yellow sweater. Michal had a broad smile on her face. "Out we go."

"Out we go," Rayla echoed, opening the door for them.

The three girls walked briskly around the pond, enjoying the wind on their cheeks as they reminisced about the many good times they'd had over the year. Finally, spent, they collapsed on a garden bench beneath the weeping willows, watching the ducks bob beneath the surface for aquatic treats.

Sherry picked up a pebble and threw it into the pond, watching as concentric circles formed around its impact point. Michal and Rayla joined her, throwing in pebbles of their own. There was something soothing about the way the ripples formed.

Rayla turned to Sherry. "Er, there's something I want to tell you."

Sherry raised an eyebrow as she looked from Michal to Rayla. Michal seemed nonchalant enough. *She clearly knows what Rayla is about to share.*

Her curiosity mounted. "O-kay ..."

"Er, I might not continue here next year. That is, I haven't decided yet."

Sherry's jaw dropped. "That's a shocker. I can't imagine school without you."

"It depends on Mom, really." Rayla blushed. "She's doing much better, and hopefully, she'll be returning to the States."

Sherry nodded. "That's wonderful news, Rayla. I'm so happy for you. But I'll miss you terribly."

Sherry thought Michal might chime in too, but Michal just threw another pebble into the water and said nothing.

"You know, when I got out of the car on my first day, I was worried," Rayla said. "Very worried." But then she flashed a soft, genuine smile. "I guess all's well that ends well."

Sherry sat very straight, her palms facing out. "You're unreal."

"Yes, you are really something!" Michal said.

Rayla laughed them off. "Nah. Things happen." She looked from one to the other. "You want to know something? There might have been a dark cloud hanging over me, but it had some very bright silver linings." She pointed to the two of them.

"And you're leaving us behind?" Sherry mock-pouted.

"I really don't know. I think this place is amazing, and I'll miss you guys so much if I do leave. It's a very difficult decision. At least Mrs. Pepper has been kind enough to give me the summer to think it over. I don't have to give her a firm answer until a week before school is due to begin." She paused. "What do you think, Sherry?"

Sherry considered. "It's not something I can answer. As much as I really wish you'd stay, I'm far happier that your mum's health is enabling you to choose. And I also get that you'd want to be closer to home now ..." She stopped short and pointed to the opposite side of the pond. "Hey, what's Bassy doing there? Why does she have such a big carrot in her hand? She's up to mischief, for sure."

"Look at her," Michal whispered. "She's coaxing a rabbit to come to her. Now what has she got up her sleeve?"

Sherry grinned. "I vote we don't tell her we saw her. We'll pretend we didn't see anything. Meanwhile, we'll be on the lookout for whatever she has in mind."

The three of them exchanged thrilled glances, and Sherry chuckled. *Is there excitement in store?*

The assembly bell rang, and the girls rushed to the main hall.

This is it—the last assembly of the year.

The hall was silent while the girls stood respectfully, waiting for Mrs. Pepper to enter. Sherry looked around, seeing the same bittersweet mix of emotions on her friends' faces.

Mrs. Pepper went over some of the lessons each class had learned that year, and urged them to take everything they had learned away with them.

"There's ample time during the holidays to practice the wonderful ideals we've discussed throughout the year. Grab the opportunities and use them well." She looked around the room. "It is absolutely essential to get your *firsts* right. But don't forget, girls, to make the most of your *lasts* too. Last impressions are lasting impressions. Make your lasts last."

She lowered her voice and focused on each girl as she spoke. Her deep blue eyes, her barely audible tone, reflected a depth of wisdom that made Sherry's heart surge with aspiration, and she bent forward to catch every word.

"Girls, more than anything: live a life of lasts.

"What do I mean by that? Every now and then, grab a 'last Shemoneh Esrei'—envision that it's your last time davening the Amidah, and daven like you've never davened before. When you meet someone, imagine it's the last time you will ever see that person. Give him your all and make him feel like a million dollars. Grab as many lasts as you can—after all, you never know when the 'last' you make will be your last 'last' for real. Girls, let's make lasts and make them last."

Make lasts and make them last. Sherry soaked in the message as she and Michal made their way out of the hall together. Rayla walked ahead with Mindy and Becky.

Sherry's mind was still immersed in the inspiring words when she noticed Michal's contemplative look. Michal gave her a smile.

"I'll miss Rayla if she decides to return to New York," Sherry whispered.

Michal swallowed. "I'll miss her too ... but a part of me hopes that she doesn't come back to Samphire." She gave a shaky cough. "You know what they say—two's company, three's a crowd."

Sherry raised her eyebrows, not quite sure what to make of that.

"You know I can be friends with more than one person at a time, right?"

Michal shifted uncomfortably. "I know. I guess since I used to be an only child, I sometimes have a hard time, um, sharing." Her face flushed red. "Not like you. You give almost too much, more than you should. Sometimes it's annoying."

Sherry started. She put a hand on Michal's arm and stopped her at the edge of the hallway. "What do you mean by that?"

Michal looked away, looking more embarrassed than ever. "Oh, I shouldn't have said anything. I forgave you already anyway."

"*Forgave* me? Forgave me for what?"

Michal tugged on her ponytail, and the ribbon came untied. "You know the writing competition? I found your story, Sherry. The real one, not the one that only got a C. I know what you did so I could win. But I didn't want to win, not when your story deserved to be shared with the world. It really hurt me that you thought I'd want you to let me win instead of trying your best. That kind of victory is no victory at all."

Sherry stared. "But you *deserve* to win, Michal! I truly feel that."

"No. I don't. And Mrs. Bergman agreed with me. She sent in your story to the contest instead of mine, though I'm sure you would have heard by now if yours had been the national winner."

Sherry shook her head. This was all wrong.

"But I wanted you to have it. I wanted you to know how much you meant to me. *Mean* to me." Her voice had risen several pitches.

Michal smiled gently and squeezed Sherry's hand. "Sherry."

Sherry frowned and looked her friend in the eye. "What?"

"I *do* know. But I don't ever want to receive merit I didn't earn. Please don't do it again."

Sherry met her friend's steady gaze. Suddenly, Michal's comments about Bassy not letting her win and the strange barbs that seemed to have nothing to do with jealousy made sense. Michal had truly been upset about what Sherry had done. But why?

For the first time, Sherry thought about how she might feel if the roles had been reversed, if she knew Michal had given up a well-deserved honor in favor of Sherry's more inferior offering. Her heart sank. She would be just as upset as Michal had been.

"Oh, Michal. I get it now. And I'm so sorry. I only wanted you to stop moping around and start enjoying yourself, and I saw how hard you were working on your story and how happy it made you, and in the end, neither of us won, so it wasn't even worth it—"

"I know. I know why you did it. That's why I forgave you already. I'm just sorry you felt you had to do it. All I wanted to do was talk about all the new things that were happening with Ma and Tatty and the move with the one person I knew would understand, and all I did was push you away."

Michal sighed. It was her turn to look at the floor. When she looked up, her mouth was firm.

"You know what? From now on, let's commit to always tell each other our secrets, no matter what. Secrets just lead to misery."

"Promise." Sherry smiled. "*Bli neder.*"

Michal smiled back.

Sherry glanced at her sister's hair. "Now bend your head and let me tie your ribbon."

20 The Last Day

The next morning, the building bustled with last-day-of-school activity. Sherry hopped from task to task with barely any time to breathe. Lockers needed cleaning, chairs had to be stacked, suitcases packed, and luggage labeled. Girls ran around in a frenzy, trying to locate their missing belongings. With all the commotion, it felt like the school was being buffeted by the ocean's waves.

Sherry noticed Bassy carrying something into the common room and nudged Michal and Rayla. Sure enough, a few minutes later, a tiny rabbit scampered behind a stack of chairs, and Bassy grinned from ear to ear.

"Bassy," Michal hissed, "didn't you learn your lesson last time? What about Mrs. Lee?"

Bassy leaned closer. "It's just a little rabbit. And besides, Mrs. Lee left three weeks ago, remember?"

Chaos ensued as the rabbit scampered around, setting the girls even more on edge. They dashed about in every direction, bumping into each other. Sherry couldn't help but giggle—it almost felt like a game of bumper cars. The other girls soon stopped being frightened and started laughing uncontrollably.

The chaos brought Mrs. Pepper out of her office. "What is going on here?"

Just then, the rabbit scurried past her shoe. She jumped backwards, then did a double-take when she saw the label attached to the creature. A small smile crept up her face and she gave Bassy a sideways glance.

"Oh, so Rabbit Two has finally turned up. I suppose it's a good thing Mrs. Lee took early leave. And that it is much too late in the year to suspend anyone."

Bassy blanched. She scooped the frightened bunny into her arms and hurried out of the room. But as soon as she was out the door, Sherry could hear her skipping steps echo down the corridor.

Baila rushed into the room, breathless, her camera at the ready. "Where's the rabbit? I want to snatch a photo of it."

"You're just a moment too late," Rayla said.

Bassy returned with empty hands and a big smile on her face.

Baila shrugged. "Never mind, I'll take a photo of the shed instead. I can't go home without a shot of our fabulous artwork. We've become good painters this year."

"Not to mention good gardeners," Michal added with a significant look at Nechama.

The girl flushed. "Yeah." She glanced at Rayla with a shy smile.

Bassy laughed. "As long as we don't become all goody-goody. Ha! As if I could ever be!"

Sherry chuckled. "You never know what time might see."

Mindy came up to the group. "We've got to go to our classroom now. Mrs. Cohen is waiting for us."

But with everyone having such a jolly time, no one seemed inclined to listen. Bassy clapped twice and the girls looked up, startled.

"We gotta go to the classroom. Come on, everyone, zoom, zoom, zoom!"

When all the girls were standing before her, Mrs. Cohen said a few parting words, to which they listened intently. She then took out a single balloon from her bag and gave it to Nechama.

"Blow it up, please."

With a look of trepidation on her face, Nechama did so. The girls burst out laughing. Written on the balloon in black ink were the words *Fly high and aim for the sky*. Nechama knotted it.

"Rayla!" she said, and batted it in her direction.

Squealing with delight, Rayla hit it away from her. As the girls tossed the balloon around the room, giggling and shrieking, Sherry noticed Baila patting her pockets with a look of distress on her face.

"I've lost my keys!" Baila yelled into the uproar.

"And I think I'm starting to lose my head," Mrs. Cohen said. "Why must you all make so much noise?"

The girls got down on their hands and knees to search for the keys, but they couldn't find them anywhere. Mrs. Bergman entered the room just then, twirling a set of keys around her finger.

"Whose keys are these?" she asked. "All they say is *Form Three*."

"There they are," Baila said with relief. "My name wore off three months ago."

She hurried forward to collect them, but Mrs. Bergman held the keyring out of her reach.

"What were you doing in the staffroom?" she asked.

"Excuse me?"

"That's where I found these keys, so I will ask again, Baila: What were you doing in there?"

"I didn't go in," Baila said. "I just opened the door to take a photo of the place where all the fun begins."

Mrs. Bergman gave an amused smile. Baila was off the hook. The teacher then turned to Sherry.

"I need to speak with you. Please come with me to the office."

Sherry's heart jumped. She exchanged glances with Michal, beckoning for her sister to join her. On their way out the door, she whispered, "What would Mrs. Bergman want from me on the last day of school?"

As they went into the office, Mrs. Bergman noticed Michal. She gestured for her to come in as well.

"Mrs. Pepper will be here shortly."

Sherry's legs trembled. "Have I gotten into trouble?"

The door creaked behind her, and Mrs. Pepper walked right in. "Trouble, did you say?" Her eyes twinkled. "Well, because of you, I received a phone call from Mrs. Taylor."

Sherry swallowed. "Mrs. Taylor? Who's she?"

"She called about the countrywide story-writing contest."

Sherry's heart beat even faster. "I thought that would have been over ages ago." She glanced at Michal. Her sister's face bore an expression of startled hope. "What... what did she want?"

"Well. She called to inform me that one of my students has won second place."

Sherry sank into the closest chair. "I won? After all that, I won? When Michal told me what she did, I thought... but I won?"

Michal came over and patted her shoulder. "What did I tell you?" She beamed. "Your story deserved to win."

Mrs. Pepper eyed the two of them. "Indeed. I believe we have two true winners in the room here today."

"And the writing was top-notch," Mrs. Bergman chimed in. "I would have been proud to have written that story myself."

Sherry blinked rapidly as her cheeks burned. "It's all so ... so unbelievable," she stammered. "I knew I didn't stand a chance with the paper I submitted."

"And that makes your win all the more commendable."

Mrs. Pepper clasped her hands in front of her and leaned on her desk. "Sherry and Michal, you have both made great strides this year. I am very proud of you. I hope you will keep going from strength to strength, and that next year will bring even greater results."

Sherry knew she was blushing. "Amen. I hope so, too." She looked at Michal and saw her happy aspirations mirrored. She couldn't wait to share her win with Ma. *I haven't gotten into too much trouble this year. Let's hope next year will be even better. I would love it to be completely trouble-free.* She laughed inwardly. *Is that even possible? We'll just have to wait and see.*

Glossary

Achakeh lo b'chol yom sheyavo—I will await the arrival of the Messiah every day

Ahavas habrios—love of your fellow Jews

B'ezras Hashem—with the Almighty's help

Baruch Hashem—thank the Almighty

Bitachon—trust in the Almighty

Bli neder—without promising

Brachah, brachos—blessing(s)

Chein—grace, favor

Chinuch—Torah education

Dan l'kaf zechus—judge favorably

Emunah—faith in the Almighty

Gemara—a volume of the Talmud

Halachos—Torah laws

Hashem—the Almighty

Hashgachah pratis—Divine providence

Hatzlachah—success

Heilige—holy

Im yirtzeh Hashem—if the Almighty wills it

Kabbalas Shabbos—Friday night prayers to welcome in the Sabbath

Keruvim—the cherubs on the cover of the Holy Ark

Kodesh—Jewish studies

Lechu Neranenah—opening Psalm in Kabbalas Shabbos, the Friday prayers to welcome in the Sabbath

Maariv—evening prayers

Mashal—parable

Mechilah—forgiveness

Melachos—the thirty-nine categories of activities that are prohibited on the Sabbath

Middah, middos—character trait(s)

Minchah—afternoon prayers

Mishkan—the Tabernacle where the Almighty's Presence resided during the Jews' forty-year sojourn in the Wilderness

Mizbei'ach—the Altar

Negel vasser—hand washing upon waking up in the morning

Netz—sunrise

Nifla'os haBorei—the wonders of the Creator

Niftar—passed away

Pesukim—verses

Purim'dik—in the spirit of the Purim holiday

Sefer—Torah book

Shabbos—the Sabbath

Shacharis—morning prayers

Shemoneh Esrei—central prayer recited three times a day, consisting of nineteen blessings

Shivas haminim—the seven species of grain and fruit that are part of the distinction of the Land of Israel

Shivisi Hashem—a poster or plaque that reminds one to think of the Almighty

Shticky—clever

Simchah—happiness

Tatty—father

Tefillah—prayer

Tehillim—Psalms

Yerushalayim—Jerusalem

Yidden—Jews

Zemiros—songs sung at the Sabbath meals